The Manicure

Charle McDaniel

Ms.WRiTE
Publications

ISBN-13: 978-0-9848890-0-6

First Printing 2011

Cover design by C Ford

Published by:

Ms. Write Publications
Rockwall, TX 75087
charlemcdaniel.com

Published in the United States of America

This book is dedicated to the many friends whose encouragement and faith filled me with the ootspah I needed to publish my first novel.

Also by Charle McDaniel

Dream Lover

Blaze

Rustic Meadows

Code Blue

A Note from the Author

Thank you for giving my words a piece of your time and a place in your life. Hopefully, this story will open your heart and your mind to the injustices of discrimination. It doesn't matter if you are straight or gay, we are who we are. All that matters is that we make a more conscious effort to treat each other with understanding and respect.

Being nice matters – today and every day.

Chapter 1

Katherine, or Katy as she was known in intimate circles, was the youngest of four children born to Frank and Mary Hopkins. The twins, Jason and Mason, were nearly five years older and Beth, the oldest, was a decade ahead of Katy in the race on life. Each child had a talent uniquely their own. Beth, cast as the lead in every performance staged by the Drama Department, was now a playwright on Broadway. Mason, an all-star quarterback, turned pro at the age of 21. Jason hired on as head coach at Lincoln High after graduating from college, due in large part for his contributions in winning four state titles while a student there.

Katy was blessed with athletic skills like her brothers and spent her youth on the sandlots and street courts right alongside of them. She was taller than most boys or girls her age and only a couple inches shorter than the twins. Because of her height and athletic abilities, she was the first and oftentimes only girl chosen to play on the old neighborhood teams.

By age twelve, Katy was a full-fledged tomboy and other kids would tease her about not really being a girl. To her brothers she was simply one of the guys. The only time she wore a dress was at church on Sundays, and she absolutely loathed the idea of wearing makeup. While other pre-teens spent hours fussing over hairstyles, Katy's long, blonde hair was always cinched in a ponytail or weaved together in a tight braid. On a priority scale, it was more important to keep it out of her face while playing sports than it was to compete in petty pageantry with her peers.

In high school, Katy was named "Outstanding Athlete" for her achievements in basketball, track, volleyball and softball. She was also class president her senior year and voted "Most Likely to Succeed" by her classmates in the 1992 Yearbook. After college, she joined the faculty at Lincoln Junior High as the new Physical Education teacher. Like her brother, Jason, it looked as though coaching would chart her course into the future.

Chapter 2

Frank and Mary had every reason to be proud parents. Their children had all grown into responsible adults, admired by all of their friends and neighbors in Lincoln, Kansas, a small, rural community about forty-five miles north of Kansas City. The census sign boasted a population of 1372. Not a big place in size, but definitely a big place in spirit.

Until college none of the Hopkins' children had ever set foot outside of Lincoln. All four were born at Mercy Hospital followed by an announcement in the Herald Banner, the town's only newspaper. They then trailed each other through the ranks in elementary, junior high and high school. For most of her classes, Katy had the same teachers as those who had taught her older siblings.

Beth left Lincoln for the bright lights of New York City right after graduation. There she met and married Benson, or Ben, as he preferred, a resident-in-training at a local hospital. He was the attending physician when she was brought into the Emergency Room after breaking her arm in a freakish fall from the stage at dress rehearsals for her first production. She was immediately drawn to the kind, young doctor and thanked him by offering a seat next to hers at their opening. Ben was smitten with her as well and they were rarely seen apart after that first show.

Frank was a crying mess on the day of their wedding, appearing more nervous than either the bride or groom. Ben's new father-in-law-to-be was noticeably unstable as he ushered Beth into the chapel. At first glance it looked as though she was clinging to his arm, but, in reality, she was holding him up, steadying him as they made their way to the altar. The twins, seated on either side of Katy, began to wager on whether their father would remain upright long enough to give the parents' blessing.

"I'll bet five bucks Dad passes out," Mason announced.

"Make it ten and you're on," Jason countered.

"You two are horrible," Katy chided. "He'll be fine. He's a little nervous, that's all."

"More than a little," Jason challenged. "Look how white he is!"

Mason leaned forward in order to see both Jason and Katy at the same time.

"I'd like to change my bet," he told them. "He probably won't pass out, but if he clams up or forgets what he's supposed to say, you each have to cough up twenty big ones."

"Twenty bucks?" Katy whined. "That's a bit steep, don't ya think?"

"I'm in," Jason said in a low voice as Beth and Frank walked past them. "But I'm going to keep my twenty on him passing out."

"Okay," Katy said, feeling pressure from both sides. "I'm in also. But I'm betting he makes it through the whole thing without any trouble."

At the point in the ceremony when the minister asks who would give the bride away in marriage, Frank became wobbly and unsteady on his feet. Several onlookers, including Jason, started to snicker.

"I should've stayed with my first bet," Mason said ruefully. "He looks like he'll be on the floor any second now!"

Katy put a finger to her lips. "Shhhhh."

Mary came forward, took Frank's hand in her own and answered for both of them, "Her father and I give our blessing to this union." After her proclamation, she turned Frank around and guided him to his seat.

"I should've known Mom would blow my chances of winning the bet," Jason muttered as he handed his brother a crisp, twenty-dollar bill. Katy reached into her purse and pulled out a wad of wrinkled cash, which she then tossed into Mason's upturned palm.

Mason unfolded Katy's money and counted it then looked at her and said, "There's only fourteen dollars here."

"It's all I've got," Katy insisted. "I'll have to borrow the rest from Mom or Dad and give it to you later."

"I can't believe you're broke again," Jason responded.

"Again?" Mason repeated. "Katy's always broke!"

Beth and Ben were exchanging vows at the same time Katy and her brothers were finalizing their transaction. Mary overheard them whispering and turned around, giving each one a "straighten-up-right-now-or-I'll-bend-you-over-my-knee" scowl. Her reaction caused Mason to giggle and Jason joined in soon after. Katy placed her hand over her mouth to stifle her own laughter. When Mary turned around the second time, their smiles evaporated, almost as if they'd been seared by the heat from their mother's wrath.

During the last part of the ceremony, the minister presented the newlyweds to the audience as husband and wife and guests on Ben's family's side of the church let out a sigh of relief. New giggles erupted from Katy and her brothers, resulting in another glaring look from their mother.

Katy kept her head down as she passed Mary in the breezeway between the chapel and the reception hall, ever mindful of the scolding that was, sooner or later, certain to take place.

In the receiving line, Beth was radiant. Frank was aglow as well but it was obvious that the flush coloring his cheeks was the result of embarrassment and not admiration for his daughter or her new husband. His legs had regained most of their strength, but if you shook his hand a little too hard, he was still sure to topple over. He stood next to Ben, who offered an occasional nudge to help him stay upright.

Katy couldn't remember a time when her sister looked more beautiful. Beth's gown was hand stitched with a white, lace bodice that framed her torso above a free-flowing skirt that trailed behind her when she walked across the floor. Baby's breath was sprinkled throughout her hair. Looking at her took Katy's breath away.

Just before the ceremony, as Katy was fastening a necklace around her sister's neck, she mentioned to Beth how pretty her gown was. Beth twirled around and gave her a quick hug then excitedly suggested that she wear the same dress at her own wedding. Katy felt an urge to refuse but held back. Instead, she smiled and turned her sister back toward the mirror with a soft "maybe so" and clasped the necklace in its place.

A short-lived premonition revealed that there would probably never come a day when Katy would wear such a dress. It was an unusual thought, but one that came and went with utmost surety nonetheless. Katy let the notion pass and gave it no further consideration.

The following year Jason married Maggie, his high school sweetheart. Their ceremony, like so many other family events, was held in the Hopkins' back yard. Frank was definitely more at ease at this wedding. He sat in the front row, winking occasionally at his beloved Mary. His arm was draped across the back of her chair and every so often he would stroke the back of her head or pat her on the shoulder. A deeper love, Katy knew, never existed.

Mason, the avowed bachelor, remained single until the age of 32 when he pledged his love for Emma, a cheerleader from his former football team. After retiring, he became a successful real estate developer in Dallas. He and Emma lived on a sprawling, 75-acre ranch north of the city with their two dogs, Mutt and Harley.

Katy dated a handful of times over the years but was never really interested in pursuing a long-term relationship with anyone that she'd been involved with. It never concerned her that she was alone. She truly believed that love would come later in life, just as it had for Mason.

Chapter 3

Katy's thirtieth birthday celebration was held at her parent's house. Her siblings were there to share in the event along with a few of her friends. Nora, her closest friend, brought her cousin, George, and his wife, Rachel, who had recently relocated to the United States from Greece. George had accepted an offer as a professor at a college in Kansas City and he and his family were staying with Nora and her husband, Steve, until they found a place of their own in Lincoln.

All eyes turned to the bronze-skinned, black-haired woman standing beside her as Nora introduced her cousin's wife. She then went on to describe how Rachel was from the island of Santorini and that she and George had met thirteen years earlier at the university library where she worked while attending classes. George was a professor at the time, to which he hastily inserted a caveat that his wife was not, nor ever had been, one of his students. Nora then spoke about their children: Dani, a 12-year-old starting junior high in the fall, and two older boys, Rafael, 16, and Rion, 15, who would be attending Lincoln High. To Katy, Rachel looked young enough to be George's daughter. She couldn't picture her as the mother of three teenage children.

Her thoughts were interrupted as Beth presented her with a fresh drink. She had unwittingly consumed several glasses of her spiked punch already, causing her mind to run a bit slower than usual. It took her several moments to process everything Nora had disclosed about George and Rachel and reach the conclusion that the age of the older two children didn't jive with the number of years they had been married. The boys were most likely from a previous union, she surmised, however, she couldn't figure out which one was the true parent. She assumed it was George simply because he looked so much older. The kids weren't there to affirm or deny – not that it would have mattered because her attention diverted to something else a few seconds later.

Nora continued to ramble on about George and Rachel and the conversation shifted entirely from Katy's big day to the couple and their pilgrimage from Greece. At first Katy didn't mind but then realized that her birthday, the event that had brought them all together, was now a mere blip on the radar screen. After downing another drink, she decided it was high time to remind everyone why they were there, so she grabbed a present and started ripping away the wrapping, making as much noise as possible in the process. To her delight, the crowd turned their attention back to her. Mary took it as a cue to fetch her birthday cake and returned with three dozen fire-tipped candles all burning brightly atop of it. This triggered one guest to start singing the Happy Birthday song. Everyone else joined in as Mary placed the cake on the table in front of Katy.

"My goodness!" Nora exclaimed when the singing subsided. "That's a lot of candles. We should probably call the fire department to come and put that out."

"Smart ass-s-s," Katy hissed, letting the "s" resonate for at least two full seconds. "Best friends forever, huh? I'm thinking forever ends today, missy!"

"Girls," Mary scolded. Her tone was both demanding and harsh. "Keep it civil. This is supposed to be a happy day, remember?"

Nora raised her glass and toasted her friend with good will, good health and good fortune. Beth elbowed her sister in the ribs and added that she also needed a good man.

Katy shot her an evil glance at the same time Mary wrapped her arm around her waist and whispered, "Don't listen to your mean, old sister, sweetie. You'll find happiness one day. The right fellow just hasn't come along yet."

Even though she had aged past the point of believing such things, Katy made a silent wish while blowing out her candles.

Whoever it is, I hope they come soon.

Chapter 4

All in all, Katy could count on one hand the number of men she had dated since college. First, there was John Trainor, whom she met in the checkout line at the Hy-Vee supermarket. They went out for several months before she asked him to move in. Three weeks later she lost interest and he was asked to leave. Then came Peter McCormick, a guy she met at a Royals baseball game. He started out normal but soon showed he had a shallow side. They only dated for a month. Next was Jeremy Jackson, who, after their first date, would park himself in front of her TV and drink beer. Their courtship lasted only a month as well.

The final contender was Mike Snodgrass, a control freak who never allowed Katy a voice in their relationship. He decided where they would go, when they would go, who they would go with and what time they would return home. When they first started dating, Mike was attentive and affectionate but then changed after they moved in together. Katy began conjuring up images of alphabetized canned goods and towels aligned by length from shortest to longest across the rack, just like in the Julia Roberts movie, *Sleeping with the Enemy*. Realizing that she might possibly face the same outcome as Julia's character, she ordered him to move out.

It had been over two years since her last boyfriend and she was content in letting at least two more pass before getting involved again. She was starting her eighth year at Lincoln Junior High and had more important things to think about than a relationship.

Coaching was her passion and one of her biggest dreams was to lead a team to the state championship. Didn't matter the sport, she just wanted an opportunity to compete at the finals and bring home that trophy. She'd come back to Lincoln with the hope of building upon the reputation she had in high school, but that had not yet been achieved. It seemed the greatest female jock from Lincoln couldn't field a winning team – in any sport!

This year would be different, she vowed. There were two new girls, Courtney and Danielle, trying out for the basketball team. Courtney was a tall, spindly girl with long arms, thick glasses and an overbite. In all truth and fairness, she was a klutz. It would take a lot of coaching to mold her into a decent player. The talent was there, however, and Katy looked forward to the challenge.

Danielle, by contrast, was a natural. She had a near perfect jump shot, was adept at handling the ball and sank an astonishing 92 percent of her free throws. With her on the team Katy felt sure they would have a winning season.

Needless to say, that hope was all but dashed as the girls suffered a crushing defeat in their opening match. They lost the second game as well, but with a much closer score. The third game, played on their opponent's court, looked to be the one that would bring Katy her first victory. With fifteen seconds left to play, Lincoln, down by one point, was in possession of the ball. Danielle had been fouled and would shoot two from the line. Given her percentages, Katy was confident she would bring it all home and clinch the win.

Danielle sank the first free throw and the crowd went wild. Katy leapt to her feet as well and her clipboard flew out of her hands, landing somewhere behind the bleachers.

The audience quieted when the referee handed Danielle the ball for her second shot. It swirled four or five times around the inside of the rim before dipping into the net and then reversing out of the hoop. The rebound was picked up by one of the Cambridge players and the crowd groaned in disappointment.

"Timeout!" Katy screamed. "Courtney! Sandy! Somebody! Hurry! Call a timeout!"

Sandy made a 'T' with her hands, which led to the official blowing his whistle. Katy looked at the clock and saw that there were still twelve seconds left to play.

"Listen up," she said as the girls formed a circle around her. "Here's what we're gonna do. As soon as the ball is put in play, commit the foul. They're not doing well on free throws, so we can hopefully get the ball for one more possession. Courtney and Sandy, we need that rebound so you two have to be all over those boards. Danielle, you stay in the back court and wait for the long pass then take your best shot. Everybody got it?"

All heads bobbed in unison.

"Ignore the crowd," she continued. "Just concentrate on the game. You can do it! Let's get out there and win this!"

They all stacked their hands on top of one another, lifted them high and shouted, "Team!"

The girls did exactly as Katy instructed and only one second had lapsed before the official blew his whistle to cite Sandy with a personal foul. He then trotted over to the scorer's table and notified them that Cambridge's Number 12 would be shooting two from the line.

Danielle waited at the opposite end of the court while her teammates lined up along both sides of the free throw line. Number 12's first shot went in smoothly and Cambridge moved ahead by one. The crowd rose to their feet again as the referee handed her the ball for her second shot.

"Miss it," Katy mumbled under her breath. "Come on, you little shit. Miss it!"

You could have heard a pin drop as the ball floated through the air toward the basket. No one was breathing; all eyes were wide open, faces frozen.

Air ball! Not even close to the basket! Lincoln still had a chance to win!

Sandy stepped out of bounds and waited for the referee to hand her the ball. When he did, she tossed it to Courtney, who, in turn, hurled it across court to Danielle. Danielle maneuvered past two Cambridge defenders, working her way closer to the basket with each dribble. Katy glanced at the clock. Six seconds remaining.

"Come on, Danielle," she whispered to herself. "Get a little closer. That's it, girl. Come on now. You're doing great!"

Four seconds.

"Okay, almost there. Don't rush it, kid!"

Two seconds.

"Go for it, Danielle. Shoot it!"

Danielle faked out her defender and pulled up for a jumper. The audience was screaming as the ball spiraled through the air.

It has plenty of height, Katy thought, and back spin. *Oh my God! We are gonna win!*

The ball spun around inside the rim and popped back out just as the buzzer sounded the end of the game. It was over. Cambridge had won.

Katy met the opposing coach at mid-court and congratulated her on the victory. She then returned to the sidelines to gather up her things before joining her team in the locker room. While she was bent over stuffing items into her gym bag, a woman stepped forward with her clipboard held tightly against her chest.

"You dropped this," the stranger announced as she tapped Katy on the shoulder. "Actually, it went flying when Dani shot that free throw."

Katy righted herself and collected the clipboard from her. "I had no idea," she said. "I must have been caught up in the moment."

They exchanged smiles before the woman replied, "It was an amazing game. They really played their hearts out. I'm sorry they lost."

"Me, too. It was a nail-biter for sure." Katy found her words trailing off as she stared into the most exquisite pair of jade-green eyes she had ever seen.

The woman nodded in agreement as Katy glanced toward the locker room and saw Danielle with her arms crossed, her foot tapping impatiently as she waited by the door. Turning back to the woman, she said, "Thanks for bringing this to me. I'm sure I never would have found it. Honestly, I probably wouldn't even have noticed it missing until sometime tomorrow." She then bobbed her head in the direction of the locker room and added, "I'd love to stay and chat but I've got to give the post-game consolation speech."

"I understand," the woman replied. "It was nice seeing you again, Katy."

And with that, Katy hustled over to join Danielle. Draping her arm around the young girl's shoulder, she accompanied her into the locker room.

Chapter 5

The loss to Cambridge was unsettling and Katy wanted to unwind a bit before going home. She thought a long drive through the country would help, as it usually did, so she turned east on Main and headed for the outskirts of town. She had driven past several intersections when a "For Sale" sign in the front yard of a small, framed house caught her eye.

"Isn't that darling?" she said aloud. It startled her that she had spoken out as there was no one in the car with her.

Good Lord, she mused. *Now I'm talking to myself! What would people think? Why I'm sure they'd think I needed a drink to calm the voices in my head. And they'd be right. A drink is exactly what I need!*

She pulled into the parking lot of the Quick Stop and turned off the engine. After opening the car door, she swung one leg around to get out then immediately changed her mind and brought it back inside. Reflecting on everything she'd been through the last couple of hours, she realized she had set the bar way too low.

I suffered a major disappointment tonight and deserve a real drink for my troubles, she reminded herself. *Diet Coke won't put Humpty Dumpty back together this time. I'm going for the gold! Cuervo Gold, that is!*

She put the car in drive and pulled out onto Main to continue heading east. As she passed the city limits sign, the woman she'd met at the gymnasium took over her thoughts.

"Nice seeing you again, Katy," the woman had told her.

She spoke as if she knew me, Katy recalled. *We must have met somewhere before but I can't remember where.*

The wheels continued to turn in her memory bank but nothing was registering. Her face then puckered into a scowl as she muttered, "I must be getting old. I remember shit that doesn't make a difference and go completely blank on the things that do. Man, I really need that drink."

Just past the intersection of Highway C and Highway A she turned into the parking lot of a bar aptly named, "Crossroads Pub." After walking inside, she plopped down on a barstool.

"Give me the usual," she told the bartender.

"And what would that be?" he challenged. "It changes every time you come in here, Katy."

"I know," she answered with a grin.

"How does a Margarita sound?"

"Like music to my ears."

"Coming right up."

She watched him lift a blender from behind the counter and pour a yellow, slushy concoction into a frosted mug. When he placed it on the bar in front of her, she gripped it with both hands, twirling it clockwise and then counterclockwise.

"Is something bothering you?" he asked.

"How long have you known me, Harry?"

"Since you were knee high to a grasshopper, I suppose. Why?"

Katy tapped her fingers on the outside of the glass.

"I need a change. I've lived in the same apartment for the past six years. I drove by a house that was for sale on my way out here. I make decent money, Harry. Maybe it's time I get my own place. That way I can do whatever I want, whenever I want."

"And what is it that you want, Katy?"

"I don't know. Something different from what I'm doing now."

"Well, if you feel that strongly then you should do it."

"Maybe I will, Harry. Maybe I will."

Katy finished her drink and left the bar then drove straight to the little house for another look. As she pulled up in front of it, she dimmed the headlights and turned off the radio so as not to disturb the neighbors then got out and leaned against the car's grill. She stared at the house for several minutes before mustering the courage to walk up and peek in the windows. There was nothing inside, save for the blinds, which were all pulled high. A full moon illuminated most of her view, enabling her to see from the front of the house all the way to the back yard. There were few interior walls, making the inside appear more spacious than it actually was.

"Oh my God!" she squealed in a high-pitched voice. "This place is perfect!"

Anxious to learn more about the property, particularly the price, she hurried back to her car, grabbed a pen and a napkin from the glove box and scribbled down the agent's phone number.

Chapter 6

Katy awoke early the next morning and immediately grabbed her phone to call the number she had jotted down the night before. She stole a quick glance at her alarm clock before dialing and the digits "6:05" glared back at her from the display. Fortunately, her sense of reality clicked in and reminded her that she should wait until a more appropriate hour to make the call. To pass the time, she drove to a nearby doughnut shop and bought a half-dozen assortment of various flavors and toppings.

Three cups of coffee and two doughnuts later the cuckoo clock in her living room, a gift from her parents that she absolutely detested but kept it on the wall out of her love for them, came to life and launched a small cast of tiny figurines twirling around in circles to an obnoxious melody while it chimed out seven loud dongs. The hour, she thought, had finally drawn nigh.

Her hands were trembling as she pressed the button for each digit. After two rings, a woman's groggy voice grumbled, "Hello?"

"Hello. May I speak with Carolyn Harper?"

"You are."

"Uh, yes, well, um, good morning, Miss Harper. My name is Katy Hopkins. I wanted to talk to you about the house at 536 Oak."

"What time is it?"

"Seven o'clock."

"In the morning?"

"Yes, ma'am."

"Don't compound things by calling me ma'am."

"Yes, mmm…," Katy responded, catching herself before repeating the word.

"What can I do for you? Katy, was it?"

"Yes, ma'am. I mean, yes. I'm calling to get some information on the house at 536 Oak."

"The office doesn't open till nine. Let me get your number and I'll call you later."

"And when might that be?"

"When the office opens at nine o'clock."

"Oh, okay. I guess I can find something to do until then."

"Try sleeping."

A moment of uncomfortable silence passed before Carolyn spoke again. "Listen," she said apologetically. "I get kinda frumpy when I'm woken up too early, so let's start this conversation again when I'm in a better mood."

When Carolyn called her back at quarter after nine, Katy had been poised over the phone and, in her haste to answer it, knocked the handset off the cradle and onto the floor. It bounced a few times before she could retrieve it. "Sorry!" she hollered while fumbling to pick it up.

"I don't know which is worse," she heard Carolyn say in a semi-stern tone as she placed the receiver next to her ear. "Having you wake me before dawn or deafening me with all that noise!"

"Sorry," Katy offered a second time.

"You said your name was Hopkins. Are you Mary Hopkins' girl?"

"Am I forgiven if I say yes?"

"Don't push your luck, kiddo."

"Right. Well then, yes, Mary is my mother. I'd appreciate it if you didn't tell her what a nuisance I've been. She'd kick my ass from here to Wichita."

"I'm sure I could handle that by myself," Carolyn quipped with that same odd blend of humor and seriousness.

"No doubt."

"Are you ready to get the ball rolling?"

"I am!"

"Why don't you come to my office and we can ride over together?"

"Can we meet at the house instead?"

"Sure. I'll meet you there in thirty minutes."

Katy pushed: "How about fifteen?"

"All right, Miss Anxious. I'll see you in fifteen."

"Thanks, Miss Harper."

"Call me Carolyn."

"Thanks, Carolyn."

Katy ended the call and sat at her kitchen table to finish off the last of the coffee and gobble down another doughnut before heading out the door. At nine thirty, she pulled up to the now familiar curb at 536 Oak. Her stomach was churning from the combination of sugar, caffeine and adrenaline all coursing through her system at the same time. Five minutes later, Carolyn pulled in behind her. Katy walked up to her and extended her hand in greeting.

"Good morning," she said.

Carolyn shook her hand firmly. "Good morning. I had a feeling you'd beat me here. Shall we take a look inside?"

Katy nodded and together they strolled up the walk. Carolyn removed the realtor's lock and opened the front door.

"I'd like to do this alone," Katy told her. "Would that be all right?"

"Of course," Carolyn replied. "I'll wait for you in the kitchen."

As she toured the property, Katy looked behind all of the doors and inspected the inside of every closet and cabinet. She flipped on light switches and ran water through the faucets to ensure they worked properly then walked the perimeter of the house to get a closer look at the foundation.

"How old is this place?" she asked Carolyn when she returned to the kitchen.

"It was built seventeen years ago."

"They've taken good care of it. How much are they asking?"

"One fifty-five, but it's been on the market for a while. I'm sure you could make an offer."

"Okay. I'm ready to make an offer."

"You don't want to look at any other houses?"

"No thanks."

"Are you sure?"

"I've never been as sure of anything in my life."

"Well then, let's go write up the contract! I'll treat you to lunch afterwards."

Katy's stomach soured at the mere mention of food, reminding her she would have been better off leaving the last doughnut for another time.

"Thanks, but I'll pass. I'm feeling a little nauseous."

"It's probably nerves. That's common for first time buyers."

Katy didn't bother to interject that it was more likely a result of poor eating habits.

When the paperwork was completed, her stomach felt better but still not quite well enough for any type of food. Carolyn offered a rain check until closing and Katy graciously accepted. After leaving the Real Estate office, she lifted her cell phone from her purse and called to share the good news with the only person programmed on her speed dial – her mother, Mary.

Chapter 7

As promised, Carolyn treated Katy to lunch when she closed on the house. It was a fantastic meal but Katy wanted to do more to celebrate her big day and decided she would splurge on some self-indulgent pampering. When she mentioned this to her mother, Mary suggested a spa visit with a full makeover. Katy thought that a bit extreme and out of her comfort zone, so she settled for a manicure instead.

She had a huge smile on her face when she entered the salon, proud of all her recent accomplishments. As she approached the counter a small, Asian woman greeted her from behind the register. Speaking with a very thick accent, the woman asked, "How you?"

"Fine, thanks," Katy responded.

"You have appointment?"

"I think so. My mom was supposed to set it up for me."

"To Lachel?"

"Excuse me?"

"Lachel," the woman repeated.

Katy cocked her head and blinked, obviously confused. With an arthritic finger, the greeter pointed to one of the manicurists seated at a booth toward the rear of the salon.

"Lachel," she echoed once more.

"I get it," Katy replied. "That must be Lachel."

The woman's head bobbed up and down as she offered her a wide, toothy grin. Katy quickly headed in that direction but then stopped when she saw her manicurist. Rachel was watching her as well and wondered if she recognized her. She was concerned Katy might have changed her mind about the appointment so she remained seated, waiting to see if she would continue toward her or turn around and leave. Katy finally came forward and sat down, her hands clasped tightly together in her lap.

"I'll need those up here," Rachel told her.

"What?" Katy seemed distracted by the comment.

"Your hands. I'll need your hands."

"Oh, yeah. Sorry about that."

Katy placed her right hand on the table while her left hand remained motionless in her lap. Rachel's touch was gentle but firm, and, as she caressed the tips of Katy's fingers, a shiver ran down her spine. Rachel noticed her reaction and smiled.

Her eyes are exquisite, Katy observed. *Mesmerizing. And what a beautiful face!*

Rachel lowered her fingertips into a bowl of warm, sudsy water then motioned for Katy to bring up her other hand. Most of her clients had told her how much they enjoyed her hand massages but Katy's eyes were glazed over and she had no reaction whatsoever.

Curious, Rachel inquired, "Is everything all right?"

"Why do you ask?"

"Because you keep staring at me."

"Oh, I'm sorry. I don't normally behave this way."

"And what way is that?"

"Weird, or whatever this is."

Rachel finished the manicure without either woman saying anything further. After applying a final coat of polish, she looked at Katy and smiled again.

"All done," she said.

"Thank you," Katy replied, forcing a smile of her own.

"My pleasure. I hope you'll come back again sometime."

Rachel waited for her to stand before doing the same. When both were upright, she looked directly into Katy's eyes and asked her, "You don't remember me, do you?"

"You look very familiar," Katy answered, her voice fading into a whisper by the end of her statement.

"I'm Dani's mother."

"Dani?"

"Danielle."

Katy looked dumbstruck, so Rachel continued.

"She plays on your basketball team."

"Now I remember! It's been bugging me since I got here! You're the woman who found my clipboard!"

"Guilty as charged."

"Sorry. I was in a mood that night. Fit of depression – you know, from the loss."

"We'd actually met prior to the game."

Now Katy was totally perplexed. "Really? Where? When?"

"At your birthday party. I'm Rachel. George's wife."

"I'm at a loss here. Who's George?"

"Nora's cousin."

Katy nodded vigorously as if that helped her remember, but, in actuality, she had no memory of meeting Rachel prior to the Cambridge game. After exchanging goodbyes, she left the salon reeling as she unsuccessfully tried to recall the night they'd met.

Why can't I remember? she wondered. *There has to be a reason.*

She contemplated her dementia (hoping it was only a temporary affliction) as she made the drive back to her apartment. Along the way she called her friend, Nora, to elicit details about the party and who all had been there. Nora reminded her that she had drank quite a bit of Beth's famous punch that night and by the time she arrived with George and Rachel, Katy wasn't drunk but wasn't far from it, either.

Thinking back, Katy realized that her entire party was a blur. Try as she might she couldn't remember a single gift she'd been given or even the flavor of her birthday cake. It bothered her that Rachel had seen her inebriated and she cringed at the thought that this lovely woman might think she drank so much that she could forget meeting her.

Damn that sister of mine! she fumed. *I could kick her in the ass for getting me hammered like that! She's lucky I was able to present myself in a better light at the Cambridge game. I'd be facing serious consequences if one of my students' parents had even the slightest suspicion that I had a drinking problem!*

Katy called her folks next. When her father answered, she blurted out, "Hey, Pop. What are you guys doing?"

"Watching TV. How about you?"

"I just got in from my manicure. I appreciate you and Mom gifting that to me."

Looking to anchor her spot as his favorite child, she added, "You guys are amazing. Have any of your kids – besides me – told you that lately?"

"Hold on a minute," he said then quickly handed the phone to Mary. "It's for you," he told her. "It's your daughter."

"Now, Frank," Mary scoffed, her blue eyes glaring at him over the rim of her bifocals. "Why do you say things like that? She's your daughter, too!"

"Not when she's gushing on like that," he countered.

Mary lifted the phone to her ear. "Hello?"

"Hey, Mom. Guess I scared Dad off again."

"Don't worry about it. He's being his typical ol' grouchy self. What's on your mind?"

"At my birthday party, do you think I had too much to drink? I met someone and don't remember it."

"Oh, sweetie, that was such a long time ago. There were lots of people that night. Too many to remember them all."

"Why did you guys let me drink so much?"

"You're making more of this than it merits. You know what they say, mountains out of mole hills. Don't let it upset you so much. Why don't you go soak in a hot bath? I'm sure you'll feel better afterwards and forget all about it."

"A hot bath. That's a good idea. Maybe it'll help me relax. I have been a bit stressed lately."

"I know you have."

"I think I'll have a glass of wine while I'm soaking," Katy added as a side thought.

A giggle slipped out of Mary as she rebutted, "You might skip the alcohol since it has such an adverse effect on your sense of recall. I'd hate for you to forget who it was that gave you such wonderful advice!"

Even though Mary couldn't see it, Katy frowned and pursed her lips. "Not funny, Mom," she grumbled. Her jovial mood then returned as she added, "I'm gonna go now, but thanks for the suggestion. Love you!"

"We love you too, Katy."

Mary put the receiver down and turned to Frank. Peering over her glasses again, she sighed, "That girl of ours really needs to get out more."

Chapter 8

Katy was preoccupied with thoughts of Rachel that entire week. The moments were fleeting since she didn't know that much about her, but her image kept flashing across her mind nonetheless.

I'll just keep myself busy, she decided. *I've got a bunch of stuff I could be doing: packing, working, moving into my new place. If I focus on those, maybe I won't think about her so much.*

And though her time was consumed with the tasks at hand, the week that followed offered no reprieve. Katy was still not able to get Rachel off her mind for more than a few minutes at a time. It became near impossible to concentrate on anything else as every day was a repeat of the day before. Eventually she came up with a plan on what she should do to remedy her situation.

I'll go see her again. Maybe that'll put my life back on track. This behavior isn't healthy, and it certainly isn't productive.

She telephoned the salon and the same Asian woman she had encountered before answered. After asking her to repeat herself several times, Katy was able to decipher that she was scheduled for the following Saturday at ten o'clock.

On the morning of her appointment she awoke to a strange fluttering sensation in her stomach that felt like kamikaze pilots taking nosedives into the walls of her abdomen. She was apprehensive about seeing Rachel and when she pulled into the parking lot the fluttering intensified and she was convinced she would toss her breakfast. Her gut felt like it was twisting into knots and her throat suddenly became as dry as the Sahara Desert. To top it off, her palms were sweating so much that they left wet spots on her pants when she wiped them to absorb the moisture.

What the hell is wrong with me? Why am I so afraid of this woman? I need to just buck it up and go inside and talk to her.

With a deep breath of resolve, she walked confidently toward the door. When she reached for the handle, however, her sweaty hands caused it to slip out of her grasp.

"Good God!" she exclaimed. "I've got to get a grip!"

The unintentional pun made her giggle and before long she was grabbing at her sides and doubling over, gasping for air as she transitioned from mere chuckling to outright hysteria. The Asian woman witnessed her apparent descent into madness and came rushing outside.

"Wasso funny?" she asked.

The question made Katy laugh harder and every time she looked at the woman, she would start right back up again. When she was finally able to calm herself and catch her breath, she answered, "I'll be all right. I just got tickled, that's all."

"Who tickle you? No one here but you, lady."

And with that, Katy burst into another fit of laughter. Store patrons and employees began to gather, gawking at the crazed woman on the sidewalk. Rachel steered her way through the small crowd and stepped outside where she spotted Katy right away.

"What's going on?" she asked. "Katy, are you all right?"

"Yes," Katy answered. "I'm fine."

Rachel looped their arms together and guided her toward the door. Upon entering the salon, she shot a disgusted look at those gathered around them.

"Show's over," she snapped. Her voice had an angry, rumbly sound to it. "You can all go back to whatever it was you were doing."

After everyone dispersed, her tone softened as she turned to Katy and asked, "What brings you here today?"

"I have an appointment."

"Really? With who?"

"With you."

"It can't be with me. I'm all booked up today."

"You're kidding! Then who's my appointment with?"

"Are you sure you have the right day?"

"I thought so. Your boss is tough to interpret at times."

Rachel leaned over the counter to grab the appointment book. Sliding her pointer finger downward as she scanned the page, she stopped when she saw Katy's name.

"Looks like you're with Martha."

"Well, that sucks," Katy whined. "I came to see you."

"She owes me a favor, so let me ask her if she'll trade."

Rachel went to Martha's station and after a relatively short deliberation returned with her green eyes twinkling and a smile so big that Katy could see nearly every tooth in her head.

"I owe her for this," she told Katy. "She pegged you as a big tipper."

"Whatever gave her that idea? Was it my torn jeans or the ragged-out sneakers? I try hard to hide my vast wealth from those less fortunate, you know."

They shared a laugh before settling into their seats.

"I'm worried this might affect my reputation," Katy added, smirking. "So, I guess I'll just leave a giant tip for you instead."

"I don't want your money," Rachel responded in a low, sultry purr.

"You don't? Well then, what do you want?"

"Your hand."

"My what?"

"Your hand, Katy. Right one first. Don't you remember?"

Rachel offered her a wink and both women smiled.

Chapter 9

Katy felt better after seeing Rachel and when she returned to work was able to put her mind back on her duties. She still had an occasional thought or two, which, thankfully, was a far cry from the all-consuming notions that had preceded them. With teaching and managing the basketball team her time was mostly monopolized with coaching practices or preparing curriculum for her classes anyway. It could be quite a load at times. She had zero time for a personal life, so her trips to the salon were the only social events on her calendar and she looked forward to each visit with great anticipation.

At every appointment she and Rachel would engage in a little more conversation, a little more eye contact and a little more probing into each other's lives. A bond was forming between them as they realized they shared similar passions, like walking hand-in-hand along a moonlit beach while ocean waves gently washed over your feet, standing on the bow of a cruise ship with your arms open wide, or making love until you didn't have enough strength left to get out of bed.

"I think we're kindred," Katy announced one day.

"Kindred," Rachel repeated. "What do you mean?"

"You know, as in kindred spirits. A union of two souls." A wave of embarrassment washed over her as she added in a timid voice, "That's what I think anyway."

"You mean like soul mates?"

"Yeah."

"I never imagined being soul mates with a friend. I thought your soul mate was supposed to be your partner."

"If that's true, then you and George are in for a world of hurt!"

"That's a terrible thing to say, Katy. I love my husband!"

"I'm sorry. I didn't mean any disrespect."

Katy could see the hurt she had caused and thought it best to leave. As she turned to go, Rachel grabbed her by the wrist and pulled her close.

"What you said is true," she admitted, her tone brimming with a range of emotions. "There are times when I feel closer to you than I do with George. Close enough to tell you anything."

Katy was shocked by her announcement. She wanted to give her a hug but thought it might stir the pot more than she had already, so she purposely responded as if it were nothing more than an off-handed remark.

"Is there something you *want* to tell me, Rachel?" she asked jokingly.

Rachel's response was dead serious.

"Oh, Katy. There are lots of things I want to say to you."

Like how miserable I am in my marriage, she confessed in silence. *That would be the first thing I would say. And then I would say that I think I'm falling in love with you but can't bring myself to tell you. Or George. Or my children.*

"Rachel," Katy prodded with a nervous smile. "Go ahead and tell me."

"Not today," Rachel answered in a whisper. "One day, but not today."

Katy decided not to push any further, sensing it would not be appropriate. Instead, she shoved her hand in her pocket and pulled out her car keys.

"I should probably head out now. I've got some more unpacking to do. If you'd like, maybe we could get together sometime before my next appointment."

"You mean somewhere other than a basketball game?"

Katy cocked her head, arched her eyebrows and flashed an impish smile, to which Rachel responded, "I would like that very much."

Unfortunately, the girls' night out never materialized and several weeks passed before Katy found time to return to the salon. Besides work, she was committed to doing things around her house, all of which depleted the little time that was left in her already scant schedule. She did miss seeing Rachel, but her priority was to get situated in her new home first and foremost.

After the basketball season ended, she spent her free time trying to squeeze as much effort into her house as possible before the start of field hockey and track. She took before and after pictures throughout the renovations to show Rachel at various school functions, which was now the only time they saw one another. Rachel was excited about the changes, but more in the opportunity to share in Katy's delight.

Her final project was to dress up the yard with a row of hedges at the front of the house and a line of rose bushes along the back fence. When she mentioned this to Rachel, Rachel volunteered her services and offered up her children as well. Katy was moved by the offer.

"Are you sure your kids will want to do this?" she asked. "My siblings and I hated it when our mom volunteered us for things, especially without our knowledge or consent."

"Of course! Dani is crazy about you! She would jump at the chance to spend more time with you. To her, you're the greatest person alive. And the boys, well, they'll do just about anything for a pizza."

"Pizza, huh? I can manage that. Can you come by on Saturday, say around eight thirty?"

"We'll be there!"

"It's a date then. See you on Saturday!"

A wide smile spread across Katy's face as she turned and walked away. Walking in the opposite direction, her kindred friend was smiling, too.

Chapter 10

After they planted the last of the hedges, the boys toted the broken branches and orphaned leaves to the trash while Katy stood on her porch with her hands squared off on her hips admiring all that they had done.

"It looks beautiful," she announced.

Rachel's sights were also focused on something she considered beautiful – Katy.

"Are we still on for pizza?" Rion asked, interrupting his stepmother's thoughts.

"Rion!" she snapped. "Don't be disrespectful!"

"But, Mom! That's what you told us!"

Katy jumped into the conversation at that point, adding, "You are absolutely right, Rion. That was our deal. I'll go call in the order. What kind of toppings do y'all want?"

"Me and Rion like pepperoni!" Rafael shouted.

"Rion and I," Rachel interjected, realizing after she said it that the grammar lesson was lost on him.

"Pepperoni sucks!" Dani hollered. "Can I have hamburger?"

"No problem," Katy responded. "I'll get one of each. Rachel, what would you like on yours?"

Rachel didn't hear the question as her mind was busy envisioning herself as a chef, strategically and erotically smearing sauce over various parts of Katy's body.

"Rachel?" Katy asked again.

The sound of Katy's voice brought her back to the present. "I'm sorry," she replied, blushing. "I was a million miles away just then. I'm not that picky, so I'll have whatever you're having."

"All righty. Pimiento and anchovies it is!"

"E-e-e-w-w-w-w-w!" the kids chimed in unison.

"Pimiento and anchovies," Rachel jeered. "For real?"

"Just wanted to see if you were listening," Katy answered with a grin.

That started a round of giggles that continued until Rion asked, "We're gonna get more pizza after we plant the rose bushes, right?"

Rachel was flabbergasted by her son's impudence but Katy took it in stride, giving him a thumbs up and telling him, "You bet! I never welch on a deal!"

As she turned to go inside, she saw Rachel tussling his hair.

"Are you crazy?" she heard her say to him. "What happened to my *real* son? The one with manners?"

With the most serious expression on his face, he replied, "He'll come back when the pizza gets here, Mama. Honest!"

Rachel groaned and shook her head. Their interaction caused Katy to smile as she picked up the phone to call in the order.

This feels good, she thought. *Like a real family. If only it were mine…*

She then invited everyone inside to wait for the pizza. Hoping it might get him back in his mother's good graces, Rion passed on the invitation and offered to start digging trenches for the rose bushes instead. He had barely gotten started when the driver arrived. When he saw Katy carrying the boxes into the house, he dropped his shovel and bolted in after her.

"That kid," Rachel muttered as he whizzed by their host. "What's a mother to do?"

"He's just a typical teenage boy," Katy answered. "I think he's adorable."

"Yeah, well don't let him hear you say that."

"Got it. We'll keep that just between the two of us."

Dani, who was standing close enough to overhear, seized the opportunity to shag her older brother. "Hey, Rion!" she yelled. "Coach thinks you're adorable!"

Rachel leaned in close to Katy and whispered, "You're in big trouble now!"

As Rachel's cheek brushed against her own, those pesky butterflies began a new flight pattern in Katy's stomach and she reacted in a way that caught Rachel's attention.

"Is something wrong?" Rachel asked.

"No," Katy answered quickly. "Why do you ask?"

"You have the same look on your face that you had the first time you came to the salon."

"I'm sure it's just hunger pangs. I skipped breakfast this morning."

Katy managed a stiff smile and Rachel gave a curious nod in return. She knew Katy wasn't telling the truth. She also knew there would be no more discussion on the subject, at least for now.

Several hours passed before the second batch of planting produced another round of pizzas. When they finally left Katy's house, Rachel and her children were all very full *and* very happy.

"I like Katy," Rion announced on the ride home.

"Yeah, she's cool," Rafael admitted reluctantly.

"I love her," Dani said. "She's my favorite teacher!"

"She is pretty special," Rachel concurred. Glancing at her reflection in the rearview mirror, she added in silence, *God help me, I love her, too!*

Chapter 11

Katy and Rachel ran into each other at a booster club rally a few nights later and picked up right where they had left off with Katy telling Rachel how much she enjoyed the freedom of living in her own place and adding that she was anxious to have her friends and family over to see what she had accomplished since moving in. Rachel suggested she have a housewarming party, which Katy hemmed and hawed at first but then after some verbal nudging on Rachel's part eventually gave in and agreed to it. Rachel offered to help her plan it and for the next two weeks they spoke almost daily to work out the details. The duration of the calls would oftentimes go from minutes to hours as one or the other would routinely venture off topic to discuss subjects not related to the party. Katy looked forward to their conversations, partly because of her enthusiasm for the party, but more for the sheer enjoyment of hearing Rachel's voice.

"I hope it turns out wonderfully," Rachel announced at the end of one of their calls.

Katy quickly rebutted, "Why would you say that? Aren't you coming?"

"I didn't want to assume that I was invited."

"Of course, you're invited! Silly woman! It wouldn't be a party without you!"

"You know, I only saw the kitchen and restroom when we were there working in your yard. The pictures are amazing, but I'd sure love to see the rest of the house!"

"Oh my gosh! I'm sorry! We were so busy that I forgot to show you around!"

"I'll let you make it up to me. Promise I'll be the first to see the place, okay? After all, I did help spruce it up!"

"You bet. The party starts at seven, so why don't you come by a little earlier and I'll give you a private tour."

"I would love that. I'll see you then. Bye, Katy!"

"Bye, Rachel."

After hanging up, Katy called her mother to let her know about the party. Mary was as enthusiastic hearing about it as Rachel and Katy had been in planning it. Next, she called Nora, Maggie and Beth, who, according to Mary, was already planning to come for a visit around that date, to relay the same information. She then topped off her list with calls to a handful of friends. Hearing the excitement in all of their voices, she had no doubt it was going to be a night to remember.

Rachel, meanwhile, was counting down the hours until she and Katy were reunited. On the day of the party, she showed up just as Katy was finishing sweeping freshly mown grass off of her sidewalk. Katy ushered her into the house and told her to make herself comfortable while she went to take a shower.

"Can I have the tour first?" Rachel pleaded. "If not, I might just get nosy and start poking around. I've seen the pictures so many times that I could probably find things on my own anyway."

"Sure, but we've got to move fast. I've only got about thirty minutes to shower and finish getting everything ready before the others arrive."

Katy poured two glasses of wine and handed one to Rachel before kicking off the tour. Standing on tiptoe, Rachel peered over her shoulder into a small bedroom decorated with southwestern-style furniture. An old, oak rocking chair was situated in a corner with a longhorn skull mounted on the wall behind it. A cowboy lariat was draped over one side of the footboard.

"I got all of this from an estate sale at the Miller farm last month," she boasted. "It's a little masculine, but I like it. Don't you?"

Rachel could smell the sweat on Katy's t-shirt as she stood next to her in the doorway. The dampness had caused it to cling to her torso, outlining her firm breasts. In a moment of unbridled lust, her senses became overwhelmed and she found it tough to concentrate, much less offer an answer to her question.

"Wow," she finally managed to say.

"Are you all right?" Katy asked. "You look a little woozy."

"I'm okay. I think I drank my wine too fast."

Katy grabbed her hand at the same time inquiring, "Do you need to sit down?"

"Really, I'm fine. Please show me more!"

"Okay then. Follow me!"

I'd follow you anywhere, Rachel thought absently. *Anywhere you wanted to take me.*

Katy was still holding her hand as she led her further down the hall past a guest bathroom and into a combination office and exercise room. A computer desk and mated bookshelves abutted the back wall with a small treadmill nearby in front of the window. Katy's sports plaques and trophies were displayed throughout the room.

"I guess this room doesn't need much explaining," she announced facetiously as she let go of Rachel's hand. Rachel nodded in agreement, still much more aware of Katy's physical presence than the décor she was calling out.

The next stop on the tour was the master bedroom, an oversized room with more contemporary furnishings than the first bedroom. Admitting that she copied the floorplan from an advertisement she saw in a magazine, Katy used the excess space to create a small reading area. A chaise lounge was nestled in a corner a few feet from the bed with a blue, velour throw folded neatly over its back. Books by her favorite authors lined the shelves of a small side table beside it, and French prints, all depicting faces of beautiful women, were staggered across the walls surrounding the bed.

Katy mentioned the significance of some of the items as she was pointing them out, but Rachel's mind had taken her somewhere else and she didn't hear a word she said. Her imagination ran wild as it conjured up images of the two of them lying naked together in Katy's bed. It was only when Katy took her hand again and led her to the master bathroom that the fantasy lost its hold on her.

Several candles were burning on the windowsill behind the bathtub, illuminating the small space with their soft, flickering lights and permeating the air with their delicious scent, all of which created an ambiance that only served to reignite Rachel's imagination.

"Now that you've had the tour," Katy said as she turned to face her, "what do you think of the place?"

In response, Rachel dreamily confessed, "I love it."

Katy placed her hand on the small of her back and escorted her to the living room.

"I'm gonna take a shower now. I shouldn't be long. There's booze in the kitchen, so claim your poison and help yourself to another drink if you want."

Rachel watched her disappear then waited until she heard the water running to return to Katy's bedroom, stopping just outside the bathroom doorway. Katy had left the door open and she could see small puffs of steam rising over the shower stall. The candles were the only source of light, creating an erotic silhouette inside the shower chamber. Her passion and curiosity now had full control of her mind and her body and she found herself unable to pull away.

She watched in reverence without regard for getting caught, remaining motionless until Katy shut off the water. She knew that she should escape back to the living room but instead was completely mesmerized, and, effectively, paralyzed. A small gasp escaped her when Katy opened the shower door and reached for a towel.

"Rachel?" Katy called out as she turned in the direction of the sound she had heard. Raising the towel to dry her face, she added, "Is that you?"

"Yes," Rachel replied, her voice barely audible.

"Did you need something?"

I need to tell you how I feel, Rachel confessed in silence. *I need to tell you that I'm falling in love with you, Katy.* But, of course, she didn't respond to her question aloud.

"Rachel?" Katy called out again as she stepped completely out of the shower. This time there was no answer, not even a faint one, for Rachel had already left the room. She wrapped the towel around her body and walked into the main part of her bedroom hoping to find Rachel there, but the room was empty.

She dressed quickly and hurried down the hall, eager to discuss what had just taken place before the other guests arrived. Unfortunately, the doorbell rang when she entered the room and the opportunity was lost. She would have to wait until after the party for an explanation.

Chapter 12

All of Katy's guests were genuinely impressed with her new home. Some brought gifts, mostly towel sets for the bathroom or some type of small appliance for the kitchen. Mary managed to sneak in a flat-screen television without Katy noticing, and Beth, always the wise ass, brought 24 rolls of toilet paper. It was intended as a joke, but Katy, in a hurry as usual, had forgotten to purchase extra rolls. Before night's end, Beth's gift had earned her highest praise.

The party finally came to an end around one o'clock in the morning. It had been a fantastic evening and Katy was elated that her family and friends had all come together to celebrate this major milestone in her life. As they prepared to leave, she gave each one a hug and thanked them for coming. She purposely avoided Rachel until everyone else had preceded her out the door.

They hadn't engaged with one another much over the course of the evening and spent most of their time on opposite sides of whatever room they were in. Katy couldn't help but wonder if she had been intentionally avoiding her. When it was finally down to just the two of them, she whispered in her ear during their embrace, "We need to talk."

"About what?" Rachel responded. But, of course, she already knew.

She felt anxious and afraid of what Katy would say. After all, she'd been caught spying on her. How would she justify her behavior? She decided to let Katy speak first before offering any explanations or excuses.

They shared only a brief glance before Rachel's gaze shifted to the floor. Katy closed the door and moved a step closer. She then cradled Rachel's face in her hands.

"Look at me," she pleaded.

Rachel didn't move. Katy put her fingers under her chin and gently lifted it upward. When their eyes met, it felt to Rachel as if she were looking directly into her soul.

"You were watching me in the shower," Katy said slowly, then added, "Why?"

Rachel shrugged her shoulders like a child being reprimanded by its parent.

"How long were you standing there?"

"Not long," Rachel answered in a voice so hushed that Katy could barely hear her.

"Why were you there?"

Again, Rachel broke eye contact and shrugged her shoulders.

Katy urged, "Please, Rachel. I want to talk about this."

Rachel shook her head rapidly from side to side, muttering, "I can't."

"Why not?"

"How can I talk about something I'm having trouble understanding myself?" The inflection of her tone made it sound more like an apology than a question.

"Just put it out there, Rachel. I'm sure that once you start talking it will all begin to make sense. If not, we can figure it out together."

"Let it go, Katy. Pretend it never happened."

"But it *did* happen."

"It's late," Rachel said, thinking it would deter her from asking any more questions. Reaching around her for the doorknob, she added, "I'm sure my kids are wondering why I'm not home yet. I had a wonderful time tonight, Katy. Thank you for inviting me to your party."

She opened the door and was about to step across the threshold when Katy grabbed her arm just above the elbow and begged her, "Don't go. Please stay and talk to me."

Tears were streaming down Rachel's face as she pulled away and ran crying into the night.

"Rachel!" Katy shouted after her. "Come back!"

She continued calling Rachel's name until her tail lights had disappeared into the darkness. Leaning against the doorjamb, a feeling of emptiness washed over her when she realized she was not going to return. Sad, alone and confused, she went inside and closed the door, slumped onto the sofa and held her head in her hands. When the sun's rays burst through the living room window hours later, she was still in the exact same position.

Chapter 13

The remainder of fall passed quickly and winter came and left without much notice. Basketball hadn't turned out as Katy hoped but spring introduced the start of field hockey and track. Coaching both sports simultaneously kept her busy, which she was thankful for because it kept her mind off of Rachel. At least to some degree.

Dani ran the quarter mile and Katy would often see both of her parents at the track meets sitting high up in the stands. Not that it mattered where they were seated. She made no effort to start a conversation and Rachel didn't either, so no words ever passed between them.

Each time she saw Rachel something stirred inside of her; something forbidden, something mysterious. She figured it best to ignore the feelings and keep things as they'd left them. No sense in dredging up things from the past. What good could come of it? And besides, who needed that kind of aggravation? Certainly not her. She had decided after the housewarming party that she had too much going on to care about such nonsense. There were classes to teach, games to coach, friends to hang out with and a family that loved her. She didn't have time to worry about Rachel or her issues.

One friend in particular who helped Katy keep her mind somewhat detached was Laura Stiles, a new English teacher who had recently moved to Lincoln. They clicked from the start and became instant friends, visiting with each other between classes and sharing an occasional lunch together in the Teacher's lounge.

Katy was drawn to Laura. Not just physically, although she was the most attractive black woman she had ever seen, but to her magnetic charm and biting wit as well. She was extremely smart to boot. Rumor had it that she was also a lesbian. In the first few weeks of getting to know one another the thought crossed Katy's mind that because they were spending so much time together others might think she was a lesbian, too.

Makes perfect sense, she reasoned. *After all, I have a horrible track record with men. And, for a while, I was practically addicted to the mother of one of my players.*

It was then that another thought occurred to her. *Maybe that's why Rachel ran off the night of the party. Maybe she thought I was a lesbian.* She pictured Rachel standing next to her shower and started chuckling to herself. *She was probably looking to see if I had a penis dangling between my legs or hair growing on my chest.*

"Hello-o-o-o-o!" Laura said, breaking into her thoughts. "Earth to Katy! Come in, Katy!"

"Huh?" Katy replied, startled. "What?"

"I've been talking to you for a while now. I thought you were ignoring me but I guess you were daydreaming."

"Sorry. I've had a lot on my mind lately."

"Care to share?"

"Not really."

"No biggie. Say, you wanna get together tonight and go out for a drink? There's a bar I heard about in Kansas City that I've been dying to scope out. Pick you up at seven?"

"Ummm, sure. Sounds great."

Laura took a few steps down the hall then stopped and spun around to add, "You'll have a blast. They say it's our kind of bar."

"What does that mean?" Katy asked, but her question went unanswered as Laura slipped into her classroom.

Our kind of bar? she pondered. *I wonder if that means it's a lesbian bar. I must be giving off some kind of lesbian vibe or something. I'll just have to straighten that out with her later. I can't have her going around thinking I'm that way.*

Laura arrived at Katy's promptly at seven decked out in black, denim jeans and a striped, long-sleeved polo shirt. Katy's green business slacks and matching jacket seemed comparatively overdressed, so she went to her bedroom and reemerged in Dockers and a loose-fitting top.

"Now you look presentable," Laura told her.

"What did I look like before?"

"Stuffy. Stuck up. Elitist. Pick one..."

"Ouch!"

"Sorry. Better that I speak the truth now than have you risk embarrassment later."

"You're right," Katy agreed. "Hey, I asked you this earlier but you ran into your classroom so fast that I guess you didn't hear me. Where exactly are we going tonight?"

"I thought I told you. It's a bar."

"I got that part. What kind of bar is it?"

"It's a women's bar, of course!"

"I had a feeling that's what you meant. I've never been to one of those."

"You're kidding, right?"

"No. The only bar I've ever been to is Crossroads."

"Wow! Have you always lived in that cocoon?"

"Pretty much."

"But you've had women to keep you company in there from time to time, yes?"

"No."

"No shit? Not even one?"

"I'm not a lesbian, Laura."

Laura paused to stare at her new friend and started nodding, shaking her finger at Katy while chuckling, "Yeah, right. You keep telling yourself that, Katy."

"It's the truth. You have the wrong impression of me."

Laura gave her a half-grin before opening the door and stepping past her onto the porch. Katy grabbed her purse and walked out behind her.

"I've never been wrong before," Laura boasted as she started down the sidewalk. When they reached the curb, she climbed into an old Buick LeSabre then leaned across the seat to pull up the handle on the passenger door to unlock it. The look on Katy's face when she latched her seatbelt triggered her to add, "She ain't pretty, but she runs well." She then flashed Katy a wink before making a U-turn to head in the opposite direction.

"Getting back to our previous conversation," she continued as she switched on her blinker to turn off of Oak. "Have you ever wanted to be with a woman?"

"Be with a woman?" Katy repeated. "Uh... not really. Probably not in the way you mean it anyway. I did think about kissing a woman once." As she made that revelation, the image of Rachel's green eyes flashed across her mind.

"And why didn't you?"

"Wasn't meant to be, I suppose."

"Well, tonight may give you another opportunity if you play your cards right."

"I told you, Laura. That isn't who I am."

"My gaydar has never been wrong before, Katy."

"Well, this time your gaydar is ka-flooey. Like I said, I'm not gay."

"Sure, you are. You just haven't owned up to it yet."

They shared small talk for the remainder of the ride. Katy was relieved to be off the subject of lesbianism, at least for the time being, but had no doubt that Laura would be circling back to it at some point.

Chapter 14

The parking lot was packed when they arrived, leaving them a fairly good distance from the building. As they walked up to the entrance, Katy saw a hand-painted sign above the door with a rainbow flag in each corner and bold, multi-colored letters centered across the front proclaiming the name of the bar as "Our Place." Another sign, typed in large font on a sheet of paper and taped conspicuously to the door itself, described the business as a homosexual establishment and identified its clientele as lesbian and/or gay. It advised those who were offended by this to refrain from entering and warned that troublemakers would be "ejected by their private parts, if necessary."

Katy's eyes darted back and forth from one side of the room to the other when they entered the bar, causing her to nearly bump into two women who were locked together in a passionate kiss. The larger, more masculine of the two had the smaller one pressed up against a wall. The sight transfixed her.

She must be trying to keep her from escaping, Katy thought. And even though the remark was mean-spirited, she surprised herself with the afterthought, *Hmmm... Maybe I should've tried that with Rachel.*

Laura grabbed Katy's arm but she didn't flinch. She was still focused on the couple.

"Katy!" she snapped. "Stop staring!"

"Sorry," Katy offered apologetically. "I didn't realize I *was* staring!"

"Well, you were. Look, my friend, gay or not, you can't be gawking at everyone in here. Try to relax. Act like you fit in."

"You make that sound easy," Katy answered sarcastically as they claimed two open barstools and sat down. While waiting for the bartender to take their drink orders, a gruff, mannish woman positioned herself next to Katy. Katy turned to face her and the woman smiled.

"Hello," the stranger said, her voice booming with what sounded like an overdose of testosterone. "Would you like to dance?"

Katy looked at Laura with a panicked expression and mouthed the words, *What do I do?*

Laura grinned and mimed back, *Dance with her!*

As soon as Katy nodded her acceptance, her suitor grabbed her hand and led her to the dance floor.

"Do you two-step?" the woman asked. Her voice was both raspy and harsh.

"Not very well," Katy admitted.

After situating Katy's hand on her shoulder, her dance partner grabbed her other hand and told her, "Just follow my lead."

Katy's first attempt at dancing with another woman was an all-out disaster. When they weren't stepping on each other's feet, their knees were banging into one another. She was convinced that both would be sporting serious bruises the following day.

"Relax," the woman told her midway through the song. Tightening her squeeze on Katy's waist, she added the suggestion "feel the music" to try and help her find her groove.

"I don't feel anything," Katy mumbled, "except idiotic."

"Aw, come on. You're doing fine."

Katy glanced around at other couples and noticed a pair dancing as badly as they were. "Look," she said, nodding in their direction. "We've met our match!"

Her partner giggled and pulled Katy closer. As she did, Katy's body stiffened.

"You're cute," the woman said. "I really like you."

Uh oh, Katy thought as her mind raced to come up with an escape plan. *This can't be good.*

The stranger then added, "I don't think I've ever seen you here before."

"It's my first time."

"First time at a bar? Or first time at this bar?"

"First time at this bar."

"Well then, welcome to the neighborhood! What's your name?"

"Lisa," Katy lied.

"Lisa. That's a pretty name. My name is Cindy."

"Listen, Cindy. I really appreciate you asking me to dance but I suck at this."

"How about a drink instead? Or we could go somewhere else. Somewhere more private."

The thought of going somewhere "private" made Katy queasy.

"I'm here with a friend," she offered to discourage Cindy's advancements. It didn't appear to work, however, because, despite her comment, Cindy took her hand and started leading her toward the front of the bar. Katy was stunned by her actions and pulled away.

"My friend is over there," she said, choosing a random direction to point her finger even though Laura was nowhere in sight. "I'll see you around."

As she hurried to get away from her, Cindy called out, "Save me a dance!"

Katy wandered around the bar until she eventually found Laura with several other women at a pool table near one of the restrooms. Moving up behind her, she poked her in the middle of her back.

"I'm ready to go," she announced.

"Now?" Laura objected.

"Yes," Katy replied sternly. "Now!"

"But we haven't even been here thirty minutes!"

"I don't care, Laura. I'm ready to go."

"But why? Look around at all the women checking you out!"

"I don't want to be checked out. I want to go home."

"All right. Take a breath and calm down. Let me finish my drink and say goodbye to my friends and I'll meet you at the door."

Katy waited under the Exit sign for what seemed to her like an eternity.

"Took you long enough," she snarled as Laura approached. "Did you expect me to stand here all night?"

"You need to chill," Laura grumbled. "It's only been a few minutes. What is up with you tonight?"

"I'm not ready for this," Katy contested in a tone that reflected both frustration and despair. "Can you just take me home?"

"Sure," Laura answered curtly. Her response was void of any emotion or inflection. She then looked into Katy's eyes and her tone quickly softened. "I'm sorry, Katy. I didn't realize you were having such a lousy time."

They walked to her car without saying anything more and remained silent for the entire drive back to Lincoln. After pulling to a stop in front of Katy's house, Laura shut off the engine and stared at the side of Katy's face for several seconds before speaking.

"What got you so upset tonight?" she asked.

"Nothing," Katy muttered softly.

"If it was nothing then why did you want to leave?"

"I told you, Laura. I'm not ready."

"Ready for what?"

Katy didn't answer, so Laura followed her up the sidewalk and waited on the stoop while she unlocked the door.

"Do you want me to come in?" she asked.

Again, Katy remained mute.

"Look, Katy. I don't know what's bugging you, but if you want me to come in you need to say it."

"Come in or go home, Laura. It really doesn't matter."

"It matters to me. I want to know what's bothering you."

Katy walked inside and tossed her keys on the coffee table before sitting down on the sofa. Laura eased in beside her and it was then that Katy finally confided, "I realized something tonight."

"What was that?"

"The very first thing I saw when we walked into that bar was those two women kissing. It looked... I don't know... Natural. Know what I mean?"

Laura nodded.

"I thought it would freak me out but it didn't. I couldn't look away."

"I noticed."

Katy sneered at her before continuing.

"I'd never seen two women kiss and it made me think of Rachel."

"Rachel? Is that the woman you were referring to earlier?"

"Leave her out of this, Laura."

"But, Katy," Laura laughed, "you just brought her up."

"This isn't about her. It's about me."

"Okay, so did something happen tonight?"

"Cruella DeVille happened. All that writhing and such. It made me uncomfortable. She reminded me of Mike, the last man I was involved with. I wasn't sure how to get away from her and you were nowhere in sight!"

"Sorry. I thought you could handle yourself."

"My first time? Come on, Laura!"

"You're right. I apologize. Will you forgive me?"

She brushed away a tear from Katy's cheek with her thumb then scooted closer and draped her arm around her shoulder.

"Please don't cry," she murmured. "I only wanted you to have a good time. I never imagined it would turn out so badly."

Her hand slid down to stroke Katy's back as she added, "I should have never left you alone tonight. What can I do to make it up to you?"

She waited for an answer but none came.

"Katy," Laura said, this time with greater urgency. "Tell me what to do! Please!"

"Kiss me," Katy whispered.

Laura immediately backed away from her. "I don't think that's a good idea."

"But I thought you liked me!"

"I do like you, very much."

Katy leaned in and kissed her squarely on the mouth. Laura found she had little strength to resist and the kiss deepened.

"Please," Katy moaned. "Make love to me."

Laura scooted even further away.

"It's not that I don't want to, Katy, but it's your first time with a woman, and, well, what about this Rachel?"

Katy tried kissing her again but Laura put up her hand to block her.

"Don't be angry," she said. "I can't. Not like this."

Katy glared at her. Her eyes were red from crying.

"Don't be angry?" she echoed. "Fuck you, Laura!" She then stood up and marched to the door and held it open to facilitate Laura's exit. "You should go," she demanded.

"Fine," Laura responded, not entirely certain what was happening but knowing for sure that Katy was serious. "Can I call you tomorrow?"

"Don't bother."

"All right then. I guess I'll see you at school on Monday."

Laura frowned as she moved past her onto the porch.

"Katy," she said, turning around. "I don't want to lose…"

Katy slammed the door in her face before she could finish and then walked to the kitchen, poured herself a glass of wine and carried it to the bedroom. She decided to take a shower, convinced that the water would wash away the effects of the evening: the very essence of Cruella, the two women kissing, the confusion she was feeling. Down the drain it would go. All of it.

She sipped her drink while waiting for the water to heat up and the more she drank the more the alcohol penetrated her mood, allowing her to release some of the stress that had built up over the past few hours. The wine and the shower both had a calming effect and after drying off she felt relaxed enough to climb into bed and go to sleep.

Dreams invaded her subconscious shortly after she dozed off and transported her back to the night of the housewarming party, to the very moment Rachel had been eyeing her in the shower.

What was she looking for? What did she see? What did she want to see?

Chapter 15

Sometime that morning, she wasn't exactly sure when, Katy's phone rang and her illusions were vanquished; however, the spells that they cast rendered her immobile. She continued to stare at the ringing phone on her bedside table but was unable to pick it up. After the fourth ring, the answering machine intercepted for her. Eventually, she emerged from her daze to see who it was that called.

The message started with, "Hello?" and then, "Katy? Are you there?"

After a brief pause, the voice on the line identified itself.

"It's Laura."

Instead of letting it finish, Katy dialed Laura's number so they could speak directly.

"Hey, did I wake you?" Laura asked.

"No problem. I'm sure I needed to get up anyway."

"Can we meet somewhere? We need to talk about last night."

Katy couldn't refute her request. She knew she owed her an explanation.

Not waiting for Katy's response, Laura added, "How about the donut shop?"

"That's fine. I can be there in half an hour or so."

"Thanks, Katy. I'll see you there."

Katy walked to the bathroom and glanced at her reflection in the mirror. Using her fingers, she brushed all the rogue hair spikes back into place.

"Aren't you a sight," she snarled at the image staring back at her.

After splashing water on her face, she brushed her teeth then shuffled over to her closet. She didn't feel pretty and it made no sense to dress up her body when she was in such a lousy mood, so she went to her dresser instead and picked a pair of sweatpants and a t-shirt as her outfit for the day.

Just before heading out the door, she grabbed a lightweight jacket and her purse. The clock on her dashboard said she would be late but she didn't care. She was amazed that she had agreed to go at all. It would have been much easier to stay in bed and pretend the previous night had never taken place.

Laura pulled into the parking lot just ahead of her. They walked into the restaurant together and were greeted by a plump, dark-haired woman who escorted them to a booth. From her seat, Katy was able to see all the way out to the street. There wasn't much traffic, just a few kids on rollerblades and skateboards occasionally whizzing by.

"I wanted to…" both women said simultaneously.

"You go first," Laura urged.

"No, you go first," Katy argued.

"Okay. I wanted to say this last night but you cut me off."

Katy's eyes were locked on her as she continued.

"When you shut the door on me, I waited on the porch for a while to see if you were going to ask me to come back inside. You didn't, so I got pissed and left. I'm glad I did. I think I probably would have said something I would have regretted."

"Laura…"

"Let me finish."

Katy motioned for her to go on.

"The more I tried to process what happened the more confused I became. I tossed and turned all night. I don't want our friendship to be over, Katy. I like you too much. I never thought about being with you – not like that anyway – and I needed time to consider how I felt about all of this.

"I decided I would like to date you but I want to get to know you better before we, you know… You should also know that I won't be a fill-in for Rachel. If we're going to be together, I want to be the only woman in your life."

She cleared her throat and swallowed hard before making her final statement.

"That's all I wanted to say. It's your turn now."

Katy responded post haste, starting with, "There was something you said before we left my house. That whole gaydar thing set me off. It made me furious."

"Why did that upset you?"

"Because you figured it out before I did."

"Figured what out?"

"That I'm gay."

"I was only trying to let you know it was okay to be yourself around me. Sorry for blurting it out like that."

"I'm the one who needs to apologize. I was a total jerk last night. I was frustrated and you were in my line of fire. Before we left the bar, it felt like my whole world was being turned upside down. And, by the time we got to my house, everything I knew about myself stopped making sense. But then I thought about the trouble I've had with men, my tomboy ways, Rachel... Everything. And you were right. I am gay."

Laura nodded as she continued.

"I was angry that my first time 'out' was with that creep at the bar. I deserve better than that. If you had been the first woman I danced with, maybe I wouldn't have freaked out like that. I don't know. I guess it doesn't matter much now.

"The one thing I do know is that I want to be loved. I mean, we all want that, right? But you need to know the truth. I really like you, but it's obvious that my feelings are tied to someone else. I don't want them to be, but I can't help it.

"I know that Rachel and I will never be together. That being said, I would like to experience love with someone who cares about me. I know that's not really fair, probably for either of us, but I'd like to give it a shot. Think you could handle that?"

"Wow," Laura said, reaching across the table to touch her hand. "That's a lot of honesty to take in all at once."

"Take all the time you need. I'm not going anywhere."

The waitress's arrival drew them away from the emotionally charged conversation. To the relief of both, they didn't return to it. After parting, Katy got into her car and pulled her cell phone out of her purse. She tapped her thumbs on the cover for several seconds before dialing. Mary answered right away.

"Mom," she said. "We need to talk."

"Is something wrong, dear?"

"There are things I need to tell you before you hear them from someone else."

Mary grabbed a small patch of hair from the back of her neck and started twirling it between her fingers. "You're making me nervous, Katherine," she said. "Are you sure everything's all right?"

"Everything is fine. Can we get together later?"

"All right. Should I bring your father?"

"No, let's meet alone. Once we've talked, we can decide how and when to tell Dad."

"I don't like the sound of this, Katy."

"I know, Mom. Just meet me at Crossroads at seven."

"But…"

"Please, Mom. I don't want to get into this over the phone."

"All right. I'll see you at seven."

Katy spent the remainder of the afternoon rehearsing what she wanted to say to her mother. After trying out several different scripted versions, she came to realize that it would be best to just let the conversation develop naturally.

Mary, on the other hand, spent the rest of her afternoon in a panic wondering what sort of trouble her daughter had gotten herself into. Her thoughts continually led her to the same conclusion: Katy must be pregnant.

Chapter 16

Katy entered Crossroads with a heavy heart. She didn't want to hurt her mother, which she suspected she would, but she knew she had to tell her what was going on in her life. She deserved to know the truth and to hear that truth from Katy.

Mary's face was solemn as she joined her at her table.

"Thanks for coming," Katy told her.

"Tell me what's going on," Mary demanded. "Are you sick?"

"No, Mom. I'm not sick."

"Pregnant?"

"What!?!" Katy laughed, glad for the comic relief her mother was unknowingly supplying. "Whatever gave you that idea?"

"I don't know, Katy. I've been thinking about this all day and it's the only thing I could come up with."

"I'm not pregnant. I wish it were that simple. It might be easier for you to hear."

"You're scaring me, honey."

Katy took a deep breath and exhaled slowly. She then took a drink of water and laced her fingers together on the table in front of her.

"I love you very much, Mom, and I know that you love me. I just hope that you'll still love me once you hear what I have to say."

"Oh, Katy, don't be silly. I'll always love you."

"Please. I need to get this out."

Mary folded her hands in her lap. Her heart was pounding.

"I'm sorry," she said. "Go ahead, sweetheart."

"Not long ago, I discovered that I had feelings for a woman. These feelings go much deeper than just friendship. I've tried to ignore them, tried to forget about them, tried to push them aside."

Mary's face was a portrait of confusion. She started to say something but Katy held her hand up in stop-sign fashion and accelerated her speech. "I came to realize that I've been repressing my true orientation. I've always been different from other girls but never knew why. Now I do. I'm a lesbian, and I need you to be okay with that."

Mary rose from her chair and stood on tiptoe, her tiny body leaning across the table until her face was within inches of Katy's.

"You listen to me, Katherine Hopkins," she snarled. "You are not *that* way. You have allowed someone to come into your life and try to convince you of something that just isn't true."

"Mom, please sit down. You're making a scene."

Mary slowly returned to her seat. Her blue eyes turned to ice as she stared into the face of her youngest child.

"I'm your mother," she said matter-of-factly. "I raised you, Katy. I would've known if you were a lesbian."

"How could you have known? I didn't even know myself until recently."

"And when did this epiphany take place?"

"Last night. I went out with a friend and…"

"Last night? Oh, Katy. You need more time than that to…"

"No, I don't, Mom. Laura helped me realize…"

"Laura? Is she your new *friend*?"

With the inflection of her tone, the word "friend" came off sounding like an insult to Katy. Or maybe that was her intention all along.

"Yes, Laura is my friend."

"Are you having sexual relations with this woman?"

Katy was taken aback by the directness of the question but answered it anyway.

"No. We haven't even dated yet. I wanted to tell you first."

"If you're looking for my blessing, that isn't going to happen. That *lifestyle* goes against everything I was taught to believe."

Katy shook her head slowly from side to side as she realized Mary had purposely emphasized the word "lifestyle" with the same disdain she had used on the word "friend."

"I know what you believe, Mother. No one is asking you to live this way. It's my life. I just wanted to know if you'll still be a part of it."

"I need to think about this, Katy."

"I respect that. I won't pressure you. I hope that you'll come to accept this in time. You are my mother *and* my best friend and I can't imagine my life without you in it. Understand, though, you're not going to change me. Good or bad, right or wrong, this is who I am."

Mary stood to leave. Katy rose from her seat and walked around to be on the same side of the table. As she leaned in to kiss her mother on the cheek, she whispered to her, "I love you, Mom."

Chapter 17

The month of May whizzed by, bringing with it the end of the school year. Katy and Laura were looking forward to the summer break as it would allow them opportunities to spend time together away from the constraints and confines of their lives on campus.

Katy loved the summers. There were always free concerts in front of the library and more times than not you'd find her sitting on her old, raggedy blanket underneath the elm tree. She planned to spread that blanket out again, only this time with Laura by her side.

Summer nights in Lincoln were beyond beautiful with stars filling the sky as far as the eye could see. Katy loved it here and couldn't imagine ever leaving the town that had given her life, given her purpose, and now, given her a chance at real love.

She felt different since coming out to her mother. Purged, in a sense, of the weight she bore in being someone she wasn't meant to be. Her overall mood changed, too. She was happier than she'd ever remembered. Things didn't bother her the way they used to. The world was genuinely a better place to be.

By her own admission, Katy let others influence her choices in the past and made some decisions simply because they aligned with what everyone else thought she should do. It wasn't necessary to control her surroundings anymore or to keep things on an even keel and behave in ways they expected of her. She felt more confident than ever and when she looked in the mirror, she was content with the reflection looking back. But she wasn't naïve. She knew there would be obstacles, personal and professional, for her and Laura to overcome in order to be happy.

They decided to wait until the school year ended before dating. Between finals and graduation rehearsals they barely had time for each other anyway, so they spent what free time they could manage talking on the phone and trying to learn more about one another. Unfortunately, each conversation only proved how little they had in common. Katy loved the beach; Laura preferred the mountains. Katy was crazy about live theater; Laura was just as nuts over Roller Derby.

During one conversation, Laura admitted that if she didn't have to work, she would spend every waking moment playing golf. Katy loathed the sport. Katy, on the other hand, liked to work in the yard cultivating her own efforts. Laura hated getting her hands dirty and owned up to the fact that she hired contractors for every project outside of her four walls. She admitted they did most of the work on the inside as well, which was justified because it freed her up for more time on the fairway.

There was also a considerable age gap between them. Laura was nearly twelve years older and preferred things that Katy likened more to her mother's choosing. Despite their dissimilarities, they pledged to find a common ground and to explore new passions that would be of interest to both.

What did work in their favor was chemistry. Seeing each other every day at school, it was all they could do to keep their hands to themselves. Once, they gave into temptation and hid in one of the lavatory stalls, making out until the bell signaled their return to class. They had agreed from the start that they would date for at least a month before becoming intimate, a vow that became harder to honor as each day passed.

The first time Katy invited Laura to stay over, both women were ready and anxious to take the relationship to the next level. When Laura arrived, they exchanged smiles and shared a warm embrace at Katy's front door.

"I brought wine," Laura said as she trailed Katy into the kitchen.

"I love wine!" Katy squealed.

"I do, too. But only white, the red stuff is too bitter."

"I agree."

"Wow! See? We have something else in common!"

"Yep, we're racking 'em up," Katy offered jokingly.

Turning to face Laura, she looped her arms around her neck. "And I'm hoping we'll find more things in common in the bedroom tonight."

"Why, Katy Hopkins! Are you planning to take advantage of me this evening?"

"With any luck."

"You have a one-track mind."

"And you don't?"

"No, but ask me after I've had a glass of wine. I get sorta snuggly when I drink."

"You mean horny?" Katy inquired with a devilish grin.

"Not horny, sensual."

"Isn't that the same thing?"

"Men are horny, women are sensual. There's a difference."

"I've so much to learn."

"And who better to learn from than a teacher!"

"Well then, let's not waste any time getting started on my lessons. I'll grab some glasses for the wine. Go ahead and take your bag to the bedroom. It's the last door at the end of the hall."

"Why don't you show me around first? You know, give me my own private tour."

Katy's arm froze in mid-air, the glasses she retrieved from the cabinet now clinking together loudly in her outstretched hand. Laura witnessed her reaction and asked, "What happened? Did I say something wrong?"

"No," Katy responded hastily to reassure her that everything was okay. Deep down, however, she knew it wasn't okay. When Laura said the words "private tour," she instantly thought of Rachel on the night of the housewarming party.

Get out of my head, Rachel! she thought angrily. *And stay in the past where you belong! Don't blow this for me!*

Laura, of course, was oblivious to the drama unfolding in Katy's mind. She thought Katy simply needed help with the glasses, so she took them from her and set them on the counter. She then reached into her backpack to retrieve a corkscrew and plunged its spiral tip into the wine bottle. The popping sound of the cork brought Katy back to the moment, forcing Rachel back into the layer of awareness just below the surface of her conscious thoughts.

"Always be prepared," Laura announced. "That's what I learned in Girl Scouts."

"I'm sorry," Katy responded. "What were you saying?"

"A corkscrew. I carry one in my bag."

"Impressive."

"Yeah, I learned it in Girl Scouts."

"To carry a corkscrew? We never learned stuff like that in my troop. We only got to pitch a tent and make a campfire and cook chili in a cast iron pot."

Laura giggled, her brown eyes catching the reflections from the overhead lights.

"They didn't teach us to carry corkscrews," she answered with a smirk on her face. "They taught us to be prepared."

"I see. So, what else do you have in that bag?"

"Secret things. And if you're nice, I just might share them with you later."

Katy filled both glasses half full then dipped her finger into one of them and spread the liquid over her lips. She dipped into the glass once more and glossed her moist finger over Laura's lips as well.

"Oh, I can be very nice," she whispered seductively.

Holding both glasses in one hand, she grabbed Laura's hand with the other to lead her out of the kitchen. Laura snatched her backpack on the way out and followed her down the hall. Inside the bedroom, Katy set the glasses on the nightstand then lowered herself onto the bed and patted the empty spot beside her. Laura flung her bag onto the floor and sidled up next to her.

"You might not believe this," she confessed, "but I'm a bundle of nerves right now."

"I'm not nervous at all," Katy boasted. "Excited, for sure, but not nervous."

She then lifted Laura's hand and placed it over her sternum.

"Feel my heart," she said. "It's about to pound right out of my chest!"

With her hand still on Katy's chest, Laura gently lowered her onto the mattress and straddled herself over her waist. Bringing her face closer to Katy's, she whispered to her, "Do you have any idea how crazy I am about you?"

"Show me," Katy purred in response.

Laura nuzzled Katy's ear then moved to kiss the side of her neck. Katy turned her head to the side, exposing her flesh to her lover's soft lips.

"Oh, Rachel," she moaned. "I've wanted this for so long!"

Laura raised herself up and an expression of shock quickly spread over her face.

"What did you say?" she asked, her tone brimming with anger. Without waiting for Katy's answer, she immediately followed with, "You called me Rachel."

"I did? I'm so sorry!"

"It's obvious your feelings for her haven't changed."

"That's not true. My feelings have changed. I don't care about Rachel anymore. I only care about you."

"I don't believe you."

"It's the truth!"

Laura left the bed and slung her backpack over her shoulder.

"I need to go."

"Please don't leave. I promise it will never happen again."

"I need some air. I can't breathe."

Laura left the room and the next thing Katy heard was the slamming of her front door followed by the roar of Laura's engine and the sound of screeching tires. A deafening silence followed. Grabbing a pillow, she pressed it against her face in an attempt to muffle the sounds of her despair as she screamed into it, "Damn you, Rachel!"

Chapter 18

Katy was consumed with a mixture of rage and angst for several days that followed. Her only solace was that it was summer, meaning she was free to go somewhere and leave it all behind. And that's exactly what she decided to do – run away to a place she could bury her head in the sand and mourn over what might have been.

But where should I go? she wondered. *Beth and Ben live in New York. They would surely take me in. Or maybe Mason and Emma would let me stay at their ranch in Texas.*

While either would provide safe distance from the mess she'd made in Lincoln, she ultimately chose Dallas. After a brief chat with Mason, she retrieved a large suitcase from her closet and packed enough clothes to last for an extended stay. She made another call afterwards and when her father answered she asked to speak with Mary right away.

"I'm leaving town for a while," she told her mother.

Silence persisted, so she continued, "I just need to clear my head."

Several seconds passed before Mary responded, "And you don't think you can do that here in Lincoln?"

"No," Katy mumbled softly.

Mary knew something must have gone terribly wrong for Katy to just up and leave. Perhaps the relationship with her new *friend* wasn't going so well. While she had secretly hoped it would fail, she would have never expressed that to Katy.

Although she was desperate to know the reasons behind her daughter's decision to leave, she knew better than to pressure her for details. Katy would talk when she was ready and not a moment sooner. She was as stubborn as a mule and forcing her to do something she didn't want to do was a big waste of energy. She decided it would be best to just wait her out.

As the night hours crept by, Katy, impatient for morning to arrive, opened her eyes at least once every hour to look at the clock. When the time to rise did finally come, it felt as if she hadn't slept in a million years. The past few days had taken their toll and she was exhausted.

Despite their recent tensions, Mary agreed to take her to the airport. This fact alone reassured both of them on a certain level, but the ride was a quiet one with Katy spending most of it staring at her hands. Truth be told, she wanted to talk but didn't know what to say or how to say it. Her emotions were erratic, bouncing her back and forth from one low place to another. Mary was experiencing similar turmoil, but when she saw the tears in Katy's eyes as she entered the terminal, she knew her own pain paled in comparison.

Katy checked her bag and passed through the security checkpoint then handed an agent her boarding pass and squeezed into a seat between two very large men. Knowing it was going to be a cramped flight, she grabbed a magazine before buckling in then tucked her arms against her sides as tightly as possible. She lowered her head and started to read the first article but fell asleep before finishing the story.

She was awakened with a jolt two and a half hours later as the plane came in contact with the runway. Her mouth had apparently been hanging open for quite some time as evidenced by the drool that had spilled over onto her chin. Her seat mates were snoring loudly; their bodies pressed snugly against hers. Since her arms were still pinned to her sides, she rubbed her chin across her shoulder to sop up the spittle.

She deplaned quickly and collected her bag from the carousel, wheeling it outside where Mason was waiting for her at the curb. He tossed it into the back of his pickup and gave her a big squeeze.

"Hey, sis," he said, grinning.

"Hi, Mason. Thanks for letting me come."

"Honestly, I thought this day would never happen – Katy Hopkins leaving Lincoln voluntarily."

"Yeah, well, things change. People change. I've changed."

"Sounds serious. It's a couple hours from here to the ranch, so I'll get a six-pack for the ride home and you can spill your guts if you want."

"There really isn't much to say, Mason."

"Come on, Katy. We haven't seen or really spoken to each other since your birthday last year. I'm sure lots of things have happened since then."

He pulled into a drive-thru beer barn a few miles from the airport, handed a twenty to the clerk and told him to keep the change then lifted a bottle from the carton and tossed it to Katy.

"Start talking," he said.

And so, she did, eventually telling him everything over the span of two hours and three beers.

Mason took the announcement that his sister was a lesbian without much reaction. What he was shocked to hear was that their mother had given her such a hard time about it. When they arrived at his house, he retrieved her suitcase and rolled it up to the porch. Instead of taking Katy inside, he motioned for her to have a seat in one of the chairs.

"Let's hang out here for a while," he told her. "The sun will be going down soon and I can't wait for you to see it. It's beautiful."

Emma, who had seen them coming up the driveway, joined them on the porch with a tray of drinks.

"Iced tea, anyone?" she asked.

"We've already had beer," Katy answered.

"Is that a 'no' for tea then?"

"I'd love some tea," Mason responded. Giving his wife a peck on the cheek, he lifted the tray from her hands and placed it on a small, wicker table.

"Care to join us?" he asked her. "We're going to sit here and ride out the sunset."

Katy glared at him while exclaiming, "Good Lord! You talk like some hokie cowboy from an old Western!"

Both women giggled at her remark. Mason, unphased by the comment, grabbed a glass of tea and lowered himself onto a swing that had been bolted to the ceiling. Emma sat down next to him.

"Mind if I tell her?" he asked Katy.

"Go ahead," she agreed. "She'll find out sooner or later anyway."

Mason relayed a condensed version of the story Katy had shared with him. Just as he had, Emma showed little reaction in hearing the news. Katy was perturbed by that and blurted out, "Doesn't this come as a surprise to anyone?"

"I think I always knew," Mason responded. "You were quite the tomboy, more so than any of the other girls in town."

"How old was I when you first thought I was gay?"

"Hmmm. Let me think about that for a minute."

He paused long enough to recall a specific memory before continuing.

"I remember now. It was at one of your birthday parties. You were probably around six or so and Tommy Levinson tried to give you a kiss. You nearly beat the crap out of him then walked straight up to Charese Noble and planted one right on her lips. Can't say that I blamed you. She was an absolute cutie pie!"

"Mason!" Emma snapped, chastising her husband for his uncouth response.

"Well, it's true," he answered in his defense. "I'd have kissed her myself if she were five years older."

"I don't remember that," Katy challenged. "Were there any other times?"

"I was pretty busy back then with sports and stuff and didn't hang around the house much. Jason might be able to tell you more. He used to comment on how close you were to some of the girls on your softball team."

"He knows, too?" Katy shrieked.

"We all suspected it. Me, Jason and Beth. We've talked about it over the years."

"What about Mom? Did she ever say anything?"

"No. I don't think she knew."

"And Dad?"

"Dad?" Mason laughed heartily. "He doesn't even know what being 'gay' means."

"Yeah, you're probably right."

"I sure hope your mom comes around," Emma said softly, as if her inner thoughts were being transformed into words.

"Yeah," Katy muttered through a loud sigh. "That would be nice."

"She loves you, Katy," Mason offered. "Give her some time to process this."

Chapter 19

Katy spent the first two days in Texas sitting on the swing and staring into the open plains that stretched out for miles past the ranch. Emma managed to convince her to go horseback riding on the third day and Katy agreed, reluctant at first but seeming to enjoy herself more as the day progressed. After the horses were put away, however, she returned to the swing. Emma worried that she might be closing herself off and shared her concerns with Mason.

"You need to talk to your sister," she told him.

"Why? What's going on?"

"She doesn't want to do anything but sit on the porch all day. The only time she gets up is when she's hungry or thirsty or has to go to the bathroom."

"She's got a lot going on right now, Emma. Maybe we should just leave her alone."

"Or maybe we should take her out for a little fun. Help get her mind off all that crap she's dealing with."

"What'cha got in mind?"

"Let's throw some steaks on the grill and then go to Gilly's later for drinks. That band we like is playing tonight. Maybe she'll meet someone."

"There aren't any lesbians there that I know of," Mason said, rubbing his chin.

"Dear," Emma answered mockingly, "you wouldn't know a lesbian if she walked up and introduced herself to you."

"You're right. I'll see if she wants to ride into town with me to pick out some steaks."

"I'll wait about twenty minutes and fire up the grill."

"That's my girl!"

Pulling her close, he wrapped his arms around her waist and kissed her on the lips then slid his hands down to her butt and gave it a firm squeeze.

She pinched him on the cheek and reminded him, "The store, Mason."

He gave her a wink as he backed away from her.

"All right," he chuckled. "I'm going."

Emma heard him speaking with Katy, followed by the rumble of the truck's engine firing up in the driveway. When enough time had passed, she went out to the back porch and emptied a bag of charcoal into the grill then tossed in a lit match and went back inside. From the refrigerator she took out three large potatoes along with ingredients to make a dinner salad. She wrapped the potatoes in foil and placed them on an upper rack on the grill to keep them from overcooking then tossed the ingredients together for the salad.

Half an hour later, the siblings returned with three humongous slabs of meat. Katy couldn't help but smile when she saw the shocked expression on her sister-in-law's face.

"You were supposed to buy steaks," Emma chided. "Not the whole cow!"

"I tried to tell him," Katy agreed. "But you know my brother. He never listens."

Emma started a pot of water to brew a fresh pitcher of tea while Mason seasoned the steaks and carried them to the grill. Their two black labs, Mutt and Harley, were tight on his heels the entire way. Both tilted their heads to one side as they watched the flames leap high into the air when he laid the meat over the open fire. A short while later, the trio was seated around the table feasting on their bounty. At one point, Mason shoved a large forkful of meat into his mouth and told Katy between chews, "We're going into town later."

"There's a great band at Gilly's tonight," Emma included to further entice her. "We always have a good time there. Would you like to come along?"

"I don't know," Katy grumbled. "I'm kinda tired."

"Come with us, Katy. Please?"

"We won't stay out too late," Mason added. "You should go with us. It'll be fun."

Katy looked at him and then at Emma. She could tell by their expressions that they were anxious for her to come along.

"Fine," she answered sullenly. "Are we going to change first?"

"I'm not," he responded. "I'm smoking hot already."

Katy saw Emma roll her eyes and shake her head.

"I'm glad you two are related," she confided to Katy. "Otherwise, I'd be apologizing right about now."

Mason belched and patted his stomach to indicate that he was full. Emma looked at Katy and rolled her eyes again. With the meal now finished, they all pitched in to clear the table. After the dishes were put away, the women disappeared to get dressed for their big night on the town.

Chapter 20

Some patrons at the bar were engaged in a spirited line dance when they arrived, content with entertaining themselves with songs from the bar's playlist until it was time for the band to take the stage. Emma hurried out to join them and immediately fell in step with the others. She was an amazing dancer, no doubt attributed to her many years as a professional cheerleader. Mason followed her but stopped short of the dance floor, opting to watch instead.

Katy thought the steps all looked simple enough for her to join in as well but then remembered her dancing fiasco at the lesbian bar and decided to let the "boot scooters," as Mason called them, continue without her. She walked to the bar to get a drink, all the while watching her sister-in-law draw the attention of everyone on the dance floor and most everyone else in the bar as well. Not long after, a woman in tight-fitting jeans came to stand beside her.

"Hey, barkeep!" the woman called out. "Can I get a longneck?"

"Coors or Bud?" he asked in response.

The woman looked at Katy and smiled before answering, "Surprise me."

The bartender reached under the counter and lifted a beer from the cooler then twisted off the cap and set it on the bar in front of Katy.

"Thanks," Katy told him. "But I didn't order this."

"He knows," the woman commented as she reached in front of her to claim it.

Katy looked into the stranger's violet blue eyes and felt an immediate attraction to her. The woman took a long drink before speaking again.

"He does that when I'm standing next to a beautiful woman," she said with a wink. "I think it gives him a boner."

When she smiled a second time, Katy remained silent, transfixed by her dark eyes. The woman mistakenly took her non-response as a sign that she had offended her.

"Sorry if what I said bothered you," she offered as reconciliation. "I'm pretty direct and typically say the first thing that pops into my head."

Her arm brushed against Katy's as she set the bottle down and Katy suddenly found it impossible to form words. She wouldn't reclaim that ability until sometime much later that evening.

"Hey!" Mason shouted as he jumped on the stool next to her. "Who's your friend?"

"The name's Paula," the woman answered, extending her hand in his direction.

Katy could feel her arm rubbing against the small of her back as they shook hands.

"Mason," Katy's brother announced to introduce himself. He then asked Paula, "Do we know one another? You look familiar."

"I have a gallery in the Arts District."

"Off McKinney and Lemmon?"

"Yeah. That's my studio."

Before Mason could say anything more, Emma squeezed in between him and Katy.

"Dance with me," she pleaded as she tugged on Katy's sleeve.

Katy resisted but that didn't deter her. Ignoring her protests, Emma drug her away from the bar. Once they were gone, Paula hopped onto Katy's stool.

"My wife and I were at your gallery last month," Mason said, continuing as though their conversation had never been interrupted. "You've got some cool stuff in there."

"Thanks!"

"How long have you been in Dallas?"

"Seven years? Maybe eight? I've lost track."

"What brought you to this area?"

"I needed to get away from my ex."

"Oh. I'm sorry things didn't work out between you."

"No need. I've moved on and so has she."

"She?"

"Yeah, man. I'm gay."

"For real? So is my sister."

"Is that the chick that was sitting next to me?"

Mason laughed before responding, "Yes, but don't call her 'chick.' At least not to her face. She's a bit of a feminist."

"She's a real looker."

"You think?"

"Definitely. The one that came and asked her to dance – was that her girlfriend?"

"No, that's my wife."

"Lucky you. She's bad ass, too."

Mason stiffened a little, both put off by her remark but flattered by it nonetheless.

"Knowing my sister as I do," he said, "she won't be gone long. Want me to introduce you when she comes back?"

"Nah, I got it from here. Thanks, Mac."

"The name's Mason," he reminded her. "Not Mac."

Paula ignored his correction and he instantly felt an uncomfortable chill fill the air between them. He tried to dismiss it as a simple case of paranoia that sometimes happens in first encounters, but he couldn't shake the feeling that something about her wasn't quite right.

Mason was standing with his back against the bar when the girls returned. Emma caught him eyeing the stranger next to him and a twinge of jealousy stabbed at her heart.

"I'm Emma, Mason's wife," she declared as she wedged herself between them. Her eyes were locked with Paula's as she spoke.

"Nice to meet you," Paula replied.

"This is Paula," Mason announced. "She owns that gallery that you like so much." He then turned to Katy and added, "And she's a lesbian."

Emma raised one eyebrow high above the other before grabbing Katy's shirttail to reel her in. "A lesbian," she echoed as she continued steering Katy in Paula's direction. When they were less than a foot apart, she put her hands on Katy's shoulders and spun her around to face her. "Have you met my sister-in-law?" she blurted while gripping Katy's belt loops to maneuver her even closer.

"I'll bet you figured out that I'm the sister-in-law," Katy muttered as she was being manhandled into place.

The blush of embarrassment turned her cheeks bright crimson as she looked away, pretending to find fascination in the color of her own shoes and the littered debris on the barroom floor that surrounded them.

"Do you live in Dallas, too?" Paula asked her.

"No," Katy said, lifting her head only slightly to respond. "I'm just visiting."

"Let's leave these two to get acquainted," Emma suggested to Mason. "The band is about to start and I know you're just dying to dance with me!"

Mason, not a big fan of dancing himself, scrunched up his face and looked to Katy for some sort of signal that she wanted him to stay. Seeing none, he relented to his wife's request.

"We'll be right over there," he announced for her benefit.

Emma slipped her hand in his as they walked toward the dance floor. And though they were more than thirty feet apart, Paula could tell that he was keeping her in his sights.

"Your brother and his wife," she said, leaning in close enough to be heard without having to raise her voice. "They're a cute couple. How long have they been married?"

"A little over three years," Katy answered, turning her head slightly to respond in a normal tone as well. "But they've been together for seven."

Their faces were touching as they spoke and Katy could feel Paula's warm breath whistling inside her ear.

"They seem really happy."

"They're as much in love now as they were when they met."

"So, tell me again what brought you to Texas?"

"Like I said earlier, I'm just here for a visit."

"How long are you staying?"

"I'm not sure yet."

"Dallas has a lot of cool places to check out. I can show you around if you want."

"I'd like that very much."

Their conversation ended when Mason and Emma returned from the dance floor but picked up again shortly after and continued until the announcement for last call came over the PA system. Paula followed them out to the parking lot and gave Katy one of her business cards along with an open invitation to come by her studio. Katy climbed in next to Emma and the two of them exchanged waves as Mason pulled away.

"What did you guys think of her?" she asked Mason and Emma simultaneously.

"She's very attractive," Mason answered.

"I think she means aside from her looks, Mason," Emma reprimanded. "Typical man. It's always about the looks. What's important is what *you* think of her, Katy."

"Well, she is pretty. Very pretty. If we're being honest, though, my first impression wasn't all that great. She's kinda pompous and a little arrogant."

Mason quickly chimed in, "That was my first impression, too."

"She might be more aloof than arrogant," Emma offered. "She is an artist after all."

"I can only imagine what her first opinion of me was," Katy said, leaning in front of Emma to stare down her brother. "Did you have to ask her if she was a lesbian? Oh, my God! Could you make me look more desperate?"

Mason could feel Katy's eyes burning a hole through the side of his face.

"For Pete's sake," he groaned. "Don't be so melodramatic, Katy. I merely asked why she moved to Dallas and she said it was because of her girlfriend."

"That's great," Katy responded. The dejected tone of her voice was unmistakable. "It figures she'd have a girlfriend. I should've known…"

"Not anymore," he interrupted. "She called her 'the ex.'"

"So, she's single?" Emma asked, though it was more of a statement than a question.

"She didn't mention anyone else."

"I guess we can assume that she's single then."

"Unless she's a player and keeps her conquests…"

"Mason!" Katy and Emma shouted together, cutting him off in mid-sentence.

Chapter 21

It took Katy nearly a week to work up the nerve to visit Paula's gallery. The first time she tried she walked past the storefront then ran back to the car and sped away. She decided to stay home the next day to regroup. On the third day she went so far as to reach for the door handle before changing her mind and fleeing back to the ranch. It rained on the fourth day, giving her fair excuse to skip any further attempts and stay in bed.

Emma watched her languish through all of it and, on the fifth day, volunteered to drive into town with her. She would be Katy's point woman, serving as the ice breaker for Katy and her new friend. With her help, they both thought, Katy would be able to summon the courage to cross the threshold and strike up a conversation. Or at least that was the plan.

Katy was supposed to wait five minutes and then join her in the studio. After ten minutes passed and she still hadn't shown up, Emma left to see what had gone wrong and found her sitting on a bench near the corner street sign.

"What happened?" she asked. "I thought we had this all worked out?"

"I can't go through with it," Katy told her. "I'm too nervous. Strike that. I'm scared to death!"

"Of what? Believe me, I know what you're going through and there's nothing to be afraid of. Just come inside with me. You don't have to say anything if you don't want to."

"How would you know what I'm going through?"

"I haven't always been married, sweetie. You think it was easy for me to approach your brother first time? He was a famous quarterback and I was just a lowly, no-name cheerleader. He no more knew who I was than the man in the moon."

"So, what did you do?"

"One of the other cheerleaders started flirting with him and I knew I had to make my move before it was too late. I simply sucked it up and took a leap of faith. And look where it got me!"

"You're right, Emma. I just need to pull it together."

"If you don't, you'll be cheating yourself. Take the chance now and you'll have no regrets about it later."

"Okay. Here I go! Wish me luck!"

The two women exchanged a quick hug before Katy stepped around her and headed for the gallery. She reached for the door handle but then stopped and turned back around. Emma offered her two enthusiastic thumbs-up, which gave her the final push she needed to go inside.

Thirty-five minutes later, she walked back to the car. Emma was nowhere in sight, so she sat in the front seat to wait for her return, anxious to share what had happened. As soon as she saw her, she launched into the details before she even had a chance to get her door open.

"Slow down," Emma giggled as she settled into the driver's seat. "You're going so fast that I missed most of that! Now take a breath and start over. Tell me everything!"

Emma punched in Mason's number and put him on speaker phone so that he could hear the news as well. Katy described every moment, starting with when she first opened the door to the very minute she left the gallery.

Emma gave her a triumphant "Hooray" when she finished. Mason, however, stayed silent.

"Is something wrong?" she asked him.

"Yeah," Katy added. "Why are you being so quiet?"

"I don't know," he said. "It's just a gut feeling, I guess, but there's something about her that rubs me the wrong way."

Katy challenged, "Why can't you just be happy for me?"

"I *am* happy for you, sis."

"Then show it, Mason. Stop being so judgmental."

"All right," he said, agreeing only because he knew it would calm her down. "But if she hurts you…"

"I'll kick her ass," Emma interrupted.

Katy gave her a disapproving look then lodged a question for both of them. "What are you two, my parents?"

Fearing more harsh judgment from her brother, Katy intentionally omitted telling them that she had already agreed to go on a date with Paula. What she didn't know at that point – but what Mason suspected all along – was that Paula was a master manipulator who would convince her to do things she would have never thought herself capable of with a total stranger.

Chapter 22

It didn't take long for Paula to open up to Katy on their date, boasting that she was one of only two women in her large circle of friends known to have been a lesbian since birth. Her sense of pride in this odd fact was obvious and she repeatedly used the term "Gold Star" to distinguish herself from the others who didn't come out until later in life. Her rantings about lesbian birthright had Katy doubting that she would still be interested if she knew that she, too, had a heterosexual past. Katy's biggest shortcoming, however, one that she would be reluctant to admit, was that she had never had a sexual relationship with another woman. Thankfully, it was way too early to confide something that personal with someone she barely knew. Without much else to contribute to the conversation, she sat quietly and let Paula do all the talking.

Paula repeatedly filled Katy's wine glass as she told her about her parents, both of whom had been killed in an automobile accident when she was six. Her grandmother was asked to sit with her that night while they went out to celebrate their tenth anniversary. Later that same evening, a uniformed officer knocked on the door. After speaking with her grandmother for a few minutes, she watched in horror as she began clutching at her chest and then collapsed into his arms. As another officer whisked her away, she saw him trying to breathe life back into her grandmother's limp body.

With no other living relatives, she ended up in foster care, and, by the age of fifteen, had already been through nine different homes. Thinking she'd be better off on her own, she ran away, shuttling from one place to the next that was willing to offer her any type of assistance. It was during that time that she formed a bond with an older, wealthy woman who invited her to come stay with her.

The woman, a painter, introduced Paula to the medium that she attributed to her amazing success. She was also her first lover. In her beginnings as an artist, her paintings were dark, brooding interpretations of the tragedies she suffered in her youth. Once she learned to harness her anger and express it more creatively, people began to take notice and she was invited to showcase her work in one of the local galleries in Tulsa. The woman that had taken her in, now jealous and hurt by the attention being showered on her young protégé, kicked her to the curb not long after. Fortunately, Paula's first two paintings were bought by an Oklahoma oilman and fetched a handsome price, endowing her with enough money to continue painting. She relocated to Dallas where her artwork continued to sell, and, five years later, bought the studio. The rest, she told Katy, was history.

Katy was flattered that Paula had felt comfortable revealing so much about herself. Throughout her stories, Paula would occasionally reach out to touch her hand or stroke the side of her face, bringing her own emotions close to the surface as well. Katy purposely chose to ignore the voice inside her head that was telling her to be cautious, warning her that things were moving too fast. She was drawn to the wounded artist and when Paula took her to bed, her feelings changed from initial attraction to all-out infatuation.

She had never felt that type of intense pleasure from a male partner and responded to her every move with a lustful hunger. It was a perfect blend of exhilaration and passion and she gave herself over to the experience entirely. At some point, she wasn't sure exactly when, she must have passed out from the wine or fell asleep because the next thing she remembered was wiggling out from under Paula's arm to gather her clothes. Her memory of what had actually transpired between them was fuzzy and she was apprehensive about what their morning conversation might expose, so she hurried back to the ranch before anyone had awakened. She managed to sneak into the house without being noticed, but then the squeaky hinges on her bedroom door caught her brother's attention and he came into the hallway to see what was going on.

"What time is it?" he asked.

"It's early," Katy answered. "Go back to bed."

"Are you just getting in?"

"I've been here a while," she fibbed. "I was just on my way to get something to snack on until breakfast."

"In your street clothes?"

Feeling guilty that she was perpetuating the lie, Katy added, "I figured since I was up, I may as well be dressed."

What am I doing? she wondered. *He's not stupid. I'm sure he knows I've been out all night. I'm sure Emma does, too. And what if they do? I'm thirty years old, for Christ's sake! I'm allowed to have an adult relationship without anyone's permission!*

In an attempt to avoid detection and the endless questions that were sure to follow, she left Mason in the hall and, being that she really *was* hungry, went on to find something to eat. He stared at her backside for a moment and then, after hearing his stomach growl, joined her in the kitchen.

Chapter 23

Every time Katy visited Paula, she was able to push Rachel and Laura farther into the recesses of her mind. Paula did show her a few places around Dallas as she had offered and even introduced her to some of her friends. To Katy, that level of attention meant that she genuinely cared for her and she was eager to show her appreciation in any way Paula asked of her.

Paula was very active in the gay community and chaired several events in the Arts District. While her social calendar remained full, she did make time for Katy whenever it was possible. Much to Katy's chagrin, though, those small time slices didn't produce many opportunities for them to be intimate. They did share one night of passion after that first date and the way their bodies came together was amazing – or so Katy thought – and she longed to experience it again. The timing of it, however, was not in her favor.

Given her feelings for Paula and the fact that her trip had already passed the thirty-day mark, she began to reconsider whether she should return to Lincoln or stay in Texas to build upon their relationship. She turned to Emma, who, not surprisingly, advised her to follow her heart. She then asked Mason for his opinion.

"Maybe I shouldn't go back," she told him. "There are lots of schools in Dallas. I'm sure I could find a teaching job at one of them."

"You're welcome to stay as long as you like," he replied, "but you belong in Lincoln, Katy. That's where your life is."

"I don't know, Mason. I've got so much going for me here."

"And what would that be? All you've got is Paula and she shouldn't be the reason you commit to Texas. Consider everything, sis. You have no money, no job, no place to call your own."

"Maybe Paula would let me stay with her."

"Is that what you want? You'd be giving up a big part of yourself to stay here, Katy."

"I guess I really need to think about this."

"Yeah, you do."

Katy kissed him on the forehead then walked out onto the deck. She settled into a chair and took in several deep, long breaths of the cool night air to help clear her mind. She hadn't spoken to anyone in Lincoln since coming to Texas, which made the decision to go back even more difficult. And now there was Paula to consider. What would she have to say about it? Since she would be the main reason for her staying, Katy wanted to know her thoughts as well. She telephoned the gallery but it went directly to voicemail, so she left a message asking Paula to call her back at her convenience.

The following day, Katy had yet to hear from her so she called again. Once more, it went straight to the machine. Twenty-four more hours passed with still no word from her. On the third day she called twice, only to have both picked up by the answering machine.

Paula had never taken that long to return her call and her intuition was telling her she needed to investigate to make sure nothing was wrong. Best case scenario, she was at some business event. Worst case scenario? Too many to consider. The only way to know for sure was to drive to the studio and look for the answer, or simply wait for her to return. She knew where she hid a spare key, so it wouldn't be a problem getting into the building.

Emma drove Katy to town and waited in the car while she searched for clues to her lover's absence. She was gone long enough for Emma's mind to become flooded with an array of fears ranging from the notion that Paula had some sort of accident and was lying unconscious to the more ominous notion that whatever caused Paula to go missing had now befallen her sister-in-law as well. She had just taken off her seat belt and was reaching for the door handle to exit the car when Katy ran out of the building. Tears were streaming down Katy's face as she yanked the passenger door open and jumped inside.

Emma was stunned and didn't have time to form a question before she saw Paula running after her, buttoning her shirt as she came toward the car.

"Roll down the window," Paula demanded, pounding on the glass.

"Leave me alone!" Katy shouted.

"Come on," Paula urged, tapping her fist on the window. "Roll it down."

"Screw you, Paula!"

"Why are you being like this, Katy? It's no big deal."

Katy grabbed the window knob and forcefully cranked the window open. "No big deal?" she shrieked. "I was worried when I hadn't heard from you, so I came here to see if you were okay. And what did I find? You… In bed with another woman!"

"I've done nothing wrong," Paula retaliated. "It's not like we were exclusive or anything."

"Why didn't you tell me you were seeing someone else?"

"I can date whoever I want. We both can."

"I thought you cared for me!"

"Look, Katy, we had some good times together, but…"

"But…?"

"It was never anything serious."

Katy grabbed the window knob again, causing Emma, who had remained mute this entire time, to wince. "Please," Katy whispered as she gave her a sideways glance. She then rolled the window up, this time with much less force than she had cranked it down, and said in a low voice, "Let's go."

"You got it," Emma responded. "We're outta here."

While Paula stood on the curb shouting out Katy's name, Emma started the engine and pulled out into the street. Sticking her arm out the window, she flipped her the middle finger then squealed the tires and sped away.

Back at the ranch, Katy disappeared into her bedroom while Emma called Mason to relay what was going on. He told her he would come home but then nonchalantly added he would be stopping by the gallery first to beat the shit out of Paula. It took Emma several minutes to convince him that an assault wouldn't fix anything. Katy's heart would still be broken and he would be of no use to her from a jail cell.

Mason packed his briefcase and hurried home. Emma was waiting for him in the kitchen.

"How is she?" he asked after giving her a hug.

"She hasn't come out of the bedroom yet."

Mason walked to her door and knocked lightly before announcing, "Hey, Katy. It's Mason. Emma told me what happened."

Silence persisted, so he pressed his ear against it to listen for sounds from within.

"Katy?" he repeated, tapping against the wood. "Can I come in?"

"Go away," she whimpered. "I want to be alone."

"Sorry, but I can't do that. I'm coming in now, okay?"

He opened the door and went inside. Katy was sitting on the edge of the bed staring out the window.

"What can I do?" he asked as he sat down next to her.

"Shoot me," she sobbed. "Put me out of my misery."

"That's a bit extreme, don't you think? She isn't worth all that."

"Please don't make light of this, Mason. I'm in a lot of pain here."

"Don't waste your energy on that bitch, Katy. She's a player and doesn't deserve someone as great as you."

"Thanks for trying to make me feel better, but you can go. I'll be all right."

He wrapped his arms around her and whispered, "I'm not going anywhere, kiddo."

He continued to hold her until her tears subsided then walked her out to the porch and sat down with her on the swing. Emma followed them out the door and watched as Katy snuggled up to him.

"I suck at love," Katy boo-hooed into her brother's shoulder.

"No, you don't," he reassured her. "You simply got involved with the wrong person. Once you find Miss Right, everything will be different."

"What if I never find her?"

Emma answered for him, saying, "You will, Katy."

Mason scooted over so that Emma could join them on the swing. They stayed there taking turns at idle conversation until the moon disappeared behind the roof of the stable. Sometime after midnight, Mason and Emma announced that they were turning in. Katy insisted she'd do the same but was still there when the rooster's crowing woke her up the next morning.

Chapter 24

"What's this?" Mason asked as he came out to the porch and saw Katy on the swing.

Katy sat upright, opened her mouth in a wide yawn and stretched her limbs to their fullest extent. "I guess I fell asleep out here," she offered in response.

It was then they heard Emma call them to breakfast. Both raced to the kitchen and were treated to a meal of eggs benedict with a side of corned beef hash. When they finished eating, Katy helped her sister-in-law clear the table.

With a smile, Emma confided, "It's nice to see you in better spirits this morning."

"Yeah," Katy agreed. "Yesterday was a real downer."

"So, what's the plan for today?"

"I need to decide whether I'm staying here or going back to Lincoln."

"We've loved having you, but I agree with Mason. Your life is in Lincoln, Katy. You may have left things in a mess but you can fix them. Running away doesn't solve anything, it only makes things worse."

"I guess it's time I face the music. Besides, if I stay here, I'd probably run into Paula somewhere and I don't think I could handle that."

"I'm not going to handle that either," Mason echoed. "I might have to punch her in the nose next time I see her just for spite."

Emma shook a scolding finger at him then turned back to Katy.

"Next time," she said, "come and stay with us just for the fun of it. Okay?"

"I will," Katy promised.

Emma called the airlines and found a flight later that same day and Katy gave her the go ahead to book it for her. While she felt melancholic about ending her trip, she was looking forward to finally going home.

Before leaving for the airport, Mason gathered her suitcase and laid it in the bed of his pickup. Emma sat between them and they filled the drive with misadventures of the Hopkins siblings and what terrible tricks they all played on one another as children.

It had been a great visit but Katy knew deep down it was time for it to be over. She had acquired numerous souvenirs throughout her trip, both physical and emotional, so the experience would not soon be forgotten.

She didn't give too much thought about Paula during her flight but instead focused on how much she missed Mary and how she hoped that their time apart had healed their wounds. Granted, it stung seeing Paula with the other woman but she was right. It wasn't love. Whatever it was Katy wasn't completely sure, but she knew Mary was the one to help her figure it out. Mary had always been her confidant and she desperately wanted to talk with her, to tell her how she was feeling and to ask her how to move forward with her life.

To her surprise, Mary was already waiting for her in the baggage claim area. Their initial embrace was warm and endearing and brought both of them to tears.

"How are you?" Katy asked, being both sincere in her own words and tentative in regards to what her mother's response might be.

"Glad to have you back," Mary replied without missing a beat. "How was Dallas?"

"Revealing. I learned a lot about myself while I was away."

Mary's eyebrows arched up with curiosity. "Anything you want to share?"

Katy answered, "Yes," but then didn't elaborate any further.

Mary stood quietly by while she collected her suitcase. As they rode the elevator to the parking garage, she decided she couldn't wait any longer for her to offer up details.

"Tell me something exciting that happened on your trip," she prodded.

"Actually," Katy started, "lots of things happened while I was there."

"Did everything turn out the way you had hoped?"

"Maybe not so much in Texas. But now that I'm home I'm hoping it will."

"I spoke to Mason after he dropped you off at the airport," Mary announced as they stepped out of the elevator. "He said it didn't come as a surprise when you told him you were gay and that he, Jason and Beth had all suspected it since you were kids. It saddened me to hear that."

Katy raised her hand to object but Mary shook her head and resumed speaking.

"He also told me I needed to get my act together or I could lose you. That hurt me to my very core. You sprung all of this on me before you left and we haven't spoken since. This has been a lot to process for the both of us. The hardest part for me was how I missed something like that for all those years. I feel like I failed you as a parent."

"No way!" Katy objected loudly. "You were fantastic parents! Are fantastic parents! I couldn't have asked for better parents than you and Dad!"

"Thank you, sweetheart. You know that I love you with every ounce of my being. Even if you are a…," she leaned in close to finish in a whisper, "a lesbian."

"I know this has been difficult for you, Mom. It hasn't been easy for me, either. Question is, are you ready to move past the shock and talk things through now?"

"Yes, I am."

"Should we tell Dad?"

Katy knew instinctively that she hadn't told him.

"Let's meet for lunch tomorrow and talk more about it then. We can order a pizza with all the toppings. We haven't done that in ages."

Once both were settled into their car seats, Mary reached for Katy's hand and gave it a little squeeze. Their conversation on the drive to Lincoln was superficial and scant at best, neither one ready to delve into anything deeper just yet. As they passed the city limits sign, Katy felt the arms of Lincoln wrap around her. Mason was right in that she wouldn't be happy anywhere else. This was where she belonged and to think any differently would be foolish.

After Mary dropped her off, she hurried into her house and flung her suitcase onto the bed. Knowing she had all the time in the world to unpack, she went to the kitchen to make herself a drink. In the door of the refrigerator was Laura's half empty bottle of wine. She pulled out the cork with her teeth and spat it onto the counter. Not bothering to get a glass, she carried the bottle to the living room.

All in all, it had been a transformative month, culminating with being accepted as a lesbian so effortlessly by Mason and Emma and her mother's pledge to continue to love her in spite of it. Since Jason and Beth already knew, and, she assumed, Maggie and Ben, those fears could be put to rest as well. The only person left to tell was Frank and she knew it was best to wait for Mary's help in bringing him up to speed with everybody else.

Chapter 25

Katy slept soundly, but when her eyes opened decided she wasn't yet ready to face the day so she pulled the covers up over her head and fell back asleep. When she awoke the second time, the red digits on her alarm clock proclaimed the time as "11:22." She'd have to get a move on if she wanted to make it to lunch with Mary by noon.

She ran to the bathroom and splashed water on her face, brushed her hair and teeth and smeared deodorant over what appeared to be a week's worth of growth under each arm then raced back to the dresser. She slipped on a pair of shorts, topped those off with a t-shirt, jammed her feet into her favorite Crocs and was out the door ten minutes later.

Mary was already at the restaurant when she arrived. She offered her a kiss on the cheek before taking a seat on the opposite side of the table. By her calculations, she still had sixty seconds to spare.

They waved the waitress off when she tried to hand them menus as they had been to Luigi's numerous times over the years and always ordered the same thing: hand-tossed, deep-dish pizza with the works and two large Diet Cokes.

"Load it up with anchovies, please," Katy told the waitress as she tucked the menus under her arm. "And extra cheese," Mary added.

"I overslept," Katy apologized to her mother after she had left. "And now I need to pee, so I'll be right back. Don't snack on too many breadsticks while I'm gone."

"Hurry!" Mary insisted. "I want to hear all about your trip!"

Katy slid out from her seat and breezed through the campsite of tables littering her path to the restroom. As she sat down on the toilet she saw there were two, small, sneaker-clad feet in the stall next to hers. Her need had been urgent, so she finished quickly and was standing at the sink when those two small feet carried their owner out into the open.

"Hey, Coach Hopkins," a young voice said.

Katy glanced in the mirror and saw Danielle standing behind her. She was stunned to see her and the look on her face clearly showed it.

"Hi, Danielle," she said, hoping her voice sounded calmer out loud than it did in her head.

"What are you doing here?"

"I'm having pizza with my mom. What about you?"

"Same."

"Oh, so you're here with your family?"

Again, Katy hoped that her words were coming out without resonating the sense of dread that she was feeling. *Shit! Is Rachel really here?*

"Rion and Rafael are playing games in the arcade and my parents are at the table." She paused long enough to wash her hands then added, "You should come by and say hi."

Katy frowned unconsciously. "Maybe some other time."

Danielle frowned, too, although she didn't notice. The teenager walked toward the door but then suddenly turned around and called out to her again.

"Miss Hopkins?"

"Yes?"

"How come you and my mom don't talk anymore? I thought you were friends."

"We were."

"Does that mean you're not friends now?"

"Not necessarily." Katy suddenly felt compelled to add, "It's just that our lives have taken different paths."

"But she misses you."

"How do you know that?"

"She told me."

"Really?" Katy's head was spinning as she repeated to herself, *She misses me?*

"Yeah. You should call her sometime."

"Thanks, Danielle. Maybe I will."

After Danielle left, Katy cupped her hands under the faucet to scoop up water and splashed it on her face in an attempt to help her recompose before leaving the restroom. She scanned the restaurant as soon as the door closed behind her and immediately zeroed in on George and Rachel sitting no more than twenty feet away from her mom. Turning sideways, she walked with her back to them, hoping not to be recognized.

But Rachel did notice. George had been talking to her but she stopped listening as her focus shifted entirely to Katy. To keep him from knowing, she pretended to be looking for the kids. It was pure coincidence that the three of them *and* Katy were all in her direct line of sight at the same time. When she did return to their conversation, she quickly cut him off by stating matter-of-factly, "I want a divorce."

"Wh-wh-what?" he stammered. The disbelief transformed him as his mouth hung open while his eyes tried desperately to connect with hers. "You can't mean that."

Rachel laid her hands over his before making her next statement. "I'm sorry, but I can't continue this charade any longer. I'm in love with someone else."

"Who? Is it someone you work with? Is it that new neighbor that moved in down the street last month? What's his name... Rick? Is it that bastard Rick?"

"No, it's not Rick."

"Who is it then?" he demanded. "Tell me who he is!" His voice was heightening.

Thinking it might soften the blow, she squeezed his hands and said in a low voice, "You don't know her."

"Her?!?" he retorted. "Are you telling me you're a queer?"

"Yes, George. I'm in love with another woman."

"Since when?"

"For a while now."

"So, our marriage was a sham?" His derision was now turning to dejection.

"No, not at all."

George shook his head vehemently. Rachel asked him to calm down and listen then slowly began to explain that she had her first lesbian experience when she was a senior in high school and then another one in college but felt pressured by her parents to conform, to get married to a man, to have children and accept the traditional role of a housewife.

George continued to shake his head as he struggled to process what she was telling him. Their children, she assured him, were reason enough that they should not have any regrets about their years together as husband and wife.

"I had no idea you were attracted to women," he said after letting the initial shock sink in. Seconds later he became agitated again, adding, "This is insane. *You* are insane if you think that you're going to be all 'gay' in front of our kids. I won't allow…"

"Don't threaten me with the children, George," she interrupted. "Our marriage has been over for years. Think about it. When was the last time you and I were intimate? The only reason I've stayed with you this long is because of the kids."

"And just what do you suggest we tell them. That you're a dyke?"

"We tell them the truth," she said, ignoring his insult. "That we're no longer in love and we're getting a divorce."

While George and Rachel huddled together discussing the failure of their marriage, Katy did her best to avoid looking in their direction but couldn't help turning her head on occasion to sneak a peek. While she couldn't hear what they were saying, the fact that they were holding hands spoke volumes. It looked obvious to her that they were engaged in a passionate conversation. Seeing them like that made her stomach churn.

"Something is upsetting you," Mary said as she noticed the sudden change in her daughter's demeanor. "What is it?"

"Nothing," Katy muttered. Hoping to change the subject, she complained, "I can't believe that pizza isn't here yet."

But the arrival of the pizza didn't improve her mood and she remained noticeably unsettled, giving Mary reason to ask again, "What is wrong, Katy? You were in such a good mood before."

"I told you it's nothing."

"And I don't believe you."

"It's personal, all right?"

"Is there anything I can do?" Before Katy could respond, she added, "I'm not asking as your mother, I'm asking as a friend. Let me in, Katy. Let me help you."

Katy swiped at a tear with her thumb as it rolled down onto her cheek.

"You're right," she confessed. "It would feel better getting this off my chest."

She started the conversation by describing what happened in Texas – editing out bits and pieces – then worked her way back in time to explain how she had messed up the relationship with Laura by calling her another person's name during their first intimate encounter. She confided everything without disclosing Rachel's true identity but the guise wasn't necessary. Mary knew exactly who she was talking about.

"Oh, Katy! It's Nora's cousin, isn't it?"

"What?"

"Nora's cousin." The next words out of her mouth were a statement, not a question. "Rachel is the woman you're in love with."

"Who told you?"

"No one had to tell me. It's been too obvious to ignore. I saw the way you looked at her at your housewarming party. And now this big change in your attitude with her being here in the restaurant."

"You knew she was here?"

"Yes. She came over to say hello when you went to the restroom."

"Did she ask about me?"

"No."

"She didn't say anything about me at all?"

"No, dear. Sorry."

"So, what do I do?"

"She's married, Katy. And as long as she's married, you have to respect that. You can't be a home-wrecker, sweetie, no matter how you feel. The right thing for you to do is to stay out of their marriage."

While Mary continued to talk, Katy stole another glance in Rachel's direction. This time, she caught Rachel looking back at her.

Chapter 26

The drive home from the pizza parlor was somber. What should have been a joyful reunion with her mother had turned out to be another low point in Katy's life.

The drive home from the pizza parlor was somber. What should have been a joyful reunion with her mother had turned out to be another low point in Katy's life.

I should go out tonight, she decided. *There's no sense in hanging around the house being miserable. Maybe I'll meet someone to help me forget all of the women in my life: Paula, Laura and Rachel.*

After finishing the list of names, she laughed out loud. *I suck at being a lesbian!*

She spent the rest of the afternoon unpacking and doing laundry then took a long, hot shower before changing into her clothes for the evening. She arrived at the bar at ten o'clock and was instantly slammed by an onslaught of nerves as she entered the building.

Am I completely nuts? What was I thinking in coming here? I know as much about soliciting female companionship as I do about defusing a neutron bomb!

Realizing she had come too far to turn back, she continued past several groups of women standing around chatting with one another. She spotted an empty stool at the end of the bar and hurried over to claim it. Soon after, the seat next to her opened up and one of the women she had seen in passing arrived to fill the void.

"Hi there," the stranger said as she sat down. "I'm Samantha. My friends call me Sam. Can I buy you a drink?"

"My name is Katy, and, sure, I'll have a Martini. Dry with two olives."

Katy never had a Martini before and, after requesting it, couldn't help but wonder why she had chosen that particular cocktail.

"Hey, barkeep, can I get a Martini for my friend? I'll have another Rum and Coke."

The bartender, a large hulk of a woman with a looming presence, nodded in return. Sam was tapping her fingers to the beat of the music playing in the background when she turned to Katy and asked, "Would you like to dance?"

"I'm not very good at it," Katy responded, cringing as she remembered the last time she danced with a woman there.

Sam gave her a smile and a quick wink. "Who cares? I'm not, either!"

After sliding off of her stool, she sprinted toward the dance floor and called back over her shoulder, "Come dance with me, Katy!"

I need some liquid encouragement first, Katy resolved, so she removed the olives from her Martini and gulped the entire drink down in one fluid motion.

"Can I get you another?" the bartender asked.

"It's been one of those days," Katy answered. "So, just keep 'em coming."

The bartender was so fast in responding that Katy stayed to inhale a second Martini and a third. After finishing the last one, she started for the dance floor. The song that was playing came to an end just as she caught up with Sam.

"You timed that perfectly," Sam offered jokingly. The next song started right away and she challenged Katy to remain by asking her, "Ready to shake your money maker?"

"All right, but I warned you."

"Warned me about what?"

"My dancing. I'm really lousy."

"Don't worry about it," Sam reassured her. "So am I!"

"Not from what I've seen."

Katy thought Sam would dismiss her comment as exaggeration but she was being genuine. She really was a very talented dancer.

"You're just being nice," Sam responded, just as she expected. Sam then backed up to Katy, grabbed her hands and placed them on her hips and began gyrating from side to side as she shouted, "Hang on!"

The alcohol was blazing its way through Katy's midsection and she felt an intense primal urge to take Sam right where they stood. Before the thought left her mind, the song ended and Sam was dragging her through the crowd back to the bar.

"Barkeep!" she shouted after returning to their seats. "Another round, por favor!"

Being a lightweight, Katy insisted, "I need to wait. I've had too much already."

"No way! Come on! It's on me!"

Sam pulled a wad of money from her pocket, peeled a twenty-dollar bill off the top and slid it across the counter to the bartender.

"Another round," she repeated.

After finishing that drink and at least two more that followed, Sam made her move, rotating Katy's stool until they were facing one another. Seconds later, she was tonguing her way past Katy's lips while at the same time wedging her hand between Katy's thighs. Katy spread her legs wider apart to accommodate, drunkenly oblivious to the fact that she was making a spectacle of herself in front of an audience of onlookers. To her, the patrons surrounding them were nothing more than a vague reality. She was feeding off her libido, and, while it might not have been the right place for sex, it was definitely the right time.

The bartender didn't care that Katy was ripe and ready for picking and rapped a beer mug on the counter to get her attention.

"Take that shit somewhere else," she told her. "This is a bar, not a motel."

"No worries, Sandy," Sam replied as she pulled away from Katy. "I gotta be heading out anyway. It's late and my girlfriend gets really pissed if I'm not home by midnight."

She then turned to Katy, adding, "You are really hot. We should hook up sometime so we can finish what we started!"

Katy was inebriated to the point that she could no longer focus. Everything in the bar was a blur. She pointed her gaze in the direction of Sam's voice and saw three floating heads. She had no idea which one actually belonged to Sam.

"Gir'fren?" she inquired in a shrill voice. "You got a gir'fren?"

"Yeah," Sam answered. "Let me tell ya, she gets pretty nasty if she thinks that I'm cheating on her. She actually beat up a couple of women she thought I was fooling around with."

Katy was incensed. If she knew which of the heads was Sam's she would have surely punched its lights out. As tempting as it was, she knew saying anything more might cause further embarrassment. Instead, she stared at her empty glass and waited for her to leave. Soon after, she decided to leave as well but then nearly took a spill as she was coming off the stool and had to grab onto the counter to avoid landing face first on the floor. It was then she realized she was a long way from home and too drunk to get there on her own. Thinking she'd sober up within a reasonable amount of time, she climbed back onto her stool, stretched her arm out across the counter and laid her head down on top of it.

"Bartenner?" she called out meekly.

"Yes?" Sandy answered.

"Can I get a cuff of coppee?"

"You need more than a cuff, honey. I'd better bring you the whole pot."

"Izzit okay if I sit here for a li'l bit?"

"You can stay until two thirty. That's when we close up."

"'Kay. Thanks. I 'preciate you being so nice to me."

"Why don't you let me call you a taxi?"

"Cuz it pro'lly cost a fortune to take me there, silly."

"Where would that be?"

"Lincoln."

"Boy, are you in luck. There's another gal from Lincoln that comes here. I think she's on the patio. I'll go see if she can give you a ride."

"Thadda be great. Hey, lady? Are you're single? I hope so, cuz I'd sure like to date someone nice as you."

"I don't think my wife would go for that," Sandy replied while pointing at the ring on her finger. "I've been happily married for sixteen years."

"Figgers. The good ones are always married."

Sandy poured a cup of coffee then dropped an ice cube in it so Katy wouldn't scald herself. A few minutes later, she returned with the other Lincoln resident in tow.

"Katy!" Laura exclaimed. "What the hell are you doing here?"

"Drinkin'," Katy boasted proudly.

"So, I've been told. Where's your car?"

"Ou'side."

Laura and Sandy exchanged glances before Sandy resumed her position at the bar.

"I'll take her home," Laura volunteered. "We'll come back tomorrow to get her car."

"Fine by me," Sandy responded. "It should be safe in the parking lot overnight."

Not directing her comment to either one of them in particular, Katy said, "Thanks, lady. I 'preciate you being so nice to me."

"Be careful," Sandy warned Laura. "I got the same line just before she asked me for a date."

"Hey, cut her some slack," Laura responded in Katy's defense. "She's brand new at this. She just recently came out."

"She's damn lucky you were here tonight or I would have had to call the cops to put her in the tank. Get her on out of here. Take her home and put her to bed."

"Will do. Thanks for coming to get me."

Laura slipped her arm around Katy's waist and hoisted her down off the stool then practically carried her from the building to her car. Once they were at Katy's, she walked her inside, undressed her and helped her into bed. She pulled the covers up to her chin, kissed her on the cheek and told her goodnight. Then she grabbed Katy's keys, locked the front door behind her and went home.

Chapter 27

Laura returned at ten o'clock and used Katy's key to let herself in, started a pot of coffee then sat down at her kitchen table to wait for her to rise. Katy wandered in twenty minutes later with the sash of her robe knotted loosely around her waist, leaving most of her stomach and chest exposed. Upon seeing Laura, she quickly closed the robe with one hand and cinched it with the other.

"What are you doing here?" she asked.

"Having coffee," Laura answered honestly.

"Please tell me we didn't…"

Laura smiled broadly, thoroughly enjoying the nervous look on Katy's face.

"No, we didn't. I merely brought you home."

Katy breathed a sigh of relief. "Thank you."

"You're welcome. How are you feeling today?"

"Like a truck hit me head on."

"It's no wonder. You were pretty smashed last night."

"Really? I don't remember much."

"That's probably best. Do you remember anything at all?"

"Dancing and drinking, way more of the latter, obviously, with a girl named Steve or Stan or something close to that."

"When did you get back in town?"

"Yesterday, I think. Or maybe the day before. It seems like such a long time ago already. How did you know I was out of town?"

"I called a few times. And I drove by…"

"Sorry I missed you." Katy gave this response automatically, like polite small talk, but when Laura said that she had missed her, too, she quickly changed the subject.

"I'm assuming we came back here in your car, right?"

"Yes. Yours is still at the bar."

"I appreciate you going out of your way like that to bring me home."

Laura walked to the coffee pot and filled a cup for Katy.

"No problem," she said as she handed it to her. "I'm sure you would have done the same for me if the situation were reversed."

"Did you stay overnight?"

"No. After I helped you into bed I went home."

"You're such a Girl Scout."

Laura smiled, triggering Katy to giggle before announcing, "I should probably get dressed now so we can go get my car."

"Okay. I'll wait here for you."

Katy wasn't looking forward to the drive to Kansas City with her. What would they talk about? They weren't on speaking terms when she ran off to Texas. Calling her by the wrong name made sure of that. And now she'd gotten herself so drunk that she had to be rescued. Neither were worth rehashing while being trapped together on a long ride.

Laura was just as apprehensive but for an entirely different reason. She pined for Katy while she was away and wanted her back in her life but was clueless on how to broach the subject with her.

A short while later they were on the road. While the radio churned out hits from the 60's, 70's and 80's, both women struggled to initiate a conversation. Uncomfortable with the silence, Katy cleared her throat to say something but Laura beat her to it.

"I know you don't know that much about me," she began, "so, I thought I'd share a few things with you. Is that okay?"

"Sure."

"Did I ever tell you how I ended up in Lincoln?"

"No, you never did."

"I lived about four hours north of here in Fort Dodge, Iowa. It's a fairly good-sized city. I taught at one of the elementary schools there."

"Why would you leave Fort Dodge to come to a small town like Lincoln?"

"I didn't have a choice. I had to leave."

"Why? What happened?"

"My parents disowned me when I told them I was gay. The only person in my family who would have anything to do with me was my brother. When he was killed…"

Laura rubbed her eyes before continuing. Katy could tell she was about to cry.

"When he was killed," she repeated, "there was no reason for me to stay."

"Oh, Laura. I'm so sorry."

Laura went on to tell Katy about her brother's life and described how his untimely death was violent, dying at the hands of a thug robbing a convenience store near his home. He was two years younger than Laura and they were the best of friends. His name was Luke. He was a fireman. He had been married for fifteen years and was the father of two children, a twelve-year-old daughter and a six-year-old son. He was killed the day before his fortieth birthday.

All throughout his funeral her parents refused to speak to her or even acknowledge her presence. She overheard her mother telling one of her friends that she wished Laura had been killed and not Luke. And so, with him gone, there was no reason for her to stay.

Having no idea where to go, she took a sheet of paper and tore it into several small pieces, penned "North," "South," "East," and "West" on four of the scraps then wrote random numbers on the remaining pieces and tossed them into two separate bowls. She pulled one slip from each bowl and when put together they read "South 250," which meant she was to travel south for 250 miles and wherever those coordinates landed her, that's where she would stay. That random pairing brought her to Lincoln.

She slept in her car while scouring employment ads in the Herald Banner, and, a few days later, saw the announcement advertising an open position for an English teacher. Getting hired, she told Katy, was a sheer stroke of luck.

Katy listened intently. When Laura finished, she reached out to touch her arm and offered her a smile. She kept her hand there until they arrived at the bar.

"Thank you for sharing that with me," she said as they pulled up next to her car.

"It's me who should be thanking you. You welcomed me right away and made my transition a whole lot easier."

"Yeah, but then I screwed it all up."

"That's in the past. Today is a new day. There's no reason we can't start over again as friends."

"I'd like that. Maybe we could get together for dinner or a movie sometime."

"That would be wonderful. Well, I guess I'll see you around. Take care of yourself."

"You do the same. Thanks again – for everything. And I don't just mean last night."

"No problem. I'll always be here for you, Katy."

Chapter 28

When Katy returned to Lincoln, she parked her car in the garage and went inside the house. Her answering machine was signaling that someone had left her a message, so she leaned over the counter and pressed the Play button. The message was from Mary.

"Hi, Katy. I was calling to see if you would like to have dinner with me. Your dad is helping Jason put up shelving and I don't feel like cooking for myself. I'm not sure where you are. Maybe you're outside or something. Anyway, call me when you get this."

Katy called her back and Mary picked up on the first ring.

"Hey, Mom. Is it too late to accept your invitation?"

"Never. Where do you want to go?"

"Somewhere light, my stomach's a little queasy."

"Are you sick?"

"Temporarily. I drank a bit too much last night and I'm feeling it today. You wanna check out that new buffet restaurant over in Smithville? I should be able to handle that."

"Okay, but you'll have to drive. Your father has the car."

"That's fine. I'm in shorts, so give me a few minutes to change. I'll be there in a bit."

An hour later, Katy was standing behind her mother in the buffet line, her hangover causing waves of nausea to rise up within her as Mary shoveled additional toppings onto an already loaded baked potato.

"That's disgusting," she said, grimacing.

"Different strokes for different folks," Mary challenged.

Katy chose a salad as her meal and they carried their trays to an open table and sat down across from one another.

"School starts next month," she announced. "I'm hoping the same girls come back for basketball. They really started coming together as a team the second half of the season. I'd like to see that hard work pay off for them by at least making it to regionals this year."

"For them or for you?"

"Both, actually."

"Will Danielle be playing again? She has such incredible talent – reminds me a lot of you at that age."

"I'm sure she will. This is her last year in junior high, you know."

"That's too bad. Is it going to bother you to see her at the games?"

"Who? Danielle?"

"No, her mother."

"I don't know. I don't think so."

"It's good that you're moving on with things, Katy."

Talking about Rachel served no purpose to either one of them, yet Mary's comment still bothered her. On a positive note, however, it provided an opportunity to see just how far Mary was willing to stand behind her statement, so Katy asked her, "Did I tell you that Laura and I are talking again?"

Thinking that her mother had no real clue who Laura was, she was surprised when she answered, "I'm glad. I like her. She seems nice."

"When did you meet her?"

"I saw you talking with her at a couple basketball games last year, so I said hello to her at the Hy-Vee and we kept running into each other after that. She told me that the two of you had become close friends and I put two and two together that she was the one that helped you realize you were a lesbian. Just before you ran off to Texas, she asked me what to get you for your birthday."

"What did you tell her?"

"I can't say. She swore me to secrecy."

"You two bonded rather quickly."

"We did. She's a wonderful person."

"I really hosed things up with her."

"If you would've stayed in Lincoln, perhaps…"

Katy cut her off. "I had to sort out my feelings."

"And did you?"

"I hope so. I can't stop the way I feel about Rachel but you were right. I can't impose myself on a married woman."

"It's what's best, Katy, for everyone. And now that you know that, you have another chance to make a go with Laura."

"You think she could forgive me?"

"She seems the kind of person who would. Stop being so hard on yourself. If you made a mistake, own up to it and move on."

"I can't believe you're okay with all of this."

"We both know it didn't start out that way. I, too, did some soul searching while you were away and decided that your happiness is all that matters to me."

"Thank you for saying that."

"You have a big heart, Katy. You deserve to be loved and to have someone special to love in return. Maybe that person is Laura."

"Maybe."

"You know, your birthday is right around the corner. You should invite her to your party this year. It would be a great way for everyone to meet her."

"That's a wonderful idea!"

And with that suggestion, mother and daughter went right back to being in sync as they started making plans for the party. With her month-long tribulation now behind her, from what Katy could tell, life in Lincoln was going to be better than ever.

Chapter 29

Katy and Laura went out as friends a handful of times before deciding to give their relationship another try. Laura needed assurances and Katy needed absolution, so they pledged to move slower the second time around. Both wanted to proceed cautiously, each having their own doubts about what lie ahead. But, with optimism chartering their course, before summer's end, their fear of being hurt had given way to hope.

Laura and Mary joined forces to lay the groundwork for Katy's surprise. She knew they were in cahoots but had no idea what they were actually plotting. Despite her many attempts, she couldn't prod either one into revealing their secret.

On the morning of her birthday, Laura showed up at Katy's house unannounced and asked her to go for a ride. Knowing Katy wasn't a spontaneous person she had to beg and plead to get her to finally go along with it. Once Katy was in her car, she opened the glovebox and pulled out a blindfold.

"What's that for?" Katy inquired.

"Don't ask," Laura answered as she slipped the mask over Katy's eyes. "Just sit back and enjoy the ride."

Katy turned her head slightly and stuck out her tongue then said with a giggle, "You are so dramatic."

"That's what makes life fun!" Laura joshed. "You ought to try it sometime."

Katy stuck her tongue out a second time.

"You may be blind," Laura told her. "But I'm not. I can see you doing that."

"Doing what?"

"Poking your tongue out at me."

"Why, Miss Laura Drama Stiles, I have no idea what you're rambling on about."

"Okay, Scarlett. Just be patient and try not to spoil the surprise. All good things come to those who wait, remember?"

"In case you hadn't noticed, I'm not a very patient person."

"That was made painfully clear the first time we went out."

Laura's response was an uncomfortable reminder of Katy's boorish behavior at the lesbian bar and afterwards, and she retaliated in a snit, saying, "At least I'm open about things. I don't keep secrets from the people that I care about."

"I doubt that, Katy. Everyone has a secret or two stashed away. They form the basis of our fantasies."

"That's way too Freudian for me to comprehend. Let's keep the conversation light today, shall we? After all, it is my birthday."

"Yes, dear."

"Whoa! We just recently started dating and I'm already getting a 'yes, dear'?"

"Yes, dear."

Katy stuck her tongue out a third time.

"Better put that thing away," Laura snickered, "before I put it to good use."

Both were silent for a while until Katy grumbled, "How far away is this place? I'm ready to come out of this blindfold."

"We're just about there. It's not that far from your house, actually. I've been driving around in circles on purpose to confuse you."

"Well, it worked. I have no freaking idea where we are."

The car came to a stop not long after that and Laura announced, "We're here." She then walked to Katy's side of the car to open her door.

"Can I take the mask off now?" Katy asked.

"Not yet," Laura answered quickly. "Let's go inside first."

"Cradle to grave with this thing, aren't ya?"

"Yes, dear."

"Enough with that!"

"Okay. Grab my arm and let's go get your surprise!"

Katy clasped her hands together around Laura's arm. Laura ushered her inside, led her to a chair and told her to sit down. Katy could hear people rustling all around her. She thought some of the voices sounded familiar, but, at the same time, couldn't place them. There was also a strange odor – strong and pungent. That seemed familiar, too.

Holy crap! she thought, wincing as she realized where they were. *It's a nail salon! Oh man, oh man! Please God, don't let it be Rachel's!*

Laura removed Katy's blindfold and squealed, "Happy Birthday!"

Katy looked past Laura at the woman standing behind her.

"Happy Birthday, Katy," Rachel echoed.

Katy's bottom lip started to quiver. Laura saw it and asked, "Are you about to cry? Your mom told me you loved manicures but I had no idea it would have this kind of effect on you!"

What should I do? Katy wondered. *Laura has no clue Rachel works here. How could she? I've never told her. I've never told anyone.*

Laura helped Katy to her feet and draped an arm over her shoulder.

"Well? What do you think of your surprise?"

Katy looked first at her and then at Rachel.

"I'm stunned," she answered. "I don't know what to say."

It was obvious that not only did Laura not know this was where Rachel worked, she also didn't know that the woman standing a few feet away was, in fact, Rachel.

"Katy Hopkins is speechless!" she remarked. "That doesn't happen very often."

Katy managed a weak smile. *How can I go through with this? If I let Rachel touch me, I'll fall back under her spell. Things are good with… with…* Laura's name suddenly escaped her. *Oh shit! I'm in big trouble now!*

"Excuse me, Katy," Rachel said, interrupting her thoughts.

"Yes?" Katy replied. Her eyes were blinking rapidly as she continued shifting her gaze back and forth between her and Laura.

"Are you ready?"

"As ready as I'll ever be, I guess."

"Let's go on back to my station, shall we?"

Laura pointed to an empty chair in the lobby area and told Katy, "I'll wait for you over there." Katy nodded sheepishly then followed Rachel to the rear of the salon.

"You're trembling," Rachel cooed as she caressed the top of Katy's hand. "Just like the first time you came here. Do you remember that?"

Katy affirmed her with a slight bob of her head.

"Hard to believe it's been almost a year already," Rachel continued as she lowered Katy's hand into the bowl.

Katy immediately pulled her hand back and snapped, "Listen, Rachel. We can't just pick up where we left off. Too much has happened."

Rachel heard the pain in her voice and responded sympathetically, "I understand."

"You ran out on me," Katy muttered under her breath.

"Pardon? I didn't hear you."

"Never mind." This time her response was louder and more guttural.

Not knowing if she should continue, Rachel leaned back in her chair.

"Do you want me to stop?" she asked.

"No," Katy growled. "My friend went to a lot of trouble to set this up for me."

"She must care a lot about you."

"Yes, she does."

"I'm glad you have such a good friend, Katy."

Rachel motioned for her hand and Katy obliged, but her renewed touch triggered her resentment and she quickly pulled away again.

"Katy," Rachel whispered, then raised her voice slightly to add, "If you don't want me to…"

"I need a minute," Katy interrupted.

The two sat idle while she collected herself. When she was ready, Katy took a long, deep breath and returned her hand to the table. Rachel smiled and a shiver ran up Katy's spine, just as it had the first time.

Seeing that they were nearly finished, Laura rose from her seat and started walking toward them. Neither Katy nor Rachel knew she was standing close enough to hear their parting remarks.

"It was great seeing you again," Rachel told Katy.

"Yeah," Katy agreed. "This was nice."

Rachel grabbed both of her hands and squeezed them tightly.

"Goodbye, Katy."

"Goodbye, Rachel."

Chapter 30

"So, that was Rachel," Laura announced after they were back in the car. She wanted Katy to look at her but she chose to stare out over the dashboard instead.

"What do you want me to say, Laura?" Katy's tone was not defensive.

"The truth. I want you to tell me what you're feeling."

"Now?"

"Right now."

"To be honest, I don't know what I'm feeling."

"Why didn't you tell me she was a manicurist?"

"Why do you think I stopped coming?"

"Your mom thought it was because you couldn't afford it. She said you stopped going around the same time you bought the house."

"The last time I talked to Rachel was at my housewarming, not long after I moved in, so I can see why she thought that."

"What happened that night?"

"Nothing happened. At least not in the way you mean it."

"I'm not implying anything, Katy. But something must have happened that night between the two of you."

Katy sighed, "I thought we were getting close."

"We are!"

"Not us. Me and Rachel. You know, back then."

"Oh."

Laura eased her car into Mary's driveway and put it in Park but didn't shut off the engine. After scooting her seat back as far as it would go, she turned to face Katy.

"Aren't we going in?" Katy asked.

"I think we should talk about this."

"Why?"

"Because I'm tired of competing with her."

"That's nonsense, Laura. There is no competition."

"Maybe not that you're willing to admit, but it's a constant struggle for me, Katy."

"What is?"

"Fighting to win your affection – to win your love."

"What are you talking about? Rachel is out of my life. Hell, she was never really in my life to begin with! Anyway, I've moved on."

"Have you? Have you really moved on?"

"Yes, I have. I thought you would have noticed that by now."

"What I've noticed is that you haven't gotten over it, you've simply gotten on with it. You tried to move on; I'll give you that. But one touch from her pulled you right back."

"I don't know what you're talking about."

"Look me in the eye and tell me you're not in love with her anymore."

Katy peered directly into her eyes but found herself unable to speak.

"Well?" Laura prompted.

Katy started to cry. "I can't do it," she sobbed.

"That's what I thought."

Katy moved closer and wrapped her arms around Laura's neck.

"Oh, Laura," she whispered as she buried her head in her shoulder. "I'm so sorry!"

Laura ran her fingers through Katy's hair then gently pushed her away.

"You can't help who you fall in love with, Katy. If we could, I wouldn't be here with you right now."

"Please don't say that, Laura. I do love you."

"I know. But you'll never love me the way you love her."

Tears were streaming down Katy's face as she settled back into her seat. She then turned to Laura and said, "I guess this is goodbye."

"I guess so," Laura echoed, her voice crackling with disappointment. "I hope you have a wonderful birthday, Katy. Please tell your mom I'm sorry I had to leave."

Katy waved goodbye as she stood on her parents' porch. Hoping to hide her sorrow behind a happy pretense, she dried her tears with the back of her sleeve then opened the door and went inside.

Chapter 31

What a mess I've made of my life, Katy thought as she closed the door behind her. *Laura's, too. How could I have screwed things up so badly in just one year?*

Mason was the first to greet her.

"So, where is she?" he asked.

"Where is who?"

"Laura, silly. Who else? I can't wait to meet her. I've heard so much about her."

Katy shrugged, "She's not coming."

"What do you mean she's not coming?" Mary questioned as she joined them in the entryway. "I just spoke with her this morning when she came to get the blindfold. She was excited about meeting the rest of the family."

"Blindfold, Mother?" Jason asked with a raised brow as he stepped into the foyer. "Perhaps you should explain that."

"Not now," Mary said to shush him. "Besides, it's none of your business."

"You probably don't want to know the answer to that," Mason interjected.

Emma worked her way into the packed hallway and gave Katy a big hug. "Happy birthday!" she squealed. "So, where is this girlfriend of yours?"

"She's not coming," Katy repeated glumly.

"I'm sure you mean she'll be arriving later," Mary insisted.

"No, Mom," Katy argued. "She's not coming."

Nora squeezed her way into the crowd and planted a kiss on her best friend's cheek. "Why is everyone standing around the front door?" she asked.

"Laura's not coming," Mason told her.

Nora looked to Katy for an explanation. "Did you two have a fight?"

"No," Katy broadcasted to the entire group. "We didn't have a fight."

Jason prodded, "So, why isn't she coming?"

Katy pondered the possible answers she might give for why her "girlfriend" was not with her. She's sick? She had a family emergency? Uh… she caught me with another woman? There was a hint of truth in that last thought but she didn't think it wise to share it with the mob gathered around her. So, she simply stated the facts as she knew them to be. "Because we aren't together anymore," she announced matter-of-factly.

"What in the world happened?" Mary asked. "Didn't she give you your birthday present?"

"She did," Katy replied. "Only it didn't turn out the way anyone expected."

"You have to do better than that," Mason said, urging his little sister to offer more of an explanation. "Spill it, missy."

"What went wrong?" Mary asked. "We both thought a manicure would be the perfect gift!"

"Did someone mention a manicure?" George asked as he, too, barged into the conversation. "My wife is a manicurist."

Katy was shocked to see him and glared at Nora to show her contempt for bringing him to her party. What she didn't know was that Mary had accidentally dropped Rachel's name when she was telling her brothers and their wives about Laura.

"Your wife is a manicurist?" Mason echoed.

A round of audible groans then passed through the crowd.

"Oh no!" Mary exclaimed. "I had no idea! You never told me she was a manicurist!"

"What's going on?" Beth asked, merging herself into the huddle moments later. "Why are we all assembling at the door? I thought this was a birthday party for Katy?"

"It was," Jason said, "until Mom blew it by sending her to see Rachel."

"I didn't know," Mary sobbed. Horrified by her part in the disaster, she raised her hands to cover her eyes and shield her from the stares coming at her from every direction.

"Who's Rachel?" Beth asked, innocently enough.

"She's the other one," Mason reminded her. "Can't you keep up with anything?"

"Sorry!" she growled in response. "It's such a Peyton Place around here."

Katy looked at George and saw that his face was turning redder by the second.

"Zip it!" Jason shouted. "Dad's coming!"

"What are you people talking about?" Frank asked as he came to stand next to Mary. "And why is everyone crowded around the door? I've got a hundred dollars' worth of steaks on the grill that will be burnt to a crisp if all of you aren't seated around the table, ready to eat in the next five minutes."

"Oh, Frank!" Mary wailed. "There isn't going to be a party!"

Frank roared, "What the hell? Will someone please tell me what's going on?"

"It's not that complicated," George responded, his voice tinged with bitter, angry sarcasm. "It seems Katy's in love with my wife so her new girlfriend dumped her!"

And so, on Katy's thirty-first birthday, she was officially thrown out of the closet and Frank was finally made aware that his youngest daughter was a lesbian.

Chapter 32

The final week leading up to the start of school was exceptionally hard for Katy as she spent a great deal of that time trying to help her mother explain homosexuality, along with her role in it, to her father. Frank didn't take the news well that his little girl preferred the company of females, even though Katy insisted she had been that way since birth. He openly blamed Rachel and Laura for converting her to a life a sin and swore that neither would be allowed to set foot in his house ("darken his doorstep" were his actual words).

Mary knew better than anyone that it would be hard for him to come to terms with Katy's orientation. She'd had a hard time accepting it herself but knew it would be even more challenging for him. In the forty-three years they'd been married, he would piously defend his religious beliefs and resisted anything that went against or contradicted them. He was a loving and generous man and a wonderful father to his children, but he was also stubborn, opinionated and set in his ways. He firmly believed that men were supposed to be with women and women with men. His Bible said so.

Mary wasn't sure she could persuade him to accept the fact that their daughter was a lesbian but knew she had to try. It was important that Katy not feel ostracized because her father was reluctant to change. There had to be a way to win him over and she set her mind on finding it.

It upset Katy that Frank was so angry. He wouldn't look at her, nor would he speak to her. She knew exactly how Laura must have felt when her parents turned against her.

Her pain and anguish reached an almost unbearable level when, on the first day of school, she passed Laura in the hall and Laura didn't return her greeting. Katy continued to say hello every time they crossed paths, yet nearly three weeks would pass before she finally reciprocated.

"Hi, Laura," she said that monumental day, truly expecting nothing in return.

"Hello," Laura said, her tone barely loud enough for Katy to hear.

"Hello!" Katy repeated excitedly. "How are you?"

"Well as can be expected."

"Does this mean you're speaking to me again?"

"Yeah, I guess it does."

"What changed your mind?"

"I saw your mom at the Hy-Vee yesterday and she told me what happened at your party. Sounds like you've had a lot of crap to deal with ever since. First our shit and then George flipping out like that."

"And now my dad won't have anything to do with me. So, yeah, you can say it was pretty much the worst day of my life."

"It sucks that it all happened on your birthday. I'm sorry."

Katy shook her head to disagree. "Why? None of this was your fault."

"Well, it wasn't yours either."

"I'm having a hard time believing that, Laura."

"Your mom seems to think your dad will come around. What was it she said to me? Oh yeah, 'Failure is not an option.'"

"That sounds like my mom."

"You're lucky to have her on your side. Are you doing all right otherwise?"

"Yeah, as long as the rest of my family stays in my corner."

"I know from experience how hard it is to be shut out by the people you love."

"I just hope my dad comes around."

"He will, Katy."

"I hope so. I miss having him in my life."

"Basketball will be starting back up soon. At least that will keep your mind occupied on something else for a while and give you a break from all the bullshit."

"Yeah. Practices start next week and I'm really looking forward to it – for a bunch of reasons, obviously."

"I need to start coming to more games."

"Are you sure it won't make you uncomfortable? Rachel will be there."

"It is was it is. Have you seen her since your birthday?"

"No."

Neither was sure how to continue the conversation after that and remained quiet until Laura broke the silence with, "I hear they're serving Chili Mac next Tuesday in the cafeteria."

"Is that an invitation?"

Before confirming, Laura wanted Katy to acknowledge her feelings. "I'm still hurt by all of this," she said. "But I know that if we're going to be friends, we have to work this out together."

Katy smiled before offering, "I'm willing to try if you are."

They shared a hug and separated to go to their respective classes. Katy walked into the gymnasium, grabbed a basketball from the equipment rack and carried it out onto the court. Fourth period bell was about to ring, bringing with it Danielle, Courtney and Sandy to spend the hour with her honing their basketball skills, just as they had the year prior.

It pleased Katy to have them back on the roster again. It gave the team maturity, confidence and continuity, all of which would surely help their chances for a successful season. She had lost one starter to high school, but the other four were returning to play under the Lincoln banner.

At their first few practices, Katy randomly paired up different teams to scrimmage against one another and was excited to see how well they all executed together. She was impressed with the skills of everyone on the court, including the newcomers. The mixture of talent was unlike anything she had ever experienced in her nine years as a coach.

The season began with a roaring start as they defeated their first three competitors. The townsfolk began prophesying that, barring any unforeseen circumstances, this group would definitely be contenders for the state championship.

The next match was against Cambridge, the team Katy feared most. Cambridge had outscored them in the first three quarters, but her girls pulled ahead in the fourth. When the final buzzer sounded, the scoreboard read, Lincoln 33, Cambridge 32.

After that teeth-clenching win, the Lincoln crowd rushed onto the floor and began high fiving one another. Katy got dragged into the melee after being congratulated by the opposing coach, and, as she tried to make her way through the pack, several people would reach out to touch her arm or offer her a pat on the back. Mrs. Willoughby, a woman she had known since sixth grade, and, who, according to nearly everyone who had ever gone to Lincoln Junior High, herself included, made the best Chili Mac in all the world, got so caught up in the moment that she cupped Katy's face in her hands and ran a trail of kisses straight down from her forehead to her chin. She was quickly replaced by Mrs. Jones, the school librarian, another long-time acquaintance, who did the exact same thing. Others followed suit, swapping out high fives for hugs, and, occasionally, a little kiss or a peck on the cheek.

Katy followed in the spirit of celebration and grabbed the person standing next to her without looking first to see who it was. Her eyes momentarily closed as she leaned in to give them a hug, and when they reopened, she discovered that her lips had accidentally landed on Rachel's. Before either had a chance to acknowledge what was happening, Bob Lyons, the boys' basketball coach, manhandled his way into their embrace.

"My turn!" he blurted out as he pulled Katy into his arms and planted a wet, sloppy kiss on the side of her face. "Congratulations on the win, Katy! Those girls of yours played magnificently tonight! This will be front page news in Sunday's paper for sure!"

Still in his grasp, Katy peered over his shoulder to look for Rachel, who had already skirted the crowd and was approaching the exit doors. Knowing she would need to hurry to catch her before she left, she peeled away from him to chase after her.

"Rachel!" she shouted. "Wait!"

Rachel stopped and turned around.

"What happened back there… I didn't know it was you," Katy said when she caught up with her. She wondered if Rachel would consider her apology proper or insulting.

"That's okay," Rachel reassured her. "Everybody was doing it."

Katy thought it best to not discuss the matter any further. Instead, she said, "Dani was incredible tonight. Most Valuable Player in my opinion!"

"Thank you, Katy. She'll be pleased to hear that."

"You're welcome. Anyway, it was great seeing you."

"It was great seeing you, too. I hope you're doing well."

"I'm all right," Katy answered, knowing it wasn't really the truth but not knowing what else to offer in its place. "How about you? How are you doing?"

"We're all good. Thanks for asking."

After a long pause, Rachel glanced at Katy's hands and added, "I'm still working at the salon. You should come by sometime. You could use a touch up."

And with that, she turned and walked away.

Chapter 33

Katy had spoken to Nora only once since her birthday and they somehow managed to avoid the elephant in the room during that conversation. She decided it was time to tell her what she had confessed to Mary and Mason.

"Wassup?" Nora squawked into the receiver.

"Just waitin' on your ass to call me," Katy answered mockingly.

"Sorry, I've been busy. How the hell are ya?"

"To be honest, my life has been somewhat crazy these past few weeks."

"So, I've heard."

"What did you hear?"

"Besides non-stop ranting from George about your supposed affair with his wife?"

"Yes, besides that."

"Well, your mom and Mason shared some pretty juicy tidbits with me at the party."

"What did they tell you?"

"Mason told me that your heartbreak person in Texas was a she, not a he, and Mary filled me in about you and Laura."

"I should've been the one to tell you all that... Well, that I'm a..."

"A lesbian?" Nora intruded. "I hate to burst your bubble, Katy, but I've known that since we were in grade school."

"So, my parents and I, we were the last to figure it out?"

"Seems that way."

"Geez…"

"I wanted to say something to you a long time ago but Mason convinced me not to. He said you needed to come to that realization on your own. I was planning to talk to you after the party, but with George being so upset and all, we just had to get him out of there. Plus, I knew you needed time to deal with your dad."

"That's still a sore subject. He won't talk to me. Not even about basketball."

"Don't worry, he'll come around in his own time. While we're on the subject of basketball, congratulations on the big win against Cambridge! Your girls served up some serious whoop-ass the other night."

"You were at the game?"

"No, I heard it from George, believe it or not."

"You know, I was really miffed that you brought him to my party."

"I know, and I'm sorry for that. They were supposed to just drop me off. Your mom insisted that they at least come in to wish you a happy birthday."

"They?"

"Yeah, George and Steve. They were supposed to go bowling that night."

"Next time I have a party, take a taxi, will ya?"

"Ha! Ha! I will for sure."

"Why don't you ask Steve to watch the baby tonight so that you and I can go catch a movie or something?"

"Love to, but can't. George is taking us to dinner."

"Okay. If you don't think it'll set him off, tell him and Rachel I said hello."

"It's just George. Rachel isn't coming."

"Oh? Is she working tonight?"

"I have no idea. We don't talk to her much anymore."

Katy shifted in her chair and switched the phone to her other ear. "Why not?"

"Haven't you heard? They're separated."

"What? When did that happen?"

"I don't know exactly. It's been a couple of months, I think."

"I saw them at Luigi's right after I came back from Texas and they looked happy. I mean, they were holding hands. What happened?"

"She told George she had feelings for someone else."

"Where is she now?"

"She and the kids are still at the house."

"And George?"

"He's been staying with us since the split."

"Wow. That was unexpected."

"You can't seriously believe that, Katy."

"Why?"

"Because, you big dope, everyone thinks she left him for you."

"Say what?"

"You heard me."

"Why would they think that?"

"Speaking only for myself, I've seen the way she looks at you – at basketball games, at your housewarming… I could tell something was going on between you that night."

"Why does everybody keep saying that? Nothing happened!"

"Maybe not physically, but you two were definitely exchanging sparks."

Katy wanted to object but Nora continued without giving her the chance. "And then George accuses you of being in love with her at your birthday party? He didn't just come up with that on his own, Katy. Someone must have said something for him to think that."

Unbeknownst to either woman at that point was that it was actually Katy's mother and not Rachel that had spilled those beans.

"I can't believe you haven't said anything about this before now," Katy challenged.

"It wasn't my place. Look, don't take this wrong, but I hope their marriage can be saved. I'm from a broken home and it sucks. I don't want that for their kids."

"My mom told me to stay away for the same reason."

"I love you, Katy, and I want you to be happy, but she's right. If Rachel does care for you, getting involved at this point would only serve to complicate things for their family. They need to work through this on their own."

"I get that. I'm not going to do anything to jeopardize their chances of getting back together. Rachel and I have nothing to do with each other and I don't see that changing anytime soon."

"Good. Let her come to you if things don't work out between them. Listen, I gotta go now. The baby's crying."

"Okay. Call me sometime."

"Will do. You take care and stay out of trouble, you big ol' lesbian."

Katy laughed at her silly name calling as she hung up the phone. She was glad that Nora had no intentions of shutting her out her like her father had. With everything else she was dealing with, losing her best friend would have surely pushed her over the edge.

Her next call was to Laura.

"Good morning," Katy announced when she picked up.

"Morning," Laura answered with a yawn.

"Did I wake you?"

"I'm just taking my time getting around this morning. The only thing I've managed so far is making coffee and reading the paper."

Katy started to tell her about the win over Cambridge but Laura kept on talking.

"Sorry I missed the game on Friday. Must have been a real tit twister."

"Your butchery of the English language never ceases to amaze me. But you're right. The girls were really on top of their game. It was close but we pulled it out in the end."

"I read that in the paper. Have you seen it yet? Your picture is on the front page."

"Because of the win?"

"No, because of your lip-lock with Rachel."

"What? No way!"

"Way, my friend. This is definitely the hottest thing to happen around these parts in a very long time! The storyline called it a post-game celebration unlike any other and said everyone was kissing everyone. Shit, girl! This is better than the Time Magazine D-Day cover!"

"Oh no! This could ruin any chances of getting back together!"

"Who? You and Rachel?"

"George and Rachel," Katy corrected.

"George and Rachel? Her husband? Are they not together anymore?"

"Yeah. Nora just told me that they split up a couple months ago."

"Well then, what are you waiting for? Go talk to her!"

"I promised I wouldn't interfere in their marriage."

"Promised who?"

"My mom – and Nora."

"It wouldn't be interfering. Not if they're separated."

"I don't know. George has had it in for me since my birthday party. And now this…"

"What? The picture? Don't fret about that. It wasn't presented in any type of 'gay' way. There were photos of other people in the article, too, not just the one of you two."

"Still, I think it's best that I avoid that family altogether. I'm Dani's coach, after all. This could get ugly on so many levels and I don't want that innocent kid to end up in the middle of all of it. I need to keep my distance so they can work through their stuff."

"I still think you should at least go talk to her."

"Not until this blows over. I'm already dealing with enough shit with my dad. He's gonna blow a gasket when he sees that article."

"Let him. That's his problem, not yours."

"You're probably right. I just hope none of this comes back on Dani."

"Give her more credit than that. She's a sharp kid."

"Guess I better read the paper to find out what kind of mess I'm in. I'll see you at school tomorrow."

Laura hurried to get her last comment in before Katy disconnected.

"I'm gonna frame that picture!"

Katy retrieved the paper from her front porch and laid it open on the kitchen table. Before sitting down to read it, she poured herself a cup of coffee and set her cell phone on the counter. She had forgotten to turn the ringer on from the night before and it continued to rack up calls the entire time she was reading the article. By the time she reached the end of the story, she had ten messages in the voicemail queue. Most of which, she would come to find out later, were from Mary.

Chapter 34

Katy thought it best to not make a fuss over the newspaper article but Mary had an entirely different opinion on how the matter should be dealt with. Unaware that the number of messages on her phone continued to grow – the greatest contributor still being Mary – she poured a second cup of coffee and carried it to the bathroom, finishing it off just before taking a shower.

She had already dried her face and was in the act of wrapping the towel around her head to keep her hair from dripping when her mother stormed into the bathroom. Mary was holding the newspaper up and waving it in the air. Katy could see that she was fuming as she snarled, "What do you have to say for yourself?"

"Uh… um…," Katy stammered as she struggled with the towel to get it off her head and cover her naked body with it instead. "How did you get in here?"

"With my key," Mary snapped angrily. "The one you gave me when you bought the place, remember?"

"I forgot you had one. You've never used it before."

"This is the first time I've had reason to."

"You should've called first."

"I did," Mary protested. She then shook the newspaper in front of Katy again.

"How do you intend to straighten this out?" she asked with an equal mix of despair and rage. "Your father is beside himself. I've never seen him so angry."

"I don't know what you're talking about."

"Of course you do, Katy. It's all over the front page!"

"Chill out, Mom. You're scaring me."

"There had better be a good explanation for this."

"It's just a picture that was taken after the game. I don't understand why you're so upset."

"You know exactly why I'm upset! This is an embarrassment, a public humiliation! What were you thinking? Have you no shame?"

"Now hold on, Mother. It was an innocent photograph. Don't read anything more into it than that."

"How can I not, Katy? You tell me you're a lesbian, then you tell me you're in love with Danielle's mother, and now the two of you are kissing all over the front page of the Lincoln Herald Banner! Everyone in the entire county is going to see this!"

"Was there a plan to keep my lesbianism a secret?"

"Don't be silly. Of course, there wasn't a plan. But you should have had more consideration for your family than this."

Deep down, Katy sympathized with her reaction and knew that her dad would have reacted the same way when he saw the picture. Mary's histrionics, however, were making her more than a little bit aggravated.

"If you're looking for an apology," she growled, "I'm afraid you'll be disappointed. It's not like I planned on getting my picture taken. I mean, did you see the other pictures? Everyone was kissing everyone!"

"So, what are you going to do? Leave it alone and hope that it will all go away?"

"That's what I'm thinking."

"I swear, Katy. If this causes your father's blood pressure to skyrocket again…"

"Then I'll take him to the hospital myself."

"Don't be smug with me, young lady."

"Then stop chastising me for things that are out of my control."

Mary shook her head and mumbled softly, "I knew this lesbian thing was going to cause trouble."

"What did you say?" Katy asked, although she had heard Mary perfectly well.

"Nothing," Mary answered scornfully. "I am going to go home now to check on your father. You might want to call later to make sure he's okay."

"I will. Thanks for stopping by, Mom."

Always a pleasure, she thought sarcastically.

Mary slammed the front door on her way out and did the same with her car door prior to speeding away. Katy spent the rest of the day brainstorming ways to minimize the impact the photograph might have on her family, on Rachel's family, and, by default, the entire community. By nightfall, she had come up with a few options, none of which made her feel comfortable or secure in their outcome. Knowing it was time to bring in the big guns, she called Beth for some sage, sisterly advice.

"That's bad news," Beth quipped after Katy's explanation. "Get it? 'Bad news?' Did you catch the pun there?"

"Be serious, Beth."

"Sorry. Well, it sounds to me like Mom is the one blowing a gasket here. Have you called or gone over there yet?"

"Are you nuts? I'd be safer walking into my own execution! I'll just wait and call her tomorrow."

"That will only piss her off more. You know how she is. I'll call and talk to her. Maybe I can calm her down. To be honest, you have bigger things to worry about than Mom and Dad."

"What do you mean?"

"Lincoln is a conservative town, Katy, with lots of Conservative Republicans afoot. I bet they're shitting in their pants right about now."

"So, what do I do?"

"For right now, I'd say ignore it and see what happens."

"That's what I told Mom."

"She would probably agree if it wasn't coming from you. Batten down the hatches, sis. You've got a bumpy road ahead of you."

"Thanks, Beth. I appreciate you helping out with Mom."

"I'll see what I can do from my side of the globe. Call me if you need anything else."

Beth kept her promise and called Mary, who, in turn, phoned Katy not long after that call ended.

"I'm so sorry," Mary blurted out when Katy answered. "I didn't mean to come down so hard on you. I'm just afraid of what this picture might do to our family's reputation."

"I know," Katy agreed. "I'm scared, too. For all of us!"

"We'll put on a united front and deal with whatever fallout there is together."

"What about Dad?"

"Don't worry, sweetheart, I'll handle your father. You go on to bed. It's going to be a long day tomorrow."

"Goodnight, Mom."

"Night, Katy. Try to get some rest, okay?"

"I'll try. Thanks for calling me back."

Chapter 35

Katy dressed for work the next morning and drove to school, all the while trying to prepare herself for the fallout that surely awaited her. Laura pulled in behind her and they walked across the parking lot together.

"How are you feeling?" Laura asked.

A scowl transformed Katy's face as she replied, "Apprehensive. Are you sure you want to be seen with me?"

"Doesn't scare me. Why are you apprehensive?"

"I don't know. It's just a gut feeling."

"Please. It's not like you slept with the principal's wife or anything. Stop worrying about it. It was nothing. Treat it that way."

"I hope you're right, Laura."

Katy couldn't help but feel that Laura had undervalued the repercussion that could come from a situation like this. She was from a big city and didn't understand small towns and the mentalities that populate them.

She spent the entire morning on edge, constantly looking over her shoulder and tensing up whenever anyone showed up at her office uninvited. Mary's premonition had proven itself true in that it was turning out to be the longest day of her life.

When the bell rang for fourth period, Dani, Sandy and Courtney came into the gym as usual. Dani was quiet and standoffish but the other two were chatting up a storm until Katy got within ten feet of them and then they fell silent as well.

"Hi, girls," she announced as she came closer.

The three didn't offer a verbal response but nodded their heads instead. Katy knew why they were behaving that way. It was the article in the paper.

"Look," she said, deciding to tackle the issue with them head on. "I know this seems weird, but it's just a story in the newspaper. Everyone was hugging and kissing each other after the game, not just me and Dani's mom, but the publisher decided to put that picture on the front page. It isn't a big deal. Please don't let anyone convince you otherwise."

"My mom says I should stay away from you," Sandy announced. "Just in case."

"And how do you feel about that?"

"I don't have a choice. I have to do what she tells me."

"What did your parents say, Courtney?"

"Nothing," Courtney answered. "The paper was still on the porch when I left for school."

"And you, Dani? Did your mom say anything?"

"No," Dani replied. "But she was crying when I got on the bus this morning."

"Dani," Katy said softly, knowing that what she feared most, Dani being caught in the middle of everything, was becoming a reality. "I'm so sorry for all of this."

"It's okay. I know the truth about what really happened."

Katy reached out to invite all three into a hug. Courtney and Dani came forward and linked their arms together around her neck.

"I can't," Sandy said, backing away. "My mom would be mad."

Katy began to sob. Dani hugged her a second time and whispered in her ear, "It's gonna be all right, Coach."

It was then that Principal Hall entered the gymnasium and came toward them.

"Miss Hopkins," he said as he approached. "I need to speak with you in my office."

"Yessir," Katy replied. Her tone was resigned. She knew what he was going to say.

She gave Dani and Courtney a final squeeze and offered all three girls a smile before leaving the gym. She followed the principal to his office and stood by the door while he situated himself behind his desk. His secretary, Mrs. Maypole, had arrived earlier and was seated in a chair to his right with her notepad and pen poised for dictation.

"Katy," he said, motioning for her to come forward. "Please have a seat."

Katy did as he instructed. After sitting down, she folded her hands across her lap. Principal Hall started in on her right away.

"I'm sure you saw yesterday's paper, or at least heard about the story. I'm hoping there is no cause for alarm, but the School Board held an emergency session last night and they've asked for an investigation into the matter. As you know, homosexuality is not widely accepted in Lincoln and while it's not expressly forbidden here at the school, it's just not…," he paused as he searched for the right word, "tolerated. I've been on the phone all day fielding calls about this."

"There's nothing to investigate," Katy contended. "It was an innocent photo taken after the game. That's all."

"I believe you, but the system has to run its course. You understand, don't you?"

"What happens now?"

"You will continue to report for work until you are told otherwise. Do not discuss this with anyone, Katy. It will only make things worse for you."

"All right. Is that all?"

"There is one more thing."

"Yes?"

"You should refrain from having physical contact with the female students to avoid any further speculations of impropriety."

Katy's jaws were flaring as she stared into his eyes and contemplated her response.

"Fine," she responded with an exasperated snarl. "Anything else?"

"No. Mrs. Maypole will draft up a report for your personnel file; however, if nothing comes of this, the document will be destroyed."

"Thank you, sir." She immediately felt like an idiot for thanking him.

"No, it's I who should be thanking you," he responded after rising up from his seat. "You are an amazing teacher and a damn fine coach, Miss Hopkins."

As he held the door open for her, he glanced over his shoulder at Mrs. Maypole to make sure she was out of earshot and added in a low voice, "I'm on your side, Katy. I hope you know that."

Laura had seen her go into his office and waited in the hall for her to come out.

"What happened in there?" she asked when Katy emerged.

"The Board is starting an investigation."

"You're kidding. On what grounds?"

"Inappropriate behavior."

"But you didn't *do* anything!"

"Doesn't matter. It's obvious they're not going to let this go."

"Don't worry, Katy. The truth will come out and all of this will blow over."

Unfortunately, there were plenty of other reasons for Katy to worry. One of which was Mildred Snodgrass, a fellow teacher at the school and also the mother of Michael, the last man she dated. More than four years had passed since their relationship ended, but his mother continued to harbor ill feelings toward her and would glare at her every time they crossed paths. Her husband was President of the School Board and they held a great deal of influence over what happened at the school, and, in the community as well. Mrs. Snodgrass was a closeted bigot and didn't care much for Laura, or any person of color for that matter, and shared that opinion quite often with like-minded members of her inner circle. She also believed that homosexuals were an abomination and needed to be wiped off the face of the earth.

After seeing the kiss and accompanying article in the paper, Mildred reacted with her typical sanctimonious righteousness and became enraged, insisting that her husband, on behalf of the school *and* the town of Lincoln, dismiss Katy outright for deviant behavior and blatant disregard for moral fortitude and common decency. Mr. Snodgrass, a minister at the First United Methodist Church, felt inclined to agree with her.

Even though she had not been privy to those details, Katy had no doubt it was the two of them that had called for the emergency session. And, she knew they had the power to make trouble for her outside of school as well. She remained on pins and needles every day after that, jumping each time the phone rang and cringing every time someone tapped her on the shoulder.

"You need to chill," Laura said in another failed attempt to calm her. "You're gonna give yourself a stroke."

"I can't help it," Katy confided. "I'm scared to death I'm going to lose my job!"

Laura didn't respond, knowing there was not much consolation she could offer in the face of that possibility.

"They're blowing this whole thing out of proportion," Katy added. "Why do people do that?"

Laura was eager to share her thoughts on this more philosophical question. To her, the answer was obvious.

"Because they're afraid of what they don't know."

"It's just a picture, for Christ's sake!"

"But they don't see it as a picture. They see this as a threat to their way of life."

"They must be the ones who left the notes on my car this morning."

"What do you mean? What notes?"

"There were only two, but they were both pretty ugly. It looked like they were trying to write some shit across my back windshield, too."

"What did the notes say?"

"Oh, you know, stupid stuff like 'Jesus Hates Fags' and 'Lincoln Loathes Lesbians.'"

"Some folks can't handle anything that challenges the way they think. It makes them uncomfortable."

"Great. So, we're all scared. Now what?"

"All you can do, really, is just continue to ride out the storm. Maybe lay low for a while. You know what they say, 'Out of sight, out of mind.'"

"But the girls have a game Wednesday night."

Laura reconsidered her statement and offered instead, "Well, then, you should go to the game. If you don't, people will think you're hiding because you're guilty. I guess you should really just try to keep things as normal as possible. If that *is* possible."

"This really blows, Laura."

"I agree."

"Will you come to the game?"

"Of course."

"Thanks. It'll be nice having a friend there."

"You have more people in your corner than you realize, Katy."

"I hope you're right."

"I know it's hard, but try to relax. I'll catch up with you later."

When Laura reached the end of the hall she turned to Katy and mimed the motions of deep breathing. Katy smiled and nodded to show that she understood.

The rest of that day and the next continued as a typical Monday and Tuesday, with the exception of more notes left on her car and in her mailbox as well. After her last class on Wednesday, she packed up the athletic equipment then decided to wait in her office until game time to avoid having to face anyone. As one hour ticked off into another, her nemesis, the contentious Mildred Snodgrass, was on the phone trying to convince the remaining Board members to all vote with her husband in favor of Katy's dismissal.

The game that night was a blowout as Lincoln captured another win by a landslide score of 54-32. They were now the only team in the league with no losses. The ever-faithful home town fans didn't rush the court as they had for Cambridge, but people came forward to praise and congratulate Katy nonetheless.

It was true, people did care about her. She could feel their love, even without the intimacy of their touch. Her emotional walls began to crumble and she was unable to hold back her tears.

Laura was the first to approach her, followed by Doc Brown, the town veterinarian whose daughter played second-string on the team. "You're an amazing coach and teacher, Katy Hopkins," he said, loud enough for all to hear. He then grabbed her hand and raised it high in the air while adding in an even louder voice, "And a damn fine human being!"

"Amen to that," Harry from Crossroads chimed in. "We heard the School Board is trying to have you fired. We're all praying for you. Our kids and grandkids adore you and Lincoln is lucky to have you!"

"Thank you," she told the crowd. "This means more to me than you'll ever know."

She then glanced in the direction of the locker room and saw Dani waiting for her by the door. As those gathered around her began to disburse, she went to join her players.

"See," Dani bragged as she came closer. "I told you everything would be okay."

"Thanks," Katy said while ruffling her hair. "Next time I'm in a pinch, I'm definitely coming to you for advice!" Draping her arm around the young girl's shoulder, they entered the locker room side by side.

Chapter 36

Katy reported to work on Monday as usual. The entire weekend had been more or less uneventful, but for a couple prank calls, and she was glad that more time had passed without adding to the aftermath. She was starting to feel more assured that the worst had passed; however, her sense of peace would be short lived. At a quarter past nine, Mr. Hall rapped on her door.

"I hate to be the one to tell you this," he said as he stepped into her office, "but the School Board decided to suspend you pending the results of the investigation. Someone at the game said they saw you acting inappropriately with one of the students. They called another emergency session last night and the vote was 5-2. I'm sorry, Katy."

"Acting inappropriately? What are you talking about?"

"It was reported that you were fondling one of the girls on your team outside of the locker room after the game."

"That's nuts! I merely put my arm around the shoulder of one of the players. Ask her! Or, better yet, ask anyone from the crowd of people that were there watching!"

"I'm sorry, Katy," he repeated. "There's nothing I can do."

"I'm innocent!" Katy cried out. "I've done nothing wrong!"

"I believe you. Unfortunately, I have to abide by the Board's decision. Gather your things now. I'll walk you out to your car."

Katy took her purse out of her desk drawer and followed him across the gym floor. A group of boys were playing a game of three-on-three volleyball and stopped when they saw them approaching.

"Hey, Ms. Hopkins!" one student called out.

"Hi, Matt," she responded.

"Where are you going?" another student asked.

"I'm going home."

"Why? Are you sick?"

Katy and Mr. Hall exchanged an awkward glance before she replied, "Yes. I'm not feeling at all well today."

Katy continued to walk behind the principal through the hallways and out the front doors. When they reached the parking lot, she turned to him and said, "Mr. Hall?"

"Yes, Katy?"

"If you really believe me, will you help me fight this?"

"There's already a petition being circulated at this very moment. If we get enough signatures, we might be able to overturn the Board's decision."

Katy offered him a half-smile and whispered, "Thank you."

"You mean a lot to a lot of people, Katy. Those of us that have lived here a long time have watched you grow up and consider you a part of our families. We won't have any problem getting those signatures. In fact, I wouldn't be surprised if you're back on the job in no time at all!"

He held her car door open until she had settled into her seat.

"If you need anything," he said while closing it, "anything at all…"

He moved away from the car and started back toward the school. After taking a few steps, he stopped. Katy saw his head droop then watched him raise his hand and wipe the side of his face with it. After lowering his arm, he lifted his head and resumed walking. His compassion and concern for her was obvious.

If anyone can help me beat this, she thought, *he can.*

Before starting the engine, she called her mother to fill her in on the day's events. Mary was livid.

"Oh, for goodness' sake!" she exclaimed loudly. "This has gotten completely out of hand! That darned Mildred Snodgrass is just such an awful busybody!"

"You think she had something to do with this, too?"

"I'm convinced of it. Some of the ladies at church were talking about it yesterday."

"I'm scared, Mom."

"This whole thing is just so ridiculous. You were doing what everyone else was doing after that game. Why are you the only one they're holding accountable?"

"That's what I keep saying!"

"It's the truth. And if the people in Lincoln can't see that, well then, they can all go straight to hell in a hand basket!"

Even though they were miles apart, Katy could visualize her mother's fist waving above her head as she shouted into the telephone. After her rant was over, Mary lowered her voice and told Katy, "I think I'll give Bill Johnson a call tomorrow."

"Bill Johnson... The lawyer?"

"Yes. Just as a precautionary measure."

"You think we need his help?"

"I'll see his mother at bridge tomorrow. I'll have her speak to him."

"Let me know what comes of that. How is Dad handling all of this?"

"He hasn't said much of anything since all of this started. I'm a little worried. I've never known him to be so withdrawn."

"Should I talk to him?"

"No, dear. He needs to process this on his own terms."

"I'd still like to drop by sometime, if that's all right."

"Why don't you come for dinner tonight? I'll whip up something special. It will give us a chance to sit down as a family and talk."

Chapter 37

Frank was on the sofa watching television when Katy arrived at her parents' house.

"Hey, Pop!" she called out. Frank made no attempt to acknowledge her.

"Is Mom here?" she asked.

She crossed in front of the television to find her mother and still got no response from her father. She continued toward the kitchen where she found Mary scooping up a handful of diced onion and tossing it into a saucepan on the stove. Tears were streaming down her face.

"Are you all right?" Katy asked.

"It's this darn onion," Mary told her.

"I said hi to Dad on my way in but he didn't answer. He just kept watching TV like I wasn't even there."

Without saying a word, Mary removed her apron and tossed it onto the counter.

"Francis Michael Hopkins!" she shouted as she marched into the living room. "You get off that couch this instant and say hello to your daughter!"

Frank didn't budge.

"Frank!" Mary screamed. "I'll not have you acting that way in this house!"

"It's my house," he argued. "And I'll act any way I damn well please, woman!"

"Don't you take that tone with me, mister!"

"What is going on here?" Katy asked.

"Your father is being an imbecile," Mary answered smugly.

"Because of me?"

"Don't be silly, Katy. It has nothing to do with you."

Frank was quick to disagree.

"Of course it does. Our lives have been turned upside down because of her. We are the joke of the town. Everyone is talking about us and laughing behind our backs!"

"That is absurd," Mary challenged. She had moved past being angry with him and was now on the verge of seething. "Katy has done nothing wrong! How can you side with those idiots?"

"I've told you a million times, I don't want to talk about this!"

"Oh, we're going to talk about this. We're going to have it out – right here, right now!"

"Maybe I should go," Katy insisted.

"Don't you dare," Mary hissed. Her eyes had narrowed into tiny slits. "I asked you to dinner, and by God, we will sit at that table together as a family!"

"I'm not hungry," Frank grumbled.

Mary pushed back: "Then you'll sit there and watch us eat. Set the table, Katy. Frank, you can get everyone a drink."

"But, but…," he stammered.

"But nothing," Mary interrupted. "I'll have a Bloody Mary to coincide with the mood I'm in. Katy? What will you have?"

"Water is fine for me," Katy answered softly.

Frank rose from the sofa and stomped across the room. Moments later, he and Katy were standing on opposite sides of the table.

"Do you see how upset your mother is?" he asked in a hushed voice. "She's crying because of you."

"That's funny," Katy answered flatly. "She told me it was because of the onion."

"That's what she wants you to believe. She's a mess, Katherine, and it's your fault."

Mary carried in a platter with three, beautifully prepared Cornish Hens and set it in the middle of the table then went back to the kitchen for the sides. In the delivery style of a sergeant at a military training camp, when she returned, she barked out the order, "Everyone sit down."

It was obvious to Katy that she was no longer concerned with being diplomatic.

"Frank, I want you to say grace."

"Mary…," he whined.

"Just do it," she demanded. "Now, let's all join hands and give thanks for our many blessings."

Frank grabbed Mary's hand but refused to take his daughter's. Katy stood up and looked directly at her mother. "This was a mistake," she muttered under her breath.

Mary heard the pain in her voice and started to cry. This time, her tears were real.

"Look at what you've done!" Frank shouted at Katy. "You've made your mother cry again!"

Mary was unable to control her fury and unleashed all of it onto her husband.

"Frank! I've never known you to be so cruel. This is your daughter, your own flesh and blood. What has happened to you? You've allowed this nonsense to consume you and I can't take any more of it – or of you!"

She then turned to Katy. "Come on, sweetie."

Katy and Frank were both looking at her with confused expressions.

"What are you saying?" Frank asked.

"I'm leaving you, Frank. I'll be staying with Katy until you come to your senses."

Katy and Frank then exchanged blank stares with one another.

"Katy," Mary said, her tone much calmer than before. "I don't trust your father to be civil with you until I return, so wait for me in the car while I go get my things. I'll be out shortly."

"Yes, ma'am," Katy answered obediently.

Frank returned to the living room and crumpled onto the sofa. Mary tried to say something else but he drowned her out by increasing the volume on the television.

Through clenched jaws, she growled at him, "You'll regret this one day."

After packing a suitcase with a week's worth of necessities, she stood in front of the television and glared at him.

"You have one week to straighten up your act, buster," she warned. "If not, the only thing you'll be watching on that thing is Divorce Court!"

Chapter 38

In their first two days as roommates, Katy's phone rang incessantly. The local radio station had picked up the story of her suspension and were calling non-stop to secure an exclusive interview with her. After hanging up on several calls in a row, Mary announced in a fit of frustration that they were no longer going to answer it. And, after seeing a news report on a Kansas City station about an unnamed teacher under investigation in Lincoln, the television became off limits as well. Katy, unsettled by all the undue attention, eagerly complied with her mother's demands.

The morning after the broadcast, a television van parked across the street from her house with a small crew of reporters and cameramen that continually paced up and down the sidewalk next to it. Every time either one of them went outside, one of the crew would come charging toward them waving a microphone.

"Hey, Hopkins!" they yelled. "Anything you want to say to the citizens of Lincoln?" to which neither of them responded.

In the midst of everything else, mother and daughter were still trying to adjust to their new living arrangement. Katy stayed quiet and distracted most of the time and would wander around cleaning her already spotless house. Mary, meanwhile, spent hours on her cell phone, hell-bent on restoring her daughter's tarnished reputation.

It was a lonely existence, one not easily tolerated. In its absurdity, the two of them found that sharing the isolation made their bond stronger than ever. They were in exile together, a place where secrets were confessed and transgressions exposed. It was in this shared seclusion that Mary began to realize how hard it must have been for Katy to live against her grain. It saddened her that she had not lived an authentic life, instead going down a path that was expected of her.

"I wish I knew you back then," Mary confessed one day as they were having lunch together.

"What do you mean?" Katy inquired. "You've known me my whole life."

"I know who you became, sweetie, but not who you should have been all along. I wonder where your life would be now if we had known early on that you were gay."

"I don't think it would've been much different."

"I do. I think you would've had the chance to be happy with someone a long time ago. You tried to be traditional – dating all those boys – and ended up wasting a good portion of your life."

"It wasn't wasted."

"But it's time you can never get back."

"Gee, Mom. You make it sound like I've got one foot in the grave. I've still got a lot of life left in me. I'm not a total loss."

The two wrapped their arms around each other to share a hug. That's when Mary glanced over her daughter's shoulder and saw one of the reporters pointing a telescopic camera lens at them through the front window.

"Everything will turn out fine," she said as she sidestepped Katy and walked to the window. Peeved by their incessant stalking, she stuck out her tongue and flipped off the reporter before pulling the drapes closed and joining Katy on the couch.

"Danielle told me the same thing," Katy said and then raised an eyebrow and gave Mary a sideways glance. "Did you just give that guy the bird?"

"Danielle is a smart girl," Mary answered, purposely avoiding her question. "I know I've said this before, but she reminds me of you at that age."

"I hope I haven't ruined her life like I've ruined mine."

"Don't be so dramatic, Katherine. Your life is not ruined and neither is Danielle's. This is merely a bump in the road."

As her mother went on telling her not to give up on herself, Katy stopped listening and fell into a daydream about the newspaper photo of her and Rachel coming to life and blossoming from the innocent kiss that it was into a full-blown make-out session. It kept playing over and again in her head, even though she tried to snap out of it. Thankfully, Mary's poke on her shoulder helped.

"Now we'll have no more of that kind of talk," Mary announced. "You hear me?"

Katy hadn't heard what kind of "talk" she was referring to but readily agreed, nonetheless. And when Mary suggested they get in the car and go for a drive, she readily agreed to that as well.

"Where would you like to go?" Katy asked.

"Let's go to Crossroads," Mary answered. "I've got a hankering for one of Harry's famous margaritas."

Five minutes later, they headed down Oak Street in Katy's car. As Katy turned onto Main, Mary glanced in the side mirror and saw that the news van was trailing them.

"Think you can lose them?" she asked.

"Mother," Katy scoffed in a laughing manner. "We aren't Thelma and Louise."

Half-laughing herself, Mary responded, "It was just a thought."

When they arrived at Crossroads, Mary asked Katy to wait in the car while she went inside alone. The door leading into the bar had barely closed when the reporters started circling her car like vultures, thrusting their microphones and cameras at her from every direction.

Katy held her hands in front of her face to block them from taking any pictures. All of a sudden, the sound of gunshot pierced the night air. She looked around and saw Harry standing in the parking lot with a pistol in his hand.

"This is private property!" he shouted to the reporters. "I suggest you get on out of here before I feel obliged to shoot you."

"You wouldn't do that," one of the men challenged.

"I own this establishment and I am legally allowed to shoot trespassers," Harry told him. "And you look to be trespassing to me."

"He's crazy!" the driver yelled. "Let's go before he pulls that trigger!"

Harry fired another round into the sky as the trio hopped into their van and sped away. When they were gone, he walked up to Katy's car and opened her door.

"Allow me," he said, extending his hand.

"Harry Olson!" Katy exclaimed. "You gun-slinging, old coot!"

"Your mother said she wanted you and her to have a margarita in peace. And what Mary Hopkins asks for, she gets. No questions. Besides, I don't like those pesky reporter types anyway."

For the next two hours, Harry ran everyone off to afford mother and daughter some long overdue, well-deserved relaxation. "We're closed for a private party," he announced to anyone coming in the door. For any that resisted, he simply lifted his pistol from under the counter and laid it on top of the bar. No other words were necessary. His message was loud and clear.

Meanwhile, Mary and Katy sipped away at their margaritas. When it was time for them to leave, Mary repaid his kindness with a peck on the cheek.

"Thank you," she told him. "For allowing us a little comfort, a little fun and a little peace and quiet. You are a gracious man, Harry Olson."

Harry was looking down at the floor but Katy could still see his face turning a bright shade of red. "It was my pleasure," he said quietly. "Don't be a stranger now, ya hear?"

The three of them walked to the parking lot together and Katy watched as he held the door open for her mother and helped her into the car.

"Awww," she snickered as they drove away. "He's sweet on you! How cute is that?"

"Harry has had a crush on me since high school," Mary responded.

"Why, Mary Hopkins! You're a big ol' flirt! I had no idea!"

"Not a word of this to your father, Katy."

"Well, I'm telling Beth at least."

"After I'm dead and gone you can tell whomever you'd like. Till then, let's just keep this between the two of us."

The drive home was a happy one and both women were smiling when Katy made the final turn onto Oak. As they got closer to the house, they saw the news van and their smiles were quickly turned upside down.

The phone was ringing as they entered the house. Mary looked at Katy with disgust when she started to pick it up and screamed at her, "Don't answer that!"

"I wasn't," Katy countered. "I'm going to unplug it." After removing the cord from the handset, she added, "I'm kinda tired, so I'm gonna turn in early tonight."

"Me, too. I'll see you at breakfast, sweetheart."

"Night, Mom. Thanks for the company. And the margaritas!"

Chapter 39

Still half asleep when she shuffled into the kitchen, Katy absentmindedly plugged the phone back in and it rang almost immediately. She instinctively picked it up without thinking and Mary frowned at her from across the counter.

"Hello?" she announced to the caller while returning Mary's grimacing expression with one of her own.

"Katy, this is Bob Lyons, you know, from the school. Have you heard anything yet about coming back? The girls have a game tonight and need a coach."

"No, the school hasn't said anything. Not to me, anyway."

"Well, darn. I just assumed the situation would have been resolved by now. I've let the girls practice with the boys this past week, but I wouldn't feel comfortable filling in for you as coach. The substitute they hired doesn't want to do it either. Is there anyone you could recommend to take your place? What about Miss Stiles?"

Katy laughed loudly.

"Laura's an English teacher and doesn't know the first thing about basketball!"

"Oh well, I just thought that… you know, since she's a… well, never mind. So, what do you want me to do?"

"Why can't you fill in for me?"

"I would, Katy, but I don't know your plays and there isn't enough time to learn them before the game."

"Let me think about this and I'll get back with you."

"Sure. Just call me here at the school."

A bunch of options were running through Katy's mind until one finally caught hold. Thinking it might solve the problem, she shrieked, "Wait a second! I have an idea!"

"Go ahead. I'm listening."

"You *are* going to coach tonight. I'll meet you at the gym in an hour and explain everything then."

"Don't you go making a fool out of me tonight, Katy Hopkins. I have a reputation of my own to live up to."

"I promise I won't. Thanks, Bob."

"All right. I'll see you in a little while."

Katy shared her idea with Mary, who agreed it was brilliant.

"That's a great plan!" her proud mother exclaimed. "How can I help?"

"You can make sure no one interferes or tries to have me ejected."

"They'll have to throw me out, too, and I definitely will not go gentle into that good night!"

"Wrong time to quote Shakespeare, Mom."

"It's times like this I realize how much I liked Laura."

"Why is that?"

"She would have known it was Dylan Thomas I was quoting, not Shakespeare."

"To-may-to, to-mah-to, Mother. Those writer types – they're all the same to me."

Mere minutes before the hour was up, Katy arrived at the school and called Bob to let her into the gymnasium through the side doors. Fortunately, the students were all at lunch so they had the place to themselves.

"What's this great plan?" he asked as they sat down on the bleachers.

"Do you have any earbuds?" she asked in return.

"What are earbuds?"

"Earpieces for a cell phone."

"You mean those Bluetooth thingies?"

"Yeah."

"I think some came with the phone but I've never used them."

"We'll need to get it set up then."

"Why do we need that?"

"Because I'm going to talk you through the game tonight."

"Can't you just sit behind the bench and tell me what to do?"

"That might get me in more trouble than I already am. You know, interfering with official school activities or impersonating a coach or some other ridiculous crap they want to charge me with. I figure this is the best shot we have, Bob."

Bob thought for a moment and said, "You're probably right. One problem, though. I don't have those earbud things on me. They're at the house."

"All right. Can you go grab my playbook? It's in the side drawer of my desk. I'll wait here in case someone walks in and I need to hide."

"Sure. I'll be right back."

Bob stepped onto the gymnasium floor and walked toward Katy's office on the balls of his feet. *No need to tiptoe,* Katy chuckled to herself. *There's no one here but us, dude!*

He returned moments later and handed her the book. She tucked it under her arm then suggested that they go fetch his earbuds to work out the details before the game.

"It'll have to be a fast trip," he told her. "My next class starts in forty-five minutes."

"Well, then," she responded while grabbing his arm. "We better get moving!"

Bob was in clandestine mode as they walked outside, using his body to shield her from anyone who might be watching. Katy thought his actions were over the top until she saw Principal Hall looking out his window. Regardless of his support for her, she figured he wouldn't want her lurking around the schoolgrounds while she was on suspension.

She moved ahead of Bob as they neared the parking lot so that he could continue blocking the view of anyone behind them. She then followed him to his house and joined him at his front door.

"If anyone sees you…," he whispered.

"We'll tell them we're having an affair," Katy whispered back. "Maybe it'll stimulate reasonable doubt for my current situation."

"You make it sound like you're on trial."

"I may as well be."

"You have come under a bit of scrutiny lately."

Katy couldn't help but respond crudely, "Ya think?"

"There's no reason to get testy, Katy. I'm on your side, remember?"

"Sorry, Bob. The stress is really starting to get to me."

Bob entered the house first and went directly to the kitchen with Katy on his heels.

"I'm pretty sure those things are in here somewhere," he told her.

He reached into a drawer next to the refrigerator and lifted out a small box. Inside where his earbuds, still wrapped in the original packaging.

"So, how do these things work?" he asked as he passed the box to Katy.

"They sync up to your phone. But first, they need to charge."

"For how long?"

Katy read the label on the box before answering.

"It says it takes eight hours for a full charge, which we don't have."

Bob glanced at his watch.

"We have almost six hours until the game starts. Will that be enough? I can leave them here to charge while I'm at school."

"That's the only choice we have. You could use mine, but then I'd have no way to get in touch with you."

Katy pulled her own earbuds out of her jacket pocket.

"I'm guessing you've never used these before."

Bob shook his head that he had not.

"Let me show you how they work." She then handed them to him with her phone. "Hook the loops over your ears and go outside. I'll call you from your house phone."

Bob walked to the front door and gave an exaggerated nod to let her know he was ready. Katy waited a couple of minutes and then dialed her phone number. When he didn't answer, she went to look for him and found him next to his garage.

"Is there a problem?" she asked.

Bob had taken off the earpieces and was holding them in his hand.

"I couldn't figure out how to turn the damn things on," he told her.

After showing him how to activate the receiver, Katy went inside to call again. This time, it worked.

"Hello!" Bob whispered as he peered around the side of his garage to make sure no one was watching. From the muted sound of his voice, Katy knew he had his hand cupped over his mouth.

"Bob, can you hear me?"

"You're coming in loud and clear."

"Good. You can hang up now."

When he rejoined her in the kitchen, he handed Katy back her items.

"Don't forget yours later," she reminded him. "One of the girls can show you how to sync them to your phone. I'll call before the game to make sure we're still good to go."

"Okay."

"We'll have better luck pulling this off if no one knows what we're up to, so don't fiddle with your ears too much. It's important that no one catches on to what we're doing."

Bob nodded that he understood.

"You better head on back to the school now. I'll see you at the game!"

"See ya, Katy."

When Katy returned home, Mary was standing in front of the stove stirring a pot of something that smelled quite delicious.

"I figured you'd want an early dinner to get things ready," Mary told her.

"Thanks, Mom. What are we having?"

"Let's call it stew. I tossed together a few things from the fridge with some canned tomatoes and seasonings."

"Doesn't sound very appetizing. I know what was in my refrigerator, and I don't think any of it belongs in 'stew.'"

"If you're that concerned, have a bowl of cereal instead. Oh wait, nix that. I tossed the milk this morning because it was chunky."

"That's gross, Mother."

"Sorry. I forgot to pick some up at the store yesterday. How is it looking for tonight? Did he agree to help you?"

"Yes, he did. You remember what you're supposed to do, right?"

"Yes, Katy. I'm supposed to be the lookout."

"I'll probably be moving around a bit. If I do, will you want to come with me? Or will you stay in one place and give me some type of signal that someone is onto me?"

"What sort of signal?"

"I don't know. Put your hand on top of your head."

"What if I wave the peace symbol in the air?"

Katy rolled her eyes. "Sure, Mom. If that's what you prefer."

Mary ladled her concoction into two bowls and set one on the table in front of her daughter. Katy took a small bite and was impressed enough to finish all of it. She scooted the empty bowl away afterwards and laid her playbook in its place. Knowing she couldn't take it with her to the game, she would have to spend what time was left memorizing plays before executing her plan.

Chapter 40

Mary and Katy arrived at the school thirty minutes before game time. After getting out of the car, Mary pulled a pair of dark sunglasses out of her purse and put them on.

"What are those for?" Katy asked.

"I'm going incognito," she answered. "I don't want anyone to recognize me."

"Incognito? Are you joking?"

"No, I'm taking this whole thing very seriously, Katy."

"Good Lord," Katy muttered. "You're in Lincoln, Mom, not Hollywood. Now put those things back in your purse right this instant!"

"All right," Mary replied, sulking. "But I want it on record that I tried to keep this on the down-low."

"On the down-low… Do you even know what that means?"

Mary rolled her eyes and mouthed the word "Whatever."

"Your objection is noted," Katy offered to assuage her. "Can we go inside now?"

Mary looked to her left across the parking lot and then to her right before locking eyes with her daughter and loudly exclaiming, "Let's roll!"

Katy walked a few feet behind her in hopes no one would know they were together. She wasn't as concerned with being in cahoots with her as she was being embarrassed by the "Jane Bond" persona that had taken over her mother's mind and body.

Keeping their heads lowered as they entered the gymnasium, they quickly scaled the bleachers until they were on the top row. Once they were seated, Katy took out her phone and called Bob.

"Hello?" he squawked. His voice sounded very shaky.

"It's me, Bob."

"Where are you?"

"In the bleachers at the north end of the gym."

"Okay. We'll be coming out of the locker room in a few minutes."

"Did you answer with the earpiece or your actual phone?"

"With my phone. I do have the things in my ears, though."

"Remember, all you have to do is tap the side to answer. Just like we practiced. Oh, and don't forget to set your phone to vibrate so it doesn't ring out loud."

"All right. I'll be waiting for your call."

"Wish the girls luck for me."

"Will do."

Minutes later, the team from Lincoln ran onto the floor and lined up for pre-game warmups. The hometown crowd rose to their feet, cheering loudly as the girls successfully landed one layup after another. Bob trailed them onto the court and was standing on the sidelines when Katy rang him again. She watched him fidget with one of the earbuds and grab his pant leg simultaneously as his phone vibrated inside the pocket of his trousers. He tapped his ear several times before connecting and then screamed loudly, "What?!?"

"No need to shout," Katy answered reassuringly.

"Sorry, you scared the bejeebers out of me!"

"Listen, before we get going, I just wanted to say thanks for doing this."

"Of course. Anything for the kids. I mean, none of this is their fault."

"I feel the same way. Just so you know, I'd fill in for you if you ever needed it."

"Thanks, Katy."

"The game is going to start pretty soon. Assuming we get the tip-off, I want the girls to run play number five. If we don't get the tip-off, let's start with zone coverage on defense and see how that goes. We can switch to man-to-man if we have to."

"Uh, Katy?"

"Yes, Bob."

"I have no idea what that play is. I never looked at your playbook."

"Let's try this instead. Use your imagination and follow along with me here, okay?"

"Okay."

"Imagine there's a large trumpet laying on its side on the floor. The mouthpiece is at center court and the flange is at the net. Dani follows the shape of the trumpet toward the net, circles back to the free throw line, then comes down the lane a second time and takes a pass from one of her teammates for a layup. Got it? Can you envision that?"

"Yes, I can!"

"Good. For the rest of the game, I'll call out plays by whatever shapes I think they most closely resemble. If you don't understand, please ask!"

"You're a genius, Katy!"

Before disconnecting, Katy provided him with the names of the starting lineup and those who would replace them should it become necessary. When she returned the phone to her lap, she noticed her mother turning her head from side to side as she surveilled the crowd for suspicious behaviors.

"See anything?" she asked her.

"Not yet," Mary responded. "I'll give the signal when something happens. How long are you going to sit here?"

"At least until the game starts. Why?"

"Why make me a lookout if you're here beside me? Where's the challenge in that?"

"Got it, Jane."

"Who's Jane?"

"Jane. That's your super-secret spy code name. Jane Bond."

"I'm only doing what you asked me to, smarty pants. Now stop distracting me and get up and move around like you're supposed to!"

"All right already. I'm going!"

"Remember to keep checking over here for my signal."

"Ten-four, Jane."

"And stop calling me that!"

"Yes, Mother."

"Don't call me that either. Someone might recognize us."

Yeah, like everybody in Lincoln doesn't know you're my mother, crazy woman!

Katy didn't want to stay in one place too long to avoid the same people overhearing her conversations with Bob. After each call to relay a new play or substitution, she would move to a different seat then check to see if Mary was trying to alert her. She glanced over at one point and saw her frantically waving a peace sign with one hand and pointing at the school security guard with the other.

She looks like she's in a time warp from the sixties, Katy thought as she giggled aloud. *Straight from the grassy fields of Woodstock right into this very gymnasium.*

When the buzzer signaled the end of the first quarter, Katy returned to her original seat to explain the presence of the man in uniform and affirm to her mother that he had not been sent by the School Board to arrest them. He was the security guard at all home games, she told her, and then, to put her even more at ease, added as a funny sidebar that he was more often off flirting with the divorcee who ran the concession stand than he was guarding the gymnasium.

Katy returned to moving around and whenever she called Bob he would reach for his earbud and pant leg at the same time. It was an obvious distraction that Katy thought others were probably noticing as well. With each call, she began to worry that they would get caught. Scanning the crowd, it appeared the only thing the spectators were interested in was watching the girls run up and down the court.

Their combined efforts were successful and Lincoln ended the game with another decisive win. As the post-game fanfare filtered onto the court, Mary and Katy snuck out to make their getaway.

"Oh, my God!" Katy squealed, pumping her fists in and out when they arrived at her car. "We did it!"

She held her hand up for Mary to acknowledge her with a high five. Adrenaline was still coursing through Mary's body and she smacked her so hard that both of them literally cried out in pain.

Chapter 41

On Monday following the game, Katy received another call from the school. Since Mary had once again disconnected her landline, this one came through on her cell phone. The caller identified himself as soon as she picked up.

"Hi, Katy. This is Principal Hall. I hope I didn't catch you at a bad time."

"No, sir. How are you today?"

"Couldn't be better. I just wanted to pass along Coach Lyons' amazing job filling in for you at the game last week. The win was quite impressive. We are all very proud of your team's accomplishments and of Bob for leading them to victory."

"I was there, sir, and you are absolutely right. Bob did a phenomenal job."

"Actually, the compliment should go to you for pulling off a magnificent hoax."

"A hoax?"

"I kept seeing flashing blue lights in Bob's ears but didn't put two and two together until I saw you cascading up and down the bleachers with your phone pinned to your ear. You are to be commended for commandeering all of the plays from your cell phone. What a masterful plan! I can't believe you pulled it off!"

Katy was stunned silent, so Principal Hall waited what he thought was a reasonable amount of time for her to respond. When she didn't, he restarted the conversation.

"Thursday's basketball game isn't the only reason for my call. I also wanted to let you know that, as of yesterday, we have collected over 2,000 signatures on our petition."

Curious as to how they were able to obtain such a high count, Katy quickly regained the ability to speak. "There aren't that many residents in Lincoln," she pointed out. "So, where did all the extra signatures come from?"

"Neighboring towns. You are admired by many, Miss Hopkins, all throughout the county. Lots of people rallied together to help you get your job back. The Board met again last night and you are officially reinstated!"

"Thank you, Mr. Hall! Thank you, thank you, thank you!"

"You're welcome. Now, let's get you back to doing the job I hired you to do. Report to my office tomorrow morning and we'll get the paperwork out of the way."

"Yessir!"

"I do have one request, though."

"What's that?"

"The next time you feel the urge to kiss a woman in public, please make sure there are no reporters within a five-mile radius!"

"That's a promise, Mr. Hall! You have my word on that!"

Katy realized that they had both just acknowledged her orientation and neither one seemed phased by it. The more import detail, however, was that she had her job back!

When the call ended, Katy immediately shared the news with Mary. They opted to tell Frank together, hoping it might repair the rift that had driven them all apart. After a quick shower and a change of clothes they drove to the Hopkins' house, where they found Frank coming out of the kitchen with a large cake box in his hands.

"What's going on?" Katy asked as she approached him.

Mary, who was right behind her, added, "I'd like to know the answer to that, too."

"I decided to have a party," Frank announced as he set the box on the dining room table. His voice had a lilt to it that neither had heard in quite some time.

"Uh, Pop," Katy contested. "There's no one here but you."

"I knew you'd come when you heard the news," he replied, grinning. "Isn't it great?"

"Isn't what great?" Mary asked.

"The news about Katy! Isn't it wonderful?"

"Who told you?"

"I was at the Board meeting last night. I went straight to the store afterwards and asked them to make a cake especially for my Katy!"

"How did you know about the meeting?" Katy asked.

"I have my ways," he answered with a sly grin as he extended his arms toward his daughter. "I know people. Now, come on over here so I can give you a hug!"

Katy fell into his embrace and Mary joined them, laying her arms on top of Frank's.

"I'm sorry for the way I treated both of you," he said. "Can you ever forgive me?"

"You were really angry with Katy the last time she was here," Mary commented as the hug came to its conclusion. "What happened to change that?"

"Well," Frank started, "the first few days after that article came out, I was hopping mad. I couldn't fathom how Katy could do something so insensitive, something that had the potential to devastate all that we, our family, has accomplished over the years. Plus, I didn't appreciate the entire town knowing our business. It made me furious that Katy's choices put us on the front line."

"But Dad," Katy said, "This isn't a choice for me. It's who I am."

"It may take a while to wrap my head around that, Katy. I was raised to believe that lifestyle is a sin. I've been doing a lot of praying these past few weeks to help me figure it all out."

Mary placed her hands on her hips and told him, "You can't pray away gay, Frank."

"You go, Mom!" Katy exclaimed.

"I've been paying attention," she boasted proudly.

"I'm not as... uh... flexible as you are," Frank confessed, his tone laced with a hint of irritation. "Maybe it's a guy thing."

"You still haven't told us what happened to change your mind," Mary prodded.

Frank was quick to offer his response.

"When you left to go stay with Katy, I started out eating sandwiches. And then, on or about the third day, I realized I was hungry for a hot meal, so I went to the diner. While I was there, I got a sense that some of the people in the restaurant were talking about our family. I couldn't make out what they were saying, but they would stop talking when they saw me looking their way. Some even pointed at me. I just knew it was all bad."

He let out a heavy sigh before continuing.

"The food wasn't bad and the price was cheap so I kept going back. I even showed up once for a midnight snack."

"I didn't think they were open past ten," Mary interjected.

"Only during the week. On weekends, they stay open till one. More for the drinkers than the eaters, I suppose."

"So, what happened to change your mind?" Katy asked again.

"Sure, sure… I'm getting to that. Well, I was at the diner one day for breakfast and a couple of guys I knew before I retired asked why I was there by myself. I told them that Mary and I had separated because of everything that was going on with Katy. They said they were sorry and I appreciated that. Then, out of the blue, they started telling stories about their gay cousins and lesbian nieces and said it didn't matter if Katy was gay. She was one of us, they said, and they cared about her, too.

"As soon as I left there, I called Mr. Hall to ask how I could help Katy get her job back and he suggested that I come to the Board meetings. At the first one, I got the feeling that someone had already convinced the Board members that Katy was evil."

I know who that was, Katy thought to herself.

"There were also some parents there that spoke up for Katy, saying they didn't care if she was gay or not. I didn't say anything, I just listened. At yesterday's meeting, Mr. Hall showed the Board members a petition with over 2,000 names of people who thought Katy should be reinstated. Even that didn't sway a couple of them and I knew then I had to say something. Well, I stood up and was gonna tell them what a good person Katy is and what a great coach she is and how much she adores her students. I was also gonna say that what my daughter did in her private life was none of their business and that they should still respect her for all that she's done for that school – and the kids – and Lincoln."

Frank lifted his glass from the table and took a long drink.

"What's all this 'I was gonna' stuff?" Mary asked. "Did you stand up and say those things or not?"

"There was a woman there that stood up at the same time, so I sat back down. She started off introducing herself as Rachel something and said that her daughter played on Katy's basketball team. I'm pretty sure she was the woman in the photograph. I also think she was the same gal that came to Katy's birthday party last year with Nora. Anyway, she accused the Board members of making a public spectacle over an innocent kiss, saying it was nothing more than that. She reminded them how impressionable kids are and how much better it would be for them to see adults being kind and respectful to one another versus trying to destroy someone for being different. And then she encouraged them to do the right thing and give Katy her job back."

Katy and Mary stared at him with their mouths hanging open, listening intently to every word he was saying. Anxious to tell them the rest of the story, Frank puffed out his chest and kept going.

"When she was finished, I stood up and looked each Board member in the eye and said, 'Amen to that!' I think that was the clincher because they took another vote after that and it was unanimous!"

The two women locked their arms together around his waist and rested their heads against his shoulders. Frank gave both of them a squeeze then took a step back as he gently pushed them away.

"That's enough of all that mooshy stuff," he declared. "Now let's get this celebration started and have some cake!"

"I'll go get a knife and some forks and plates," Mary offered.

"I'll do it," Katy announced. With so much that had happened, she needed to step away for a minute or two to let it all sink in. Before leaving the room, she turned to Frank and said, "Thank you, Dad. It means a lot that you were there for me."

"You deserve every bit of it, Katy. I'm sorry it took me so long to come to my senses. You are very important to me. I love you and I'm proud of you. I know I don't say it very often, but it's always in my heart."

Chapter 42

Katy reported to Mr. Hall's office the following morning as instructed. He followed her in with a large cup of coffee and placed it on his desk just as the first bell rang to start classes.

"Come with me to the outer office," he told her. "I have something important I need to take care of before we get down to business."

Katy followed him through the door that separated his office from Mrs. Maypole's.

"Fran," he announced as he approached his secretary's desk. "Would you set up the PA system for me? I have something I want to say to the students."

"Yes, Mr. Hall," she answered with a smile.

Katy leaned against the corner of her desk and watched as she orchestrated various settings on the control panel.

"It's ready," she announced when she had finished. "Remember to push the button on the microphone when you want to speak and release it when you're done."

"Thanks, Frannie."

He stepped forward, lifted the unit from its base and pressed the button.

"Attention, students," he proclaimed loudly. "This is Principal Hall. I know you are already in class, but there is something important I wanted to share with all of you."

Katy stood erect, almost as if she had been called to attention.

"It is with great joy that I announce the return of Coach Hopkins," he continued. "She will be resuming her regular duties as of today, so please help me welcome her back!"

Loud cheering could be heard from classrooms down the hall within seconds of his releasing the button.

"Hear that?" he said to Katy. "That is all for you. Never doubt you are an important part of this school. We appreciate all that you do, all that you have done, and all that we know you will accomplish in the future. Congratulations on your return!"

Tears were pooling in Katy's eyes as she sobbed, "Thank you, sir."

Handing her the microphone, he prodded, "You should be thanking them as well."

Katy took a deep breath before pressing the button.

"Students," she began, surprising herself that she could actually get the words out. "First off, I want to thank all of you for your support. I appreciate the faith you have in me and I look forward to spending the remainder of this year with you."

She then moved the microphone closer to her mouth and shouted, "Go Lincoln!"

Children's voices began to sound, softly at first, gradually gaining volume with each chant. "Go Lincoln! GO LINCOLN! *GO LINCOLN!!!*"

Katy returned the microphone to its stand just as Mr. Hall asked Mrs. Maypole to bring him the disciplinary report that had been written to substantiate the School Board's investigation and her resulting suspension. While his secretary rummaged through a pile of papers on her desk, he escorted Katy back to his office. After delivering the document, the two women smiled as they watched him tear it into several small pieces and toss the remnants in the trash. Katy thanked both of them then left the office and was met by more than a dozen students in the hallway waiting to greet her. Leading the pack was Dani.

"I told you it would all work out," she said as Katy approached. "We never stopped believing in you, Coach."

"We?"

"Yeah. Me and my mom. My brothers, too."

Dani wrapped her arms around Katy's waist and she automatically responded by laying her hands on top of the teenager's shoulders.

"Be careful, Miss Hopkins," Mr. Hall warned in a low voice. "You don't want to give those naysayers any more ammunition."

Katy pulled back and let her arms fall to her side. Before the mood could dampen, Mr. Hall put one hand on Katy's shoulder and the other on Dani's.

"You better get back to class now," he told Dani, then added for the other students gathered around them, "That goes for all of you. We are all excited to have Miss Hopkins back with us, but she has a lot of work to catch up on. And, if you don't get back to class, so will you!"

Dani's face was beaming as she looked at Katy and said, "I'm so glad you're back!"

"So am I," Katy replied, smiling in return. "So am I."

Katy was back in rhythm with her students in no time at all but knew the ultimate test of acceptance would be fourth period. When the bell sounded, she was quick to join Dani, Courtney and Sandy on the court. Courtney was the first to speak.

"Did you hear we won the game without you last week?" she asked Katy.

Dani elbowed her in the ribs and grumbled, "That's mean! Don't say stuff like that!"

Before Courtney could respond, Katy reassured both of them, "I'm glad you won. I was actually in the stands watching."

"You'll be coaching our next game, though. Right?" Sandy challenged.

"Wild horses couldn't keep me away."

The look on their faces told Katy that she was once again a part of their lives.

"Unfortunately, I can't hang out with you girls today," she said apologetically. "I've got lots of paperwork I need to take care of. You're more than welcome to stay and practice on your own if you want, though."

She felt an incredible urge to bring all three together in a hug but then remembered Principal Hall's warning and instead offered them a smile and a wave before returning to her office. From her desk she watched Dani dribble a ball toward the net and realized how much she looked like Rachel. That, of course, immediately brought her to the forefront of her thoughts. Knowing the newspaper photograph had sent her own world into a tailspin, she wondered if it had done the same in Rachel's life, and, if it did, she wanted to lend her support to combat whatever fallout she might be dealing with because of it. Just as Rachel had done for her. Given that they hadn't spoken to one another since the Cambridge game, she decided to express those feelings in the form of a note. After tearing a blank sheet out of her sports journal, she grabbed a pen from her top drawer and began to write.

> Rachel,
>
> My father told me what you said at the Board meeting and I wanted to thank you for everything you did to help get my job back. I am forever in your debt.
>
> My life was turned upside down by all of this and I can only imagine it did the same to yours, too. As you have helped me, I am here for you as well. My hope is that we can put this behind us and move forward with our lives.
>
> I'm here if you ever want to talk.
>
> Warmest Regards, Katy

She folded the note, tucked it inside an envelope and peeled the backing from the adhesive strip to seal it inside. On the front of it, she scrawled, "Rachel."

Her plan was to give Dani the note to deliver on her behalf but she had already left for her next class, so she walked around her office while contemplating other options. She had the envelope in one hand and was tapping it against the palm of the other the entire time she was pacing.

I could give it to Dani at practice, she reasoned. *I think I can trust her not to read it. But, then again, I know I would. The sheer curiosity would drive me nuts.*

The more thought she put into it, the more she realized her best option was to give the note to Rachel in person. She was mentally crafting a plan on how to do that when Mr. Hall walked into her office.

"I thought I'd stop by to see how you're doing," he said. "How is everything going?"

"I'm still trying to get caught up on paperwork. Other than that, everything is fine."

"Making any progress?"

"Some."

He saw the note in Katy's hand and could clearly read Rachel's name on the outside of the envelope. Pointing to it, he inquired, "I'm assuming that is part of the paperwork you're referring to?"

On impulse, Katy automatically shifted her hands behind her back to conceal the letter, even though she knew he had already seen it.

"Rachel was the woman photographed with you, correct?" he inquired.

Katy nodded to affirm.

"Very well," he commented, then added with a grin, "When you give it to her, make sure there are no photographers around."

Chapter 43

Katy rushed out to deliver the note as soon as basketball practice ended. The panic she felt as she turned into the salon's parking lot was paralyzing, so she stayed in her car and waited for the same courage that had guided her hand to write the note to return and usher her inside. It became more evident with each passing moment that it wasn't going to happen, so she did what any other nervous woman in her situation would do. She ran to Rachel's car and secured the envelope under the wiper blade then ran back to her own car and hunkered down behind the steering wheel, praying the entire time that she had managed it without being noticed.

Raising her head up high enough to see over the dashboard, she watched as Rachel and Martha exited the building and walked toward Rachel's car. Martha arrived first and immediately snatched the envelope out from under the wiper blade.

Son of a bitch! Katy fumed in silence. *Don't you dare read that, you nosy broad!*

Martha turned away from her, preventing her from seeing what she was doing. Her heart leapt into her throat as her panic changed to desperation.

Damn it, Martha! Don't make me get out of this car!

Rachel turned in a full circle as if she were inspecting the cars in the lot.

"Mother of God," Katy groaned aloud as she scrunched farther down into her seat. "I'm gonna die from embarrassment anyway, so you may as well take me now and get it over with, Lord."

She scooted down as far as she could, earnestly wishing she had the power to make herself invisible. Suddenly, there was a knock on the window.

"Katy?" Rachel asked. "What are you doing in there?"

"Hiding," Katy answered. Her face was flushed as she rolled down the window and confessed, "Which, you may have noticed, I'm obviously not very good at."

"Why are you hiding?"

"I didn't want you to see me."

"Want me to pretend that I didn't?"

"Would you? Please?"

"Sure. Can I keep the letter?"

"What letter?"

"The letter you left on my windshield. I know it's from you."

"Terrific. Should I just tell you what it says?"

"Thanks, but I'd rather read it for myself."

"Better hurry before Martha does."

Rachel smiled and Katy felt a tingle run down her spine.

"I talked to Dani before practice and she's beside herself that you're back at school. She hasn't been this happy in a long time."

"Thank you for speaking to the Board. I really appreciate it."

"Your dad was a big influence as well."

Rachel laid her hand on Katy's shoulder and gave it a gentle squeeze.

"I'd better be getting home," she said. "I'm sure my kids are starving."

Katy wanted to respond but every semi-intelligent response she might have hoped would come out evaporated before she could say it. Instead, she voiced the first thing that popped into her head.

"What's for dinner?" she blurted out after Rachel had moved a few steps away.

Rachel spun around and gave her a puzzled look.

"Excuse me? I didn't quite hear what you said."

Real smooth, Ex-Lax. Why don't you just remove your tongue and beat yourself over the head with it?

"That's probably best. Just forget it."

"All right then. Good night, Katy."

Rachel advanced a few more feet and Katy spoke again.

"What I meant to say was, would you have dinner with me?"

Rachel looked back over her shoulder and replied, "I can't. But thanks for asking."

That went over like a lead balloon, Katy scolded herself. *What an idiot I am! What was I thinking even writing that note in the first place?*

On her way home, she made the last turn onto Oak just as her cell phone rang. She answered the call but didn't say anything right away.

"Hello?" the caller inquired. "Katy? Are you there?"

"Oh, hey, Laura."

Laura could immediately tell by the less than enthusiastic greeting that something was wrong.

"You sound bummed. I thought you'd be ecstatic being back at school and all."

"I am."

"Are you sure about that? Doesn't sound like it to me."

Katy let out a heavy sigh before offering up an explanation. In a dejected tone, she told Laura, "I saw Rachel a little while ago."

"How did it go? Did you make any progress?"

"Hardly. We're farther apart than ever."

"What happened?"

"I don't want to go into it on the phone. Can we meet somewhere and talk?"

"Uh… I've got company. We can catch up tomorrow, though."

"All right then. I guess I'll see you at school."

Katy sounded even more sullen and that worried Laura.

"Let's do lunch tomorrow," she offered in atonement for blowing her off. "With all that's been going on, we haven't really talked all that much. We need to catch up."

Katy pulled into her garage and shut off the engine.

"Fine," she said. "Go be with your company. I'll see you tomorrow." She then ended the call before Laura had a chance to say goodbye.

Knowing Mary usually went to bed long before she did, she hurried into the house, hoping for a chance to visit with her before she turned in for the night. After locking the deadbolt, she was greeted with the deafening silence that comes with living alone. Mary had left a note on the table telling her that since all was well again, she had gone home to be with Frank.

Now feeling lonelier than ever, she decided that music would be the best remedy to restore the happy mood her day had started with. Thumbing through her CD collection, she came across Carole King's "Tapestry" and knew there was no need to look any further. Unfortunately, each track had lyrics that put her right back into a funk. She had no idea how to process what she was feeling and the songs were only making it worse. Since Laura was entertaining and her parents were reuniting, she continued down her mental roster and stopped at the next name on her list.

"You sound upset," Nora told her after they exchanged hellos.

"Can we talk?"

"Sure. What do you want to talk about?"

"Not what, who. I need to talk about Rachel."

"I'd rather George not overhear me talking about that. Wanna meet somewhere?"

"George is still there?"

"He's my cousin, Katy. Did you really think I would put him out on the street?"

"Sorry. I didn't know."

"None of this is his fault. Rachel is the one that wanted out of the marriage."

"Maybe I shouldn't be talking with you about her."

"Don't be silly. I love Rachel, but I can't – and I won't – turn my back on George."

"I know."

"Do you want me to come over there?"

"Sure. Or I can meet you somewhere."

"I'll just come there. Let me get the baby tucked in and I'll be right over."

"Thanks, Nora."

Katy put two bottles of Chardonnay in the freezer to chill. When Nora arrived, they talked and drank until the wee hours of the morning, emptying both bottles in the process. Before she left, both were in agreement that Katy had put herself out there enough and that the next move, if there was to be one, should be on Rachel.

Chapter 44

Katy arrived at the school not long after Nora left and found Laura reclining in her chair with her feet propped up on her desk.

"You look like hell," Laura said in a tone more callous than sympathetic.

"Yeah? Well, you don't look so hot either."

"I didn't get any sleep last night. What's your excuse?"

"Same."

"Really? What were you doing all night?"

"Talking with my friend, Nora. And you?"

"Oh, Katy! I met the most amazing woman and I'm already thinking about asking her to move in with me!"

"Wow! That's a little sudden, don't you think?"

"When you're in love, what difference does time make?"

"You are such a hopeless romantic."

"Something you should aspire to be."

Katy scrunched her face before asking, "How well do you know this woman?"

"Well enough to have her move in. You know about the U-Haul thing, right?"

"Huh-uh."

"Oh yeah. I forgot you've only been a lesbian for like an hour."

"Whatever. Skip the sarcasm and tell me what it means."

"Boy are you a dud when you're tired!"

"Laura…"

The warning bell sounded, cutting her off.

"I've got to run or I'll be late," Laura told her. "We're still on for lunch, right?"

"If I can stay awake that long. Look, Lucy, you've got some 'splainin' to do!"

Tired as she was, Laura picked up on Katy's cue and whined like Lucille Ball, "Oh, Ricky!" then darted out the door and across the gymnasium floor.

Knowing her first-period students usually took at least ten minutes to change into their gym clothes, Katy moved her chair close to her desk and rested her head on her arms, thinking she could sneak in enough time for a quick nap. She shut her eyes and fell asleep almost immediately. Two female students entered her office not long after, one of them so concerned with what they were seeing that they started tapping their finger on the top of her head.

"Miss Hopkins?" she asked meekly.

"Is she all right?" inquired the other.

"I think she's dead," the first girl answered. "Maybe we should go get Mr. Hall."

Katy lifted her head, causing both girls to run screaming from her office.

"There is so much angst in seventh grade," she muttered as her head dropped back onto her arms.

The combination of fatigue and too much alcohol had sapped her strength and she had to force herself to stay awake until the end of class. During second-period's dodgeball match, she couldn't even muster enough energy to blow her whistle, so she delegated it to Sally Horton, a bossy pre-teen who found it necessary to sound off at least once every five seconds whether the activity called for it or not.

She stayed on the bleachers for the majority of the next two periods to reserve what was left of her dwindling stamina for lunch with Laura. She wanted to know more about her new friend, fearing all too well that the news would most likely be painful to hear. At eleven fifty-five, she trudged into the teacher's lounge. Laura strolled in two minutes later. Katy was sitting at their usual table, snoring softly with her chin resting on her chest.

"Sorry I'm late," Laura proclaimed loudly as she sat down next to her. When Katy's eyes began to open, she added in jest, "Did I wake you, sleeping beauty?"

Katy arched her back and stretched her arms out wide.

"Why don't you go out to your car and take a nap?" Laura suggested. "That's what I do when I'm tired. I just recline the seat and set the alarm on my phone."

"I may try that. I doubt I'll make it through lunch, much less the rest of the day."

"You should go out there now. We can talk later."

"You're not getting rid of me that easily, Laura. I wanna hear about this new friend of yours. I'll hold my eyelids open if I have to!"

"You may have to prop mine open, too. That woman kept me up all night!"

Katy cringed and forced a smile.

"So, you have a girlfriend now?"

Mildred Snodgrass came into the room just then, and, not wanting to get caught in the same lesbian trap that had befallen Katy, Laura leaned across the table and lowered her voice to keep their conversation out of earshot. Luckily, the elderly teacher was only there to retrieve her lunch from the refrigerator. On her way out, she turned her nose up at both of them.

"She's more than a girlfriend," Laura confided after Mildred had left.

Katy tried not to react in any obvious way. Instead, she remained stoic as she went off topic and asked Laura to explain the whole U-Haul thing.

"It's sort of a running joke in the lesbian world," Laura admitted. "If the first date goes well, on the second date one of the two women shows up with a fully-loaded U-Haul, ready to move in. I never thought it would happen to me, but I'm here to tell ya, it's for real! I'm thinking about asking her to come live with me!"

"Really? How many dates have you been on?"

"Five so far. She's the one, Katy. I just know it. She is my Rachel."

And with that declaration, any hint of jealousy Katy may have had was gone. She could see how heartfelt her friend's excitement was over this new woman in her life.

"I can't wait to meet her," she said. "The girls have a game tomorrow night, so how about we all get together on Friday?"

"Ooohh… Not Friday. I'm staying over at her place."

"How about Saturday?"

"Sheeeesh. Saturday's out, too. She wants to go shopping in Kansas City and maybe catch a movie afterwards. We'll be tied up all day. And after that, well, you know…"

"Sunday?"

"We're golfing in the morning but can probably meet you sometime that afternoon. Does that work for you?"

"I guess. I mean, if that's all you can spare."

Laura arched her eyebrows a couple times, gave Katy an impish grin and admitted, "We actually spend most of our time between the sheets."

"Ugh," Katy groaned. "Too much information, Laura."

"You asked. Hey, I'm too tired to eat so I'm gonna head out to the car. You coming?"

"I would love to, but I can't. I've got to get my next class set up for volleyball."

Laura nodded and they stood up together to leave. As they were walking out, Laura accidentally bumped into Mr. Hall, who had come there looking for Katy.

"How are things going, ladies?" he asked.

"Fine, sir," they chimed in unison.

"Glad to hear it. Katy, when you have a sec, I'd like to visit with you in my office."

"Sure," she responded. "Is it all right if I come by after next period?"

"Are you busy now?"

"I guess not." Her answer was nearly inaudible as she pondered, *What now?*

Laura was thinking the same thing. After he walked away, she turned to Katy and said, "I hope it's nothing serious. You just came back to work, for Christ's sake!"

They exchanged hugs before Katy made the solo trek to the Principal's office. Mr. Hall greeted her at the door then closed it behind them once she was inside.

"Have a seat," he said as he moved to stand in front of his desk.

"Is there a problem?" Katy asked while lowering herself into a chair.

Mr. Hall folded his arms across his chest before offering his response.

"Let's hope not. Mrs. Snodgrass was in my office earlier to discuss another possible complaint against you."

"What have I done now?"

"She was leaving an appointment and saw you in the parking lot with the woman from the photograph."

"Good God! Is she following me?"

"We've talked about this before. It's the *appearance* of impropriety that could get you into trouble, Katy. And, your timing stinks. The Board's feelings about this are still too fresh. My advice is to stay away from that woman until this completely blows over."

"Stay away from what woman? Mrs. Snodgrass?"

"You know who I'm talking about."

"This is nuts."

"Listen. I don't care if you and your friend are gay and neither do the majority of teachers here at the school. And, as evidenced by the number of signatures on the petition, the community isn't much concerned with it either. However, Mr. Snodgrass is president of the School Board and they have a lot of clout in this town. They could make it nasty for you."

"Fine," Katy mumbled under her breath. "But I still say this is nuts."

She left their meeting feeling more frustrated, angry and resentful than ever. It was obvious that lesbianism at her school was not going to be as accepted as her reinstatement led her to believe. Still, whether the interest in her private life was fair or not, the ordeal had mentally and physically depleted her and she refused to dwell on it any longer.

Basketball practice ran longer than usual and she stayed after to catch up on more paperwork. At eight thirty, she ate a quick dinner then stripped off her clothes and crawled into bed. Exhaustion anchored her body in place and sealed her eyelids shut for the next nine hours.

Chapter 45

Katy walked into her kitchen to start a fresh pot of coffee and saw that the light on her answering machine was blinking. After filling her mug, she took a few sips and pressed the Play button.

"Coach Hopkins," a female voice said. "This is Dani."

Katy furrowed her eyebrows and stared at the machine.

"I hope you don't mind me calling," Dani continued, "but I really need to talk to you. Please call me back at 555-4116. It's important. Thanks."

A beep signified the end of the message and a digitized voice informed her that the call had been recorded at "9:42." Knowing she had to hurry to get to work on time, she finished her coffee, washed her cup then showered and dressed and dashed out the door. Her cell phone was on the passenger seat, an oversight from her exhausted state the night before to put it back in her purse. She opened the cover and saw that there was a missed call from the same number that Dani had left on her answering machine.

It's too late to call her back, she decided. *I'll wait and talk to her at fourth period. I hope it isn't bad news. I couldn't handle any more of that, especially if it's about Rachel.*

She pulled into her parking spot and spotted Laura waiting for her on the sidewalk in front of the school.

"What happened with Principal Hall yesterday?" Laura asked when she joined her.

"Snodgrass saw me talking to Rachel the other night."

"And...?"

"And she reported it."

"So now it's a crime for you to speak to another woman? That's insane."

"I thought so, too."

"She must really have it in for you. I wonder why that is?"

"Probably because I broke up with her son. Good gosh! That was eons ago! I guess she's still carrying a grudge about it."

"So, what now?"

"I don't know. One thing's for sure – I'll be damned if I let that woman put me back in the closet! I just came out, for heavens' sake!"

Both heard the bell for first period and raced toward the building.

"Fuck," Laura muttered. "I'm going to be late again. It's the third time this month!"

"We're only in the second week of the month, Laura."

"Don't give me a hard time, Katy. I'm tired. I swear that woman is trying to kill me! She's wearing me out!"

"Doesn't your friend work?"

"Her name is Rebecca, and yes, she has a job. She's a librarian in Kansas City."

Katy broke into a full smile, showing all teeth like the Cheshire Cat.

"She's a *librarian*?" she asked snidely, exaggerating the last word for special effect.

"Yeah. Why do you say it like that?"

"That is perfect! What an ideal pairing – an English teacher and a librarian!"

"I never thought of it that way," Laura laughed. "How ironic is that?"

"So, your librarian is a wild child, huh?"

"Yes, she is. She brings over these romance books and…"

"Uh, uh," Katy interrupted, shaking her hands in front of her face. "No, no, no. I don't need to hear your bedtime stories."

Still giggling, Laura responded, "Okay. Well, here we are at my door." Peering in through the window, she added, "Looks like they're getting along just fine without me."

"Ladies," a voice boomed behind them. "Nice to see you could make it in today."

They turned to see Mr. Hall closing the distance between them at a rapid pace.

"Sorry we're late," Laura offered apologetically. "It was my fault."

"This isn't your first offense this month," he responded. "Is it, Miss Stiles?"

"I don't believe it is, sir."

He flashed his famous fatherly smile and commented, "Wouldn't it be impressive to your students – as well as to other faculty members – for the two of you to be in the classroom *before* the bell?"

"Yessir," they answered together.

"Let's practice that in the future. Shall we?"

Both nodded their affirmation before he moved past them and continued down the hall. Laura snuck into her classroom as Katy headed for the gym. When she arrived, her students had already started choosing teams for crab soccer. Glancing past them, she saw Dani waiting by her office door.

"I really need to talk to you," Dani announced as she came toward her.

"Can it wait till fourth period? I don't want you to be late for class."

"I don't care if I'm late. I need to talk to you."

"Is everything all right?"

"It's my mom. Something's wrong with her."

"What's going on? Is she sick?"

"I don't think so. I think she's just very, very sad."

"Maybe she's sad because of your dad and their separation."

"No, that's not it. She talks to my dad every day. She cries late at night, Coach. I can hear her through the walls. It was really bad last night."

"Have you asked her what's wrong?"

"Yeah. She says I'm too young to understand."

"I'm sure she'll be all right, Dani."

"Would you talk to her? Please? Maybe she just needs a friend right now."

Katy laid her hand on Dani's shoulder, but then thinking Mrs. Snodgrass might be skulking nearby, quickly pulled it away.

"Look, Dani, you know about the article in the paper. Some people are saying…"

Dani cut her off. "I know what they're saying and none of that matters to me. All I care about is my mom."

"You may not know this, but I've been advised to stay away from your mother."

"What? Why?"

"How can I put this…" Katy slowed her voice while trying to choose her next words carefully. "It could have a negative impact on my career."

"What does that mean?"

"There are people who don't want me and your mom to be friends and those people have a lot of influence at the school. If I go against them, I might lose my job."

"I guess my mom was right. I am too young to understand any of this."

"Talk to your dad, Dani. Maybe he can help her."

"I did. He told me you're the reason she cries. That's why I wanted to talk to you. If you're the one making her cry, then you're the one who has to make her stop."

The urge to take Dani in her arms was tearing at Katy's heart. All she could do was stand there and watch the young girl suffer.

"I wish I could, Dani, but I can't. I'm so sorry."

When Dani lowered her eyes, Katy looked past her at the students on the gym floor. The soccer game had already started and was getting rowdier by the second.

"Listen," she told Dani. "Go to class. We'll talk more during fourth period. Okay?"

Willing to risk the ire of Mildred Snodgrass, she reached her hand out to touch the young girl's face but Dani turned away from her. She was shocked by her reaction and felt a stabbing pain in the pit of her stomach.

"Dani," she said softly. "I promise…"

"Yeah," Dani interrupted, then added as she turned to leave, "Thanks for nothing, Coach."

Katy walked toward her students but kept her eyes on Dani. She still had her in her sights when a large, rubber ball came flying towards her from out of nowhere.

"Hey!" she shouted as she raised her hand to deflect it. "Y'all need to watch those kicks and keep the ball on the court! You nearly knocked my head off!"

Chapter 46

The girls finished their basketball season with zero losses and were slated to play Overland Park for the regional title. Winning that match would automatically guarantee a seed at the championship tournament in Topeka, so, to boost their skill level before the game, Katy introduced two new plays. Everyone managed to master them with little or no confusion, except for Courtney, who seemed to be having difficulty focusing on anything since her most recent visit to the orthodontist.

"My braces are killing me," she complained to Katy. "My mouth hurts all the time!"

"Have your mom give you baby aspirin before the game," Katy recommended.

Her suggestion worked and Courtney was relatively pain free when they took to the court. She played her best game that night, leading her team with 16 points and assisting on many of Dani's 12 points as well.

Lincoln won the game, 40-32. The hometown fans who had traveled to Overland Park to cheer them on rushed the floor afterwards as usual, but Katy only availed herself to congratulatory words and handshakes, fearing what might happen if she didn't. She had planned to sneak off to the locker room after the game ended, hoping to avoid another smear campaign in the paper and start her nightmare all over again. The opposing coach was not aware of all the drama she had been through and wrapped her arm around Katy's shoulder while they congratulated one another. Behind them, Katy could hear the click of a camera's shutter as someone took pictures during their embrace. After they separated, she closed rank on the photographer.

"Get what you want?" she asked angrily as she came to a stop in front of him.

The man peered out from behind the camera and smiled.

"It's me, Katy," he said. "David Jones. We went to school together."

"David? Wow, it is you! I remember you used to take pictures for the yearbook. I should have known you would end up a professional photographer. Please don't tell me it was you who took the picture that got me into all that trouble."

"Unfortunately, yes. I never meant for it to turn out like it did, Katy. That's why I'm here. I'm running another article that, Lord willing, will rectify the first one."

"You really think that's possible?"

"I do."

"I'll let you believe that for both of us then. Regardless, I will be looking forward to seeing the new story."

"I promise to do everything I can to make this right. After all, it was my fault it happened in the first place."

"I appreciate that, David."

Katy hurried to the locker room where several girls armed with an array of water-filled balloons and water pistols (check that, water assault rifles) were waiting to ambush her. A few were packing heat in both hands. There was no means to escape, so she stood her ground until all of their weapons were emptied. When the battle was over, she was drenched from head to toe.

Other girls not engaged in the attack were screaming and running around popping each other on the butt with their towels. Their loud shrieks caught the attention of Mrs. Snodgrass, who, not surprisingly, was prowling just outside the door. In a huff, she barged in and marched right up to Katy.

"Don't you dare say a word," Katy snarled as she approached her. "Or make a scene. They are just having fun, so let them be."

"I heard yelling," Mrs. Snodgrass told her. "I had to make sure everyone was okay."

"As you can see, Mildred, everyone is fine."

"Yes, I can see that. I was merely concerned."

The scowl never left Katy's face as the older woman continued.

"Well, then, Miss Hopkins. By all means, enjoy the celebration with your team." As an afterthought, she held out her hand and added, "Congratulations on your victory."

Katy ignored her gesture as she walked past her and opened the door.

"Goodbye, Mildred," she responded flatly.

After crossing the threshold, Mildred turned back around and repeated her earlier sentiment. "I was only doing what I thought was necessary to protect the children."

Katy wanted to lay her out on the very spot where she stood but restrained herself for the benefit of the girls, several of which had formed a half-circle behind them. All were staring wide-eyed to see what would happen next.

"I believe I speak for most of Lincoln when I tell you that picture in the newspaper damaged us as a community," Mildred continued in a low voice that only Katy could hear. "We will never be the same because of it. The effect this could have on the children is…"

Katy raised her hand to stop her from saying anything further.

"I will say this only once," she growled, "so pay attention. Regardless of what that photograph meant to you it has no significance in the way I teach or how I interact with my students. Your vindictiveness, hatred and petty intolerances took this to a level where it didn't belong."

Mildred shook her head from side to side emphatically as she rebutted, "I think it would be best for you to take your brand of teaching somewhere else. You are influencing these children to believe that homosexuality is okay. Well, it isn't. Behavior such as yours may be acceptable in the big city, but it will never be tolerated in Lincoln."

"I'll thank you to take your opinions elsewhere," Katy refuted as she closed the door in her face. When she turned around, she saw that the half-circle of girls had grown to the entire team. Rather than offer them an explanation, she shooed them off to take showers, instructing them to join her at center court after they were dressed.

Katy waited in the tip-off circle until all of the girls were gathered around her before doling out their praises.

"I am super proud of each and every one of you! You guys were amazing tonight!"

She then motioned for the hometown crowd to join them.

"I also want to give a shout out to everyone from Lincoln who came to support us. This victory is as much yours as it is ours. Girls, take some time to celebrate this win with your friends and families. I'll wait for you on the bus."

When she stepped away, the team was quickly engulfed by allegiant fans who had been waiting patiently for their turn to congratulate them. Katy smiled as she overheard one of the fans call out, "We're going to state!" She then continued toward the exit to fetch the driver to bring the bus around. Along the way, she unexpectedly ran into Rachel.

Rachel cocked her head and said to her, "You're all wet."

"I was ambushed after the game," Katy explained. "They got me good, didn't they? Not a dry patch anywhere on my body!"

Rachel reached for Katy's hand and her butterflies launched into another aerobatic mission inside of her stomach.

"You have done so much for those girls," Rachel said as she gave it a gentle squeeze. "Thank you for being such a great role model."

While her compliment was intentional and sincere, her true motive was not simply to say those things but to feel Katy's touch, something she longed for every time she was in her presence. And, in that moment, her sadness in not being with the woman she loved waned ever so slightly.

They continued holding hands until the sighting of Mildred Snodgrass forced them apart. In that brief connection, however, their feelings for one another were allowed to be expressed without threat of retaliation or condemnation.

Chapter 47

Katy slept in later than usual on Sunday but was still anxious to see the new article from David and went directly from her bed to the porch to retrieve the paper. One of the neighbors across the street waved at her and she responded in kind before bending over to pick it up. She sat down on the front steps and spread the paper open across her lap. The front-page headline, printed in bold, capital letters read:

KUDOS FOR KATY AS LINCOLN
CLOBBERS OVERLAND PARK

There were two pictures under the title, one of the Overland Park Coach with her arm around Katy's shoulder and the other of Mildred smiling and waving a closed fist high above her own head.

She must have thought she won the battle between us, Katy thought amusingly.

The full-page article showered Katy with accolades and high praise for leading her team to an impressive win. She was credited as well for orchestrating the unprecedented behind-the-scenes effort with Bob Lyons in defeating Lenexa weeks earlier. David quoted Mr. Hall as saying that her plan for the Lenexa game was "sheer brilliance and a testament to her love for her students and her passion for coaching."

"Katy is one of the finest teachers in Lincoln," he went on to say. "We are proud to have her on staff at Lincoln Junior High."

Many people in Lincoln suspected that Mildred Snodgrass was the primary – if not sole – contributor in igniting and continuing to fuel the controversy that had gotten Katy into so much trouble. David suspected it, too, so he included a picture of the two of them talking near the locker room door. In small, italicized font, the caption under it stated:

Peace Talks Underway?

Katy read the entire story then stood up, folded the paper and tucked it underneath her arm. She was a couple of steps from her front door when her cell phone started ringing in the pocket of her robe. After answering it, she wedged it between her neck and her ear so that she had a free hand to open the door.

"Hi, Katy. It's Laura."

"Hey, Laura."

"Did you see the article in the paper yet?"

"Yeah, I just finished reading it."

"Was that a great story or what?"

"I thought so. Maybe I'm off the hook now."

"Are you kidding? After that, I'm sure you'll be voted in as Lincoln's next mayor!"

They shared a quick laugh followed by a loud sigh from Katy.

"Is everything okay?" Laura asked.

"I saw Rachel after the game. I miss her, Laura. I mean, I miss the old Rachel."

"Are you two ever gonna work things out?"

"I honestly don't think that will ever happen."

"I wish there was something I could do." She paused momentarily then added, "I've got an idea! Let's do something fun today – something to get your mind off of her. Rebecca and I just got in from playing a round of golf. Why don't you meet us for lunch?"

"I don't know…"

"Come on, sad sack! She's dying to meet you. Plus, it'll do you good to get out and be with happy people today."

"You're probably right."

"Of course I am! We'll go someplace quiet so you two can get acquainted."

"Okay, I'll go put some clothes on."

"Awesome. We'll get cleaned up and head your way in just a bit."

After ending the call, Laura turned to Rebecca, who was lying beside her in the bed.

"Katy is miserable," she said. "There has to be something we can do to help her."

Rebecca thought for a moment then suggested, "Let's take her back to the salon."

"What?"

"I'll make an appointment for her to go see Rachel. If they have some time alone, maybe they can talk things out."

"That's a terrific idea!"

Laura wrapped her arms around Rebecca's neck and kissed her firmly on the lips. Rebecca slipped her the tongue and within seconds they were tearing each other's clothes off to have sex. It didn't occur to either of them until afterwards that they had forgotten all about Katy.

"When were you planning on coming to get me?" she shouted into the phone when Laura finally called. "I've been waiting for you this whole time!"

"Sorry," Laura apologized, her tone reflecting both embarrassment and humility. "We got sidetracked. Give us an hour or so to get ready and I'll treat you to an early dinner instead. Will that square things up between us?"

"It better be some kind of fantastic meal – that's all I've got to say."

"You can choose the restaurant and pick whatever you want from the menu."

"All right. Don't forget me this time."

"On my honor as a former Girl Scout, I give you my word that I won't forget you."

Laura and Rebecca arrived at Katy's house an hour later. Laura introduced the two strangers to one another after Katy joined them in the car.

"Thanks for the invitation," Katy said as she positioned herself in the middle of the back seat. Hoping her next words would be taken as a joke, she added for Laura's benefit, "I guess you got tired of hearing me whine and decided to fill my mouth with food so you wouldn't have to listen to me complain anymore."

"Wouldn't you if you were me?" she responded curtly.

Shocked by the flippant remark, Rebecca fired back, "That was kinda rude, don't you think?"

"Katy knows I'm just playing."

Rebecca turned to Katy and asked, "Did you know she was playing?"

"Sometimes I do," Katy answered, "and sometimes I don't."

"Why do I feel like I'm being ganged up on?" Laura grumbled.

"You need to be nice to her," Rebecca offered in Katy's defense. "She's been through a lot lately and needs some compassion – and a fine steak dinner!"

"Thank you!" Katy exclaimed as she offered a smirky grin to Laura's reflection in the rearview mirror.

Knowing her fate had been sealed, Laura vented, "I can see this budding friendship between the two of you is going to cost me a lot of money."

To support that claim, Katy added, "And I have just the restaurant in mind."

In a loud whisper that both Rebecca and Katy heard, Laura muttered, "Ka-ching, ka-ching."

As fitting punishment, Katy chose one of the top-rated restaurants in Kansas City as repentance for Laura's bad behavior. Once seated, she and Rebecca took turns ordering from the appetizer menu, causing Laura to wince with every stroke of the waiter's pen. Her reaction was even more pronounced when he recorded their entrée choices.

Though the conversation was lively and free-flowing throughout their meal, Katy's friends kept a silent vigil over their plan to reunite her with her one true love.

Chapter 48

Topics at dinner covered a wide range of subjects such as Rebecca's backstory, how she and Laura met at the bar, Katy's first introduction to Rachel at her birthday party and the clipboard incident following the Cambridge game, the kiss that nearly decimated her career, Mrs. Snodgrass and her penchant for ridding the world of gays and lesbians, and, Laura made sure to add, all people of color, Katy's wanderlust trip to Texas, plus a variety of random stories from each of their lives.

The final tale, told by Katy as Laura was pulling out her credit card to pay the bill, was that she was giving the girls a break from basketball practice for a couple of days to recover and rest for the upcoming state championship tournament. The next day, Rebecca took full advantage of that little tidbit to schedule Katy's manicure appointment for the following evening.

Still unaware of their plans, on Tuesday, Katy received a call from Laura not long after she had gotten home from school. Before she had a chance to say hello, Laura asked her, "Have you changed out of your work clothes yet?"

"I just put on my sweats," she answered.

"Go get dressed," Laura demanded. "Right now."

"Are you serious?"

"Yes. Rebecca and I have a surprise for you."

"Really? Why?"

"Because we like you. Let's just leave it at that. You don't have to get all gussied up. The place we're going is casual."

"All right. What time should I be ready?"

"Half an hour from now."

"Are the two of you going to get sidetracked again?"

"We'll try our best not to. Can't swear to that, though."

Laura started giggling and Katy could hear Rebecca laughing in the background.

"There is one more thing I need to tell you," Laura added.

"What's that?"

"I'm bringing the blindfold."

Katy cringed as she returned the phone to its cradle, recalling what happened the last time Laura made her wear a blindfold. Feeling confident that she wouldn't do that to her a second time, she began looking forward to the trio's reunion with excitement and anticipation.

"You remembered the blindfold, right?" Rebecca asked Laura when they pulled up in front of Katy's house.

"It's still in the glovebox from the last time," she confirmed. "I'll have her put it on when she gets in the car."

Just then, Katy came barreling down the sidewalk toward them.

"I'm ready!" she squealed after climbing into the back seat.

"Hold on there, Lone Ranger," Laura joshed. "You've got to don your mask before we go anywhere."

"Is that thing really necessary?"

"It is," Rebecca answered for both of them. "We don't want you to know where you are until we get there."

"All right," Katy grumbled. "But surely you remember how things turned out the last time you made me wear that thing."

"Kinda hard to forget," Laura agreed. "However, today is a new day, filled with new adventures and surprises."

Katy continued to complain as Rebecca helped her with the blindfold.

"I still can't believe you took me to the salon that day. What a nightmare experience that ended up being."

Laura stared into the eyes of her partner and Rebecca could clearly see the signs of dread on face. Situating her lips next to Laura's ear, she reassured her, "It'll be fine. Don't worry!"

"What are you two whispering about?" Katy asked.

"Just some last-minute details," she answered hastily.

Laura still looked unsettled as she eased the car away from the curb, so Rebecca leaned across the console to kiss her on the cheek.

"We're doing the right thing," she whispered.

"I hope so," Laura whispered back.

Fifteen minutes later, the car came to a stop and Laura shut off the engine.

"We're here," she announced.

Katy wasted no time in groping for the blindfold to take it off.

"Great! That means I can get rid of this thing now."

Both front seat passengers screamed at the same time, "NO!"

"O-o-okay," Katy answered slowly.

"Sorry," Rebecca expressed more calmly. "You have to leave it on until we get you situated. We don't want the surprise blown ahead of time."

Laura walked around to open the back door on the passenger side to let Katy out.

"Grab my arm," she told her as she was exiting the car.

Rachel moved next to Katy. Knowing nail salons produced smells that Katy might recognize, she lifted a small bottle of cheap perfume from her purse and sprayed it directly onto the front of Katy's jacket.

"Hey!" Katy gagged, choking through the mist. "What are you doing?"

"I'm just freshening up a bit," she answered. She gave Laura a wink and added, "I forgot that I bought this new perfume and wanted to try it out."

"Did you get any on you? Or did you spray it all on me?"

"Quit'cher bitchin'," Laura argued. "A little perfume isn't going to hurt you."

The Asian woman came forward to greet them as soon as they entered the building. Before she could say anything, Rebecca pressed her finger against her lips to let her know to remain quiet. She then held up a piece of paper that had "Rachel" penned in black magic marker across the front of it. The woman pointed a crooked finger toward the rear of the salon. Rachel was sitting at her station reading a paperback book.

"It smells funny in here," Katy commented.

"What does it smell like?" Laura asked nervously.

"Hard to say. Mostly what I smell is that perfume. That is some powerful stuff."

"Thanks," Rebecca chuckled then quickly covered her mouth to stifle a laugh. "It's my new favorite!"

Laura led Katy to Rachel's station and stopped in front of her table. Rachel peered up from her book with a perplexed look on her face.

"Hello?" she asked, though it came out as more of a challenge than a greeting.

"We brought our friend in for today's special," Laura told her. She then stuck her hand out to command Rachel's silence. Rachel nodded that she understood.

"We'd like the blindfold to stay on for now," Rebecca added.

Rachel nodded again as Laura lowered Katy into her seat and guided her hands to the table. At that instant, Katy knew exactly where they were.

"Wait a cotton-pickin' minute!" she shouted while tugging at the blindfold. "I know what you're up to!"

Laura hollered, "Surprise!" at the same time Katy yanked the mask off of her head.

Rachel and Katy froze in their seats, staring at each other from across the table.

"What have you done?" Katy bellowed. The inflection in her voice told Laura that an answer had better be forthcoming.

"We did what was best for you. For both of you. Now, you two sit right there and work this thing out. Oh, and go ahead and give her the manicure while you're at it. I'm paying for it, after all."

Laura and Rebecca exchanged smiles as they watched Katy and Rachel continue to stare at one another. Assured that they had done all that was necessary to bring the two together, they walked away and claimed two empty chairs in the waiting area.

"What did she mean?" Rachel asked after they had left. "What are we supposed to work out?"

Even though Katy had already figured out what her friends were up to, she still told Rachel, "I have no idea."

Chapter 49

Rebecca and Laura were seated less than twenty feet away and would occasionally glance up from their magazines to see how things were progressing. That effort was short-lived, however, as the space between them heated up and they began engaging on a more personal level, their attention now focused on one another instead of Katy and Rachel.

"It's okay," Laura told the other patrons in the waiting area. "She is my girlfriend."

Rachel was watching them and said to Katy, "Your friends seem quite affectionate."

Katy scrunched up her face and shrugged her shoulders.

"They think they're in love."

"And you don't?"

"It's so sudden. They haven't known each other that long."

"Looks to me like they've known each other forever."

"They've only been dating a few weeks so they're still in the honeymoon stage."

"So, they're officially a couple?"

"I suppose. Why do you ask?"

"For a while, I thought you two were an item – you and the shorter one."

"Who? Me and Laura? Why would you think that?"

"She brought you here for your birthday, remember? And every time I saw the two of you after that, you seemed pretty tight."

"We were pretty tight at one point."

"What happened?"

"I don't feel comfortable talking about that."

"Sorry."

"Let's just say it was a moment in my life that I'd rather put behind me."

The two sat quietly until Katy broke the silence by asking, "Are you coming to the tournament in Topeka?"

"Yes," Rachel replied, then chuckled as she added, "Dani is so excited she already has her bag packed."

"Where are you staying?"

"George reserved our room at the same hotel the other girls are staying at."

"Oh," Katy responded. Sliding down further into her chair, she muttered, "I guess you and George are back together then?"

Rachel's reaction was immediate.

"Heavens, no! Our divorce becomes final in two weeks. He just made arrangements for us. He can't come. He's teaching that weekend."

"That was nice of him."

"He's a sweet man, really. And a lot less angry than when I originally told him…" She stopped herself from finishing. "I just mean he's more considerate of my feelings now. Believe me, it didn't start out that way. Plus, he loves his daughter, much the same as your father loves you."

She could see the sides of Katy's mouth slowly draw upward.

"It's nice to see you smile again," she admitted. "I've missed that."

Laura and Rebecca had resumed reading their magazines, yet, when Rebecca stole a quick glance in their direction, she saw them smiling at one another.

"I think it's working!" she said after giving Laura a nudge with her elbow.

By the time Laura turned her head to look, Katy's smile had faded, followed shortly thereafter by the disappearance of Rachel's. Disappointed that she had missed it, she went back to her magazine.

"Can I ask you something?" Rachel asked Katy.

Katy nodded to agree.

Rachel set aside her nail file and laid her hands over Katy's. "Are you happy?"

"Most of the time," Katy answered. "Are you?"

"Yeah. Most of the time."

Their conversation ended after that. When the manicure was over, they walked to the waiting area where Laura and Rebecca were once again entangled in a passionate kiss.

Rachel cleared her throat to get their attention and said, "Excuse me!"

"Come up for air," Katy chimed in after her. "We're all finished."

Laura opened one eye and peered around the side of Rebecca's face. Katy waved her fingers in front of her and said, "All done. We can go now."

The two women separated and rose from their seats. Rachel pulled a Kleenex out of her pocket and handed it to Laura.

"What's this for?" she asked.

"Lipstick smudges," Rachel told her. "Lots of them."

Laura dragged the tissue across the edges of her mouth but overlooked the streaks on her front teeth. The red blobs stood out like blood stains on a white t-shirt when she smiled and inquired, "Is that better?"

Katy answered with a sneer, "Much."

Knowing she was about to leave, Rachel touched Katy's arm and said, "It was great seeing you." She then looked at Laura and Rebecca and added for their benefit, "Thanks for bringing her."

Rebecca smiled and offered, "It was our pleasure."

"We can bring her back tomorrow," Laura inserted jokingly.

Rachel looked directly at Katy when she gave her response to Laura's suggestion.

"Bring her back anytime."

Rebecca and Katy left the salon, leaving Laura behind to settle the bill. After joining them in the car, Katy reached over the seat to give her a hug.

"Thank you," she whispered.

"It was Rebecca's idea," Laura contended. "But don't hug her. It makes her horny and she'll just want to have sex with you."

"I thought you said women were sensual and only men were horny?"

A sly grin came over Laura's face as she confessed, "I lied."

Rebecca quickly steered the conversation in a different direction.

"It's obvious that woman is crazy about you," she told Katy.

"Rachel?" Katy inquired. "How can you tell?"

"By the way she looks at you."

"Then why did she turn me down when I asked her to have dinner with me?"

"Maybe there was another reason for the refusal. Keep asking. I turned Laura down the first time, too." Her gaze then switched to Laura as she purred, "And look at us now!"

"I don't think I could handle another rejection."

"Then let her make the first move."

"What if she's not interested?"

"From what I saw this evening, she is very much interested. Trust me. You two are destined to be together one day."

Chapter 50

Katy spent the rest of the week strategizing for the upcoming tournament. More than anything she wanted to bring the championship trophy back to Lincoln so she could flaunt it at the School Board and anyone else who doubted her abilities as a coach. In her mind that trophy would restore not only her credibility, but her dignity and pride as well. And, as an added bonus, be the perfect thorn in Mildred Snodgrass' craw.

For Lincoln to win, mistakes had to be minimized as much as possible. She detailed the movements of each new play and made the girls repeat them over and over in practice. By the end of that final scrimmage, they were a finely-tuned machine. Katy worried more that she would cause a loss by failing them as a coach rather than missteps the girls might make during the course of the tournament.

Early that Friday morning, Katy, the players and a few faculty members boarded the bus for Topeka and were deposited in front of the arena two and a half hours later. A lump formed in Katy's throat as she took her first steps into the building.

Oh, my God! she exclaimed in silent amazement. *I can't believe this is happening! We are really here at the State Finals!*

The girls trailed behind her one by one, their eyes darting back and forth as they marveled at the banners of previous winners suspended from the overhead rafters. A fifty-foot scoreboard and large television screens filled the spaces between the pennants.

"Hey, Coach!" Sandy yelled.

"Yes?" Katy answered.

"This place is huge! I've never seen anything this big in my life!"

"Me either!" Courtney chimed in.

"See what it looks like from the seats," Katy suggested. "Pick any section and look back down here at the floor."

Dani tagged along as the girls split up, all going in multiple directions while Katy stood in the middle of the court.

"You look kinda small!" Courtney shouted from a row about 75 feet away.

"Yeah," Dani yelled from her section. "You look like a bug!"

It was the first time Dani had spoken to Katy in over two weeks. While she wasn't exactly sure what it might signify, it pleased her to be acknowledged and brought a smile to her face nonetheless.

"Wow!" Sandy hollered from somewhere Katy couldn't determine. "She looks like a flea from up here!"

"All right, girls," Katy called out. "I just wanted to show y'all where your games will be played. Everybody back on the bus now so we can go meet your parents at the hotel."

"What time are they playing?" one of teachers asked as they were walking out.

"I'm not sure yet," Katy replied. "There is a coaches' meeting with the Tournament Director at eleven o'clock. I'm assuming I'll find out then."

Everyone scrambled back into their original seats on the bus, all the while chatting at a feverish pitch. The hotel was only five blocks from the arena and the girls had barely settled down when the bus came to a stop. A bellhop positioned himself near the door and extended his hand to each girl as they came down the stairs.

The parents all traveled separately and paired up with their daughters in the lobby, except for three girls whose parents hadn't arrived yet, one of which was Dani. It had been decided beforehand they would remain in Katy's custody until they were reunited. Within the span of fifteen minutes, the group whittled down from four to just Dani and Katy.

"My mom should be here any minute," Dani said, more for her own assurance than Katy's. Unsure if she was still angry with her, Katy didn't verbally respond but smiled and nodded instead. It surprised her when the young girl spoke again.

"She had to take Rafael to the doctor this morning."

Out of genuine concern, Katy asked, "Is he all right?"

"He's fine. He needed a physical to play soccer."

"My brother told me that Rafael is one of the best players on the team."

"How would he know?"

"He coaches at the high school."

"Oh."

Impatient for Rachel to arrive, Dani didn't add anything further and fixed her eyes on the lobby doors as if her mom might magically walk through them at any moment. The fact that she had spoken to Katy at all gave her a renewed sense of hope that things would soon go back to normal between them. To test that theory out, she decided to restart their conversation.

"I'm hungry," she announced. Seeing that she had Dani's attention, she added, "Are you? We could go somewhere and get a bite to eat while we wait."

"I don't have any money."

"My treat."

"But what if my mom comes and I'm not here?"

"Call her and tell her we'll be at the restaurant across the street. She can meet us there."

Dani pulled her phone from her backpack and flipped it open. She dialed Rachel's number then held it next to her ear.

"It's not doing anything," she told Katy.

"Let me see it."

Dani tossed her the phone and then plopped down onto an oversized chair.

"Your battery is dead," Katy said after examining it. "Here, use mine."

She left her with her phone and went to scope out items in the vending machines.

"Want a pop?" she asked as Dani entered her mom's digits on the keypad. "They've got Pepsi, Root Beer or Dr. Pepper."

"No, thanks," Dani answered then immediately said afterwards into the telephone, "Are you coming? I'm with Coach Hopkins."

Silence followed while she listened to Rachel's response.

"We're in the lobby at the hotel," Dani told her mother. "Yes, I'm being good. Coach said she would take me to get something to eat."

Staring at the back of Katy's head, she muttered, "Okay," then walked up to her and handed her the phone. "She wants to talk to you."

Katy placed the phone against her ear. "Hello?"

Now it was Katy's turn to remain silent. Dani nudged her out of the way to see what other goodies were in the machines. The wide assortment made her stomach growl.

"I will," Katy said finally. "We'll be at the Denny's across the street."

Another pause, and then, "Okay. See you in a little while."

"When is she coming?" Dani asked after the call ended.

"She'll be here in the next twenty minutes or so."

"Did she say anything else?"

"Yeah. She told me to keep an eye on you until then."

"She treats me like a kid," Dani groaned, shaking her head.

Katy giggled before answering, "That's because you *are* a kid!"

Chapter 51

Dani spotted Rachel as soon as she entered the restaurant and rose from her seat, waving her arms in the air and yelling, "Mom! We're over here!"

As Rachel came toward them, Katy felt her butterflies revving up for another flight.

"Are you hungry?" Dani asked her after she'd sat down.

Rachel smiled and replied, "An omelet sounds good to me."

"We just placed our order," Katy told her. "I'll get the waitress to add yours as well."

Katy waved at the server to get her to come over. When she arrived, she positioned herself next to Katy.

"Did you need something else?" she asked.

"I'll have the veggie omelet," Rachel told her. "And a cup of coffee, please."

"And for your sides?"

"Hashbrowns and sour dough toast," Rachel concluded.

After finishing their meals they returned to the hotel, stopping at the front desk to register and pick up room keys. George had requested a non-smoking room when he made the reservation, but a glitch in the software mistakenly assigned them to a smoking floor. The clerk quickly exchanged it and handed Rachel a new card key. The original room was two floors above Katy, but this twist of fate now had them almost directly across the hall from one another. When the elevator stopped on their floor, Rachel invited Katy to come to their room to visit for a while. She politely declined then excused herself to settle in and glance over her notes before the meeting with the Tournament Director.

There were twelve teams on the roster vying for the coveted winner's trophy. At the coach's meeting the Director reminded everyone they were playing a round-robin, double elimination schedule, meaning each team had to lose twice before they were out of the tournament. When asked if anyone wanted to use the court for practice prior to opening ceremonies, all hands went up simultaneously. A schedule was made and each team was assigned a thirty-minute block of time. He then handed out copies of the brackets so that everyone could keep track of when and where their teams played.

Katy looked at her copy and saw that Lincoln was scheduled to play Shawnee in the first match at six o'clock. She had previously told the parents to reconvene in the lobby at noon so that she could relay what she learned at the meeting. When they were all together, she passed along the information then added that she had reserved the practice court for one o'clock and wanted the girls on the bus fifteen minutes prior. Her next comment was specifically for members of the team.

"I have no idea what Shawnee plays like, but there's no reason to doubt our ability to win. All we have to do is execute the same way we have all season. I don't want to wear you out before the game, so our practice this afternoon will be more for floor shooting and free throws. At the most, we might run one or two quick scrimmages."

While she managed to calm the girls' nerves down quite a bit on the bus ride over, hers were all over the place when they entered the stadium, causing her to tremble to the point that she had to steady her pen with both hands to add last minute comments to her journal. When finished, she shoved it into her bag and joined her team on the court. Forty minutes later, the girls were back at the hotel to stay with their families until it was time to return for the opening ceremonies at five thirty.

Dodge City had a bye in the first round and the brackets showed that Lincoln would play them the following morning, given that they won their first match. Their practice was the last one scheduled before opening ceremonies, so Katy told Courtney's father that she was going to watch them and asked him to make sure the girls were all on the bus at the appropriate time.

At five o'clock, everyone from Lincoln was back in the arena. Parents and faculty members, Bob Lyons being one of them, and rightfully so, Katy reasoned, since he played a big part in getting them there, all found seats fairly close together. Katy led the girls to a different section reserved for the teams that were scheduled to play.

They sat through most of the opening ceremonies before Katy routed her team to the locker room to get ready. Fifteen minutes before gametime, the girls sprinted onto the court in their new uniforms. The old suits were hand me downs from previous teams that had become tattered and worn after years of repeated use. Through various fundraisers that included car washes and bake sales, they raised one third of the cost to purchase new ones. The Booster Club pitched in another third, and the remaining balance was gifted by Frank and Mary Hopkins.

Lincoln won the tip-off to start the game. At halftime they were ahead by six points and held the lead until the end, igniting the crowd with the first victory of the tournament. Their supporters, now numbering more than just parents and faculty, joined in the spirit of celebration as they rallied around all the players and Katy to congratulate them on the big win.

"Great game!" one person in the crowd shouted.

"Lincoln all the way!" yelled another.

The merriment preceded them to the hotel, where the staff had posted signs in the lobby acknowledging them as the winners of that first match. In addition, they had set out large trays of assorted cookies and several bowls filled to the rim with fruit punch. Before the festivities ended, one of the moms offered to wash all the uniforms and told everyone where they needed to drop them off. Katy spoke afterwards to let everyone know who and when they were playing next.

"Our next game is against Dodge City at eight tomorrow morning," she announced. "Everyone needs to be dressed and on the bus by seven fifteen. Got it?"

Parents and players all shook their heads simultaneously.

"We don't need anyone getting stomach cramps during the game," she continued, "so, make sure you're finished with breakfast by six thirty. Rest up tonight and I'll see you on the bus tomorrow morning."

Katy stayed up reviewing the notes she had taken at Dodge City's practice until well after midnight. That paid off as they won the match, which resulted in their advancing to the next tier in the winner's bracket. She was ecstatic, as were the girls, their parents, and all of the new Lincoln fans that had driven down that day to support them. Before leaving the arena, Katy informed everyone about their next scheduled matchup.

"We play Topeka at noon. That's only a few hours from now. If you're planning on getting something to eat, keep it light. Have a sandwich or a salad, or maybe some yogurt and fruit. You can have a bigger meal afterwards."

She waited for confirmation that everyone understood before speaking again.

"Leavenworth is playing next and, in my opinion, they're most likely our toughest competition in this tournament, so I'm going stay and watch their game. I want all of you suited up and back at the arena by no later than eleven fifteen."

"We'll be there, Coach!" Sandy pledged for the entire team.

"I can't even begin to tell you how proud I am of each and every one of you," Katy boasted. "And you should be extremely proud of yourselves as well!"

"We're proud of you, too, Katy!" one parent shouted, followed by a chorus of voices echoing the same sentiment.

Katy looked into the sea of smiling faces and made a wide sweep with her hand.

"All of the credit goes to these girls. I was as much of a spectator as the rest of you. Y'all get outta here now and I'll see you this afternoon. Don't be late!"

She waited for them to leave before finding an open seat near mid court. Going on a hunch that her team would play Leavenworth at some point in the tournament, she paid close attention to their style of play and watched in awe as they masterfully annihilated their opponent. She was confident her girls could beat them, but only if they played hard all the way through to the final buzzer.

Chapter 52

From what Katy was told by another coach who had watched one of her games and one of Topeka's, both were relatively equal in terms of talent. Katy also made note of the fact that Topeka was part of a larger school district and faced tougher competition in their home league, which could give them an advantage. Being local, they had a huge fan base, which was yet another advantage. In tight games, that alone could swing the momentum in the final moments of play.

She spent a fair amount of time in the locker room rallying her team before the match and their enthusiasm showed as they trotted onto the court pumping their fists up and down in the air. The number of baskets they made during warmups impressed her, and she hoped that consistency would transfer to the actual game. That hope was realized as they scored on nearly every shot taken in the first period. Despite the impressive start, Lincoln was down by six at the half. In the locker room, Katy had only two things to say to her team: "Continue to play your best" and "Have some fun out there!"

Her advice was well received and the girls made a comeback to tie the game in the final seconds. After two overtime periods they squeaked past Topeka and won by a single basket. Now, there were two teams left in the winner's bracket: Leavenworth and Lincoln, who would face off at six o'clock that evening.

The bus ride to the hotel was an equal mixture of elation and exhaustion. The girls had played their hearts out and Katy could see the result of that effort was taking its toll. Knowing their energy levels were nearly tapped out, she rose from her seat to offer some encouragement for them to keep going.

"I know you're tired," she said. Her voice was calm, neither loud nor soft, and the girls turned their attention to her right away. "But just remember, being here is one of the most amazing things that will ever happen in your life. I know, because, years ago, I was right where you are now; however, the team I played for let the fact that they were tired keep them from giving it their all and we lost the tournament. Don't make that mistake. Dig deep inside of you to find that strength for one more game. I know you can do it!"

Katy exited the bus first and offered each girl a high five as they exited, occasionally shouting out, "We can do this!" The smiles she got in response assured her they were going to give it their best shot.

After a quick shower and change of clothes, she walked back to the arena. The buzz around the tournament was that Salina was the team to watch and she was anxious to see why. They had only six players on their roster, and Katy learned that two had fouled out in their first match. The remaining four weren't able to hold up against five defenders and they lost to their opponent.

She arrived shortly after the game started and it quickly grew more intense as the two teams battled it out on the court. Both had an incredible lineup of talent, but Salina's point guard was beyond exceptional. Her hands were lightning fast as she repeatedly stole the ball from Emporia's players, most often from outside shooters. Her ball handling and passing skills were phenomenal as well and she was credited with ten assists in the first period. Katy knew that if they kept their foul count in check, they could win their way out of the loser's bracket and claim their spot in the championship match.

At halftime, she went to the concession stand to purchase a hot dog, a bag of chips and a bottle of water and carried them back to her seat. The wiener was devoured in three bites, each one leaving her with bloated cheeks and mustard stripes on the sides of her mouth. The chip bag was emptied seconds later.

She was in the act of stowing the trash under her seat to throw away after the game when a hand tapped her on the shoulder and a voice behind her said, "We figured you'd be here watching another game and not taking care of yourself, so we got this for you."

She looked up and saw Rachel with a hot dog and a drink in her outstretched hands. Dani was standing next to her with a bag of chips.

"I wanted to make sure you had something to eat," Rachel told her. "I knew you'd get so wrapped up in all of this that you'd forget."

"Actually, I..." Katy said before cutting herself off. She then continued after a brief pause, "You're right. I completely forgot. Thanks, you guys!"

Rachel sat down beside her while Dani climbed over the row to a seat behind them. It was clear they weren't going to leave until she ate something, so she plucked a few chips from the bag and held them in front of her face, took a deep breath and shoved them into her mouth. They kept their eyes on her until she emptied the entire package.

"Well," she said as she crumpled the bag in her hands. "That filled me right up!"

"You need to eat the hot dog, too," Rachel ordered.

Katy lifted the bun from the paper tray and moaned.

"Rachel..." she whined.

"Eat!" Rachel commanded.

Katy managed to finish the hot dog, this time slower and in twice as many bites as the first one. Afterwards, she licked her lips and used the napkin to wipe the sides of her mouth.

"Okay," she said, forcing a smile. "I'm officially full."

"Good," Rachel said. "We'll leave you to your duties. Come on, Dani. We can catch the shuttle back to the hotel if we hurry."

Dani stood up and patted Katy on her head. There was a big grin on her face as she mugged, "Who's the kid now?" Before Katy could answer, she placed two fingers next to her eyebrow and flipped her a salute, adding, "See ya later, Coach."

Katy turned her focus back to the game, which ended with Salina toppling Emporia by twenty-two points. Lincoln's game wasn't for another two hours, so she walked back to the hotel, breathing in the cold winter air and checking out the sights along the way. Not realizing how tired she was, once she was in her room she collapsed on the bed and slept until the ringing of her phone forced her eyes open an hour later.

It was Mary, calling to see how things were going. Katy quickly caught her up on all that had happened in the tournament so far.

"That's wonderful," Mary cheered. "But I'm more interested in hearing how things are going between you and Rachel."

"Nothing to report on that front," Katy told her. "We're here for the tournament, Mom. Nothing else."

"I was just curious how the two of you were getting along."

"We're getting along just fine. If anything changes, I'll be sure to let you know. In fact, you'll be the first call I make."

"Okay then. I'll let you get back to whatever it is you were doing."

"Thanks. I'll talk to you later."

Chapter 53

Tired as they were, the Lincoln girls played well and defeated Leavenworth by a score of 38-36. It was a close game with back-and-forth scoring, quick execution of plays and rapid ball movement, but the Lincoln girls had a little bit more oomph in them than Leavenworth did. They took Katy's advice to heart and showed it by giving everything they had from start to finish. To acknowledge and celebrate their arduous journey throughout the tournament, Katy brought everyone together in the lobby one last time before they all turned in for the night.

"You did it!" she shouted excitedly. "I knew you would! And now, you're playing for the championship! Our game is at noon, so you've got plenty of time tomorrow to get out and do something before then." As a post script, she added, "Just don't have too much fun and wear yourselves out!"

Courtney's father came up to her afterwards and asked, "Which team do you think will win the loser's bracket tomorrow?"

"Well," Katy started. "Selfishly, I'm hoping it'll be Leavenworth since we've already beaten them. Honestly, though, I think it'll be Salina. Leavenworth is good, but, in my opinion, Salina is better. That being said, it's the last chance for either of them to stay in the tournament, so both are gonna come out swinging. It'll be a good game, that's for sure. Either way, I know our girls are ready to take on the winner!"

"Thank you, Katy."

"For what?"

"For everything you've done for those girls. For being a great mentor and a great teacher. And for just being an all-around great person. My daughter is lucky to have you in her life."

Katy gave him a hug and said, "Thank you! That really means a lot!"

The crowd had thinned down to just a handful of people at that point, so Katy bid those remaining goodnight and left them to continue mingling. Her mother's comments regarding Rachel came to mind as she passed her room and saw that her light was on. She thought about knocking but then decided against it and continued on.

It was after midnight when she finally crawled into bed. Excited and nervous about playing in the championship match she tossed and turned for hours, glancing at the clock on the bedside table every thirty minutes or so to see what time it was. The last time she looked, the digits "5:15" glared back at her.

The Salina-Leavenworth game starts in three hours, she reminded herself as she rolled onto her back and pulled the covers up to her chin. She held her eyes tightly closed for a few moments and then opened them again.

Who am I kidding? I'm not gonna get any sleep, so I might as well get up.

She went to the restroom, leaving the light on afterwards as she traveled across the room and opened the curtains. It was still dark out, so she switched on a floor lamp to add more light. She then filled the coffee pot with water from the bathroom sink, poured it in the carafe and sat on the bed watching an infomercial for some brand of vacuum cleaners she'd never heard of while it brewed. Halfway through her second cup, someone knocked on her door.

"Who is it?" she asked, startled.

"It's me," the visitor announced from the hallway. "Rachel."

Katy disengaged the lock and opened the door.

"Is something wrong?" she asked.

"I can't sleep. I didn't want to disturb Dani so I went downstairs but the lobby was deserted. I saw your light on and heard the TV…"

"Come in," Katy interrupted. "I'd offer you some coffee but I finished it off already. I can call down to the desk and get more."

"I'm good, but thanks for offering."

"I know why I can't sleep. Why can't you?"

"I've got a lot on my mind."

"Problems at home?"

"Not really."

"At work?"

"No. It's personal." Rachel intentionally lowered her voice for that comment, and, not quite ready to make eye contact with Katy, stared instead at the woman on TV tossing a fistful of potting soil onto a patch of white carpeting.

"I didn't mean to pry," Katy said, pretending to turn her attention to the sales pitch as well.

"You're not prying. As a matter of fact, my thoughts…" Rachel paused long enough to raise her eyes to meet Katy's. "My thoughts," she repeated, "are about you."

"Me?"

"I need to tell you something. Something I should've told you a long time ago."

She picked up the remote and clicked off the TV then sat down on the side of the bed and motioned for Katy to join her. Katy moved closer but did not take a seat, choosing instead to remain standing a few feet away.

"Are you afraid to sit with me?" she asked.

"I don't know what I'm feeling right now," Katy answered honestly.

"I'm not surprised. I've never given you reason to…"

She paused again to brush away a stray tear then whispered more for her purpose than Katy's, "I promised myself I wouldn't cry."

Katy felt an urge to say something but stayed firm – and silent – in her spot.

"I left my husband because of my feelings for someone else," Rachel continued. "I never told anyone who that other person was. Not even George. It's you, Katy."

That triggered Katy to ask, "Why didn't you say anything before now?"

"There were lots of reasons. First, I had my kids to think about. Their father and I had just separated and I had to make sure they were okay with that before moving on to someone new. And then there was Laura. I thought the two of you were together and I would never put myself in the middle of someone else's relationship. The biggest reason, though, was that kiss. I didn't like my private life exposed like that. It was hard on me and even harder for my kids. People were leaving nasty messages on my phone and Dani was being bullied at school. Even the boys had to deal with the fallout from it."

"I'm so sorry, Rachel."

"Like I said, I never told George who I was in love with, but he suspected all along it was you. It infuriated him that I wouldn't confirm or deny it. Nora told me he even tried to get you to admit we were lovers at your parents' house in front of your family!"

"That was the day my dad found out I was gay."

"And what a horrible way that was for him to find out. George was angry, but that didn't give him the right to act so cruelly. Another reason I didn't say anything before now was because of what that photograph did to you. Professionally, I mean. It was crazy how something so innocent came so close to destroying your career. Beyond comprehension, really. I can only imagine what a catastrophe it would have caused if I'd declared my love for you while all that was going on.

"After that, I gave up thinking it would ever happen and convinced myself we would never be together. I was sad, lonely and miserable. Even my kids noticed."

"Yeah, Dani came to me asking for help."

"She did?"

"She said you were crying a lot and that George told her it was because of me."

"He had no right to say that to her. He was using her to try and flush out your true identity. Looking back, I guess it's a good thing you didn't get involved."

"What exactly did you say to him?"

"I told him the marriage was over and that I was in love with another woman."

"When did you tell him?"

"That day at the pizza parlor. I saw you there with your mom and I knew I had to own up to my feelings. I couldn't put it off any longer. He moved out later that same week."

"I saw you two there and I thought…"

"I knew you had misinterpreted what you were seeing. I could see how upset you were. I wanted to come to you, to hold you, but I couldn't. Not with George and the kids there. When you looked at me again, I had hoped you'd see the truth in my eyes."

"I couldn't see anything but my own pain."

"I know and I'm sorry, Katy."

Rachel rose from the bed to stand in front of her.

"So," she began again, tentatively, "what are your feelings now?"

"Afraid, confused, excited…"

"I meant about me. What are your feelings about me?"

"Those are my feelings about you."

Katy took an intentional pause before speaking again.

"You know," she finally blurted out, "I felt something the first time you touched my hand at the salon and I've thought about you nearly every day since. When did you know you had feelings for me?"

"At your birthday party."

"Last year? Really?"

"I couldn't take my eyes off of you."

"But I was wasted."

"True, you were a little drunk but I thought it was cute – that *you* were cute."

"Wow. That was so long ago."

"It was. And my feelings kept growing stronger every time I saw you. I knew I was in love with you at your housewarming party and it took everything I had to not join you in the shower that day."

"I wish you would've told me then what was going on."

Rachel held out her hands, which Katy then took in her own.

"I'm telling you now," she confessed.

Katy smiled and gave her hands a little squeeze. Rachel leaned forward and kissed her on the lips. It was a sweet, fulsome kiss and Katy was electrified by it.

"I've wanted to do that for a long time," Rachel admitted after they separated.

Katy pulled her into her arms and whispered, "So have I."

When their lips came together again, Katy nearly lost her balance and latched onto the corner of the desk to steady herself.

"Maybe we should sit down," Rachel offered.

She ushered Katy to the bed and gently lowered her onto the mattress. As their lips met for the third time, Katy leaned back and pulled Rachel down on top of her. Her arms wrapped around her waist at the same time Rachel pleaded, "Wait."

"Wait?" Katy panted while dropping her arms to her sides. Her heart was pounding so hard that she could feel it pulsing against her temples.

"I want our first time to be special," Rachel told her. "Not some quickie in a hotel room. Can we just hold each other? Would you be okay with that? I've waited a long time to be with you, and I'm willing to wait a little longer if I have to."

Katy exhaled loudly before responding, "I understand." She then took several deep breaths to help her heartbeat return to a normal cadence.

They snuggled up to one another and before long both were fast asleep. They were still wrapped in each other's arms when the alarm on Katy's phone went off. Katy left her in the bed and went to use the restroom. Rachel was straightening the covers when she returned.

"I'd better go wake Dani," she told Katy.

"Will I see you again before the game?"

"We could meet downstairs for breakfast, but first I want to tell Dani what's going on. I don't want her hearing it from someone else, especially her father. She takes a while to get going in the mornings, so I'll call you when we're on our way."

They kissed goodbye and Katy stood in her doorway to watch her travel the short distance to her room. Before going in, Rachel blew her a kiss.

Chapter 54

"Wake up, sweetheart," Rachel said after giving Dani a gentle nudge.

Dani grumbled and pulled the covers over her head. Rachel moved the blanket and stroked the side of her face.

"Come on, Dani. It's time to get up. You've got a championship to win today."

"No," her daughter moaned. "I don't wanna."

"I told Coach Hopkins we'd meet her for breakfast, but I wanted to talk to you first. Come on, Dani. Wake up."

Dani sat up and blinked a few times before rubbing the sleep from her eyes. Rachel sat down next to her and set about telling her the truth – all of it. When she was finished, Dani asked, "Does Dad know?"

"He knows I want to be with another woman. He just doesn't know who it is."

"I dunno, Mom. I think he does."

"Well, not officially. I am gonna tell him. I need to tell the boys, too. Before telling anyone, though, I had to talk to Coach Hopkins to see if she felt the same about me."

"Does she?"

"Yes, Dani, she does." A huge smile spread across her face, but then, seconds later, she turned serious again. "So, you're okay with all of this?"

"Sure, Mom. Why wouldn't I be? I like Coach Hopkins."

"Remember how the kids teased you about the picture in the paper? Well, some of them may give you an even harder time about this."

"They're stupid. I never pay attention to those freaks."

"Some adults are gonna have a hard time with this as well."

"Well then, they're stupid, too!"

Rachel touched Dani's face and whispered, "I love you, kiddo. I am so lucky to have a daughter like you."

"Does this mean you won't be sad anymore?"

Rachel couldn't hold her emotions any longer and burst into tears. Dani knew they were tears of joy, but couldn't resist teasing her nonetheless.

"Geez, Mom! I suppose now you'll be crying all the time because you're happy. Is Coach gonna be crying, too? I don't think I can handle that. One of you crying is enough."

Rachel leaned forward and gave her a kiss on the cheek, which Dani quickly wiped off with the back of her hand.

"Hey!" she snapped. "Cut that out!"

Katy had already showered and dressed and was waiting for them in the breakfast lounge. She had just poured herself a second cup of coffee when Rachel called to say they were on their way. Dani was still dressed in her pajamas when she claimed the seat across from her.

"I'm starving," she announced as she plopped her elbows down onto the table.

"Go through the line and get whatever you want," Rachel suggested.

"Aren't you coming?"

"Katy and I are going to stay here and talk."

"Didn't you two do enough of that already?"

"Dani," Rachel said sternly. "Go get your food."

After Dani trotted off, Katy asked, "How did it go?"

"Surprisingly well."

"No problems then?"

"No. None."

"Think it will go as smoothly with the boys?"

"I hope so. I'm the only mother they've ever known. Their birth mother abandoned them when Rion was a baby. I don't want them thinking I'm going to do the same thing."

"And George?"

"He already thought it was you, so I'm sure it won't come as a shock. Nora says he's doing a lot better now. I really think he's trying to move on. He told her that he appreciates the fact that I didn't get involved with anyone right away."

"So, what happens now?"

"Let's just take things one day at a time and see where that leads us."

Dani returned with her plate piled high with an assortment of pancakes, scrambled eggs, bacon and toast. Before taking her first bite, she glanced back and forth between the two of them and asked, "Are you guys done yakking yet?"

"Yes," Katy giggled. "We're finished."

"What are we doing after this?" she asked as she plunged her fork into the eggs.

"I'm sure Coach Hopkins has things to do before the game," Rachel answered. "You and I can find something to do until it's time to go to the arena."

Katy glanced at her watch and saw that she needed to leave to make it in time for the Salina-Leavenworth tip-off.

"I'm gonna watch the game between the teams in the loser's bracket to see who we play this afternoon," she told them. "I'll catch up with you guys later."

Dani raised her fork and tipped it in her direction, dropping a few egg morsels onto the table in the process. "Later, Coach," she mumbled through a mouthful of toast.

Katy smiled and offered them a quick wave before leaving.

Chapter 55

Katy had been right in predicting the outcome of the loser's bracket as Salina dealt a heavy blow to Leavenworth with a twelve-point victory. Throughout the game she took copious notes to help prepare for Lincoln's next – and, hopefully, final – showdown of the tournament.

Having been awake for most of the night, she decided to take a nap before meeting with the Tournament Director and Salina's coach to go over details for the championship game and for a second game, if it came to that. Regardless of whether it was one game or two, the Director also wanted to pass along the order of events for the trophy presentation that would take place immediately afterwards.

When she returned to the arena, she saw that the court had already been staged for the match. The first two rows of bleacher seats behind each team were blocked off for the players' parents, and there were signs taped to the back of each player's chair with their name and jersey number.

The door to the Director's office was locked when she tried to open it, so she went back to the court to wait. Thinking she was alone, she trotted out onto the floor punching and jabbing her fists like Sylvester Stallone in the movie, *Rocky*, while at the same time belting out the tune, *The Eye of the Tiger*. She was unaware that David, the photographer from the Herald Banner, had come early to ready his equipment and check lighting levels. It was his good fortune that he was there to capture her on film – happy and carefree, open and expressive.

After lifting a basketball from one of the racks she dribbled it toward the hoop and executed a layup that clipped the backboard before passing cleanly through the net. She then carried the ball to the top of the free throw line, bounced it twice and landed a perfect jump shot.

For the next few minutes, she shot from different places on the court and every one scored. David captured everything so the people from Lincoln could see her in her glory. She'd competed in two state competitions in high school but never made it to the finals. This was her first trip to the winner's circle.

With little more than an hour until the championship game, she spent a quarter of that time with the Director and Salina's coach going over pre-game and post-game details. As they were leaving his office, Katy saw her players filtering into the arena alongside their parents. Each had a look of amazement blanketing their faces. It was moments like this David treasured, capturing candid shots that immortalized the emotions of his subjects. His finger remained on the shutter until the memory card beeped at him that it was full. He quickly changed it out and started all over again.

The girls followed Katy into the locker room while everyone else selected their seats on the sidelines, chatting amongst themselves as they waited for the game to start. David moved his equipment closer to the court and set up his tripod, then mounted the camera and latched on the zoom lens. After aiming the camera in the direction of the locker room, he sat down to wait with the others.

He took pictures in rapid succession when the girls ran onto the court, rotating the camera from side to side as they passed in front of him. When Salina's team entered from the opposite side of the arena, he took only a few pictures of them then switched back to his hometown team.

Rosters were announced over the loudspeaker. Being that they were the only team left in the winner's bracket, Lincoln was presented first. For each name called, that player would travel to the tip-off circle as their parents were asked to stand and be recognized as well. When it was Dani's turn Rachel stood alone, prompting other parents to rise to their feet and stand with her. After finishing Lincoln's roster, the same type of acknowledgment was made for the Salina team.

Courtney won the tip-off and Lincoln scored on the first possession. Salina evened up the game at their end of the court right away, and so it went the entire first half with Lincoln scoring and Salina matching them point for point. At halftime, the score was tied. Salina moved ahead by four in the third period and halfway through the fourth increased their lead to six. Katy used her timeouts wisely, speaking encouragement into her players at each break.

With one minute left on the game clock, Lincoln had whittled the lead down to two. They had possession of the ball and the entire crowd was on their feet, screaming loudly at the top of their lungs. The noise level was deafening. Katy waved and screamed at Sandy to call a timeout but she didn't hear her.

Valuable seconds ticked away before Dani finally caught sight of her running along the sidelines, flapping her arms as if she were trying to fly.

"Timeout!" Katy yelled at her.

"Timeout!" Dani echoed to the official.

The referee blew his whistle and the crowd silenced. There were now less than twenty-five seconds on the clock. Players from both teams came off the floor and huddled around their coaches.

"Does everybody remember the new play I showed you last week where Dani and Sandy cross in front of the net and post up on opposite sides of the court?" Katy asked the circle of jerseys surrounding her. All heads were bobbing up and down that they did.

"All right," she continued. "When you go back out there, I want you to run the new play. Keep playing smart and don't let them shake your confidence. You know how to win. Now, get out there and kick some Salina butt!"

"Yeah!" Sandy roared.

"Let's do it!" Courtney shouted.

The girls all laid their hands on top of Katy's and raised them high, shouting, "Go Lincoln!"

Matching the skill of seasoned professionals, the Lincoln five executed the play perfectly and made the basket to tie the score. Very little time had expired, and now Salina was in control of the ball – and the clock.

Salina's point guard advanced the ball just inside the half court line and stopped, dribbling in and out between her legs while precious seconds ticked away. Katy was about to call for a final timeout when Sandy charged her and stole the ball. Dani raced down the court with her and got a perfect bounce pass within five feet of the basket. The layup rolled off of her fingers and cleared the net just as the buzzer sounded the end of the game. The hometown crowd ran screaming onto the floor to congratulate them. Katy headed straight for the basket, scooping Dani up in her arms and lifting her off the ground.

"Oh, my God!" she screamed. "Dani! That was brilliant! Sandy!" She quickly spun around to find her. "Where's my beautiful Sandy?"

"I'm here, Coach!" Sandy called out.

"Get over here!" Katy yelled.

Katy lowered Dani to the floor and gave Sandy a hug so tight that it nearly knocked the wind out of her. The rest of the team circled around them as David continued to point and shoot his way in and out of their huddle.

"Wow!" Katy exclaimed, her head towering over everyone around her. "You did it!"

Rachel muscled her way through the crowd to get to her daughter and immediately wrapped her arms around her. "I am so proud of you!" she squealed, clutching her tightly. Then, to the other players, she added, "I'm proud of *all* of you!"

She glanced at Katy and the two exchanged smiles. With Dani in tow, she moved beside her and without so much as a word between them put her hand behind Katy's head, pulled her close and kissed her on the lips. Other parents were busy celebrating with their children, not at all concerned with the passionate embrace taking place a few feet away from them. In short time, many followed suit and were kissing their spouses or significant others as well.

A few fathers lifted their daughters onto their shoulders and began marching them around the court. Others fell in line behind them, creating an impromptu parade. The last two people Katy saw joining the procession were Principal Hall and Mr. Snodgrass. As her eyes followed them, she caught sight of her parents standing in the bleachers waving their arms at her. The only person noticeably absent was Mildred Snodgrass, who, Katy would learn days later from the rumor mill at Mary's church, was currently living apart from her husband.

The fans who stayed behind in Lincoln were on hand to welcome them home. Some had parked near the city limit sign to cheer the bus as it came into town while others set out folding chairs, lining both sides of Main Street for several blocks. Trucks were parked with the tailgates lowered, their passengers seated atop the cabs or on chairs in the beds for a better view of the returning champions.

Horns blared and headlamps flashed as the bus passed in front of them with waves of applause rippling through the crowd like horse hooves on a racetrack. Overwhelmed with the sheer magnitude of it all, Katy could no longer contain her emotions.

"Here you go, honey," the driver said, pulling a tissue from her pocket.

"Better give me the whole box," Katy sobbed.

The driver slowed the bus to a crawl and shouted to her passengers, "Go ahead and open the windows, girls! Let's show these folks how much you appreciate them!"

Arms and heads began extending out the side windows as the crowd continued to cheer. The driver brought the bus to a stop so that Katy could acknowledge them as well. When the door opened, she came down the stairs carrying the trophy and everyone rose to their feet to give her a standing ovation.

Chapter 56

The owner of the newspaper wanted to run a special edition to honor the event, so David and his staff worked late into the night to put it all together. Seven o'clock Monday morning, every house within the city limits had a copy at their front door.

David created a four-page storybook and photo album of the Lincoln players, their parents and Katy taken at various times throughout the competition. Dani's winning shot appeared on the front page with a headline that read:

LINCOLN WINS STATE!

Page 2 opened with a photo of some parents staring wide-eyed and open mouthed as a ball floated through the air in front of their faces. At the bottom of Page 3 was a picture of Katy's and Rachel's kiss, this time, without any fanfare. Unless you were looking to call it out, it was just one of the many photographs featured in the article.

Mary skimmed over the story quickly and rushed to the bedroom to share the news with her husband. "Frank!" she shouted. "Frank! Wake up! They wrote a special paper for our Katy!"

She grabbed his spectacles from the headboard and put them on her own face as she sat down next to him. She spread the paper open across her lap to read the full article and would occasionally make little throaty sounds and utter an occasional, "Oh, my!"

Laying on his side facing away from her with the blanket tucked up under his chin, Frank would ask after each outburst, "What is it?"

Mary didn't answer. Instead, when she was finished, she folded the paper and laid it and his glasses on the bedside table, grinning from ear to ear as she left the room. She then went to the kitchen and poured each of them a cup of coffee. He had fallen back to sleep by the time she returned, so she carried the cups back to the kitchen and called Katy.

"Yes?" Katy answered in a hushed voice.

"Why are you whispering?"

"I'm in class, Mom."

"Did you see the paper this morning?"

"What paper?"

"The Herald Banner! They wrote an article about the tournament!"

Katy shuddered as she recalled the kiss with Rachel after the championship match. Fearing the same outcome the previous kiss had caused, she exclaimed in a nervous voice, "Oh shit! Rachel and I… Are we on the front page?"

"I believe the picture you're referring to is on Page 3."

"You're joking, right?"

"David did a real nice job. Filled up four pages!"

"Can you bring me a copy?"

"Wouldn't it be better to wait until you get off work?"

"I'd rather not wait. Could you bring it to me? Please?"

"All right. I'll be over once I get up and around."

Katy paced back and forth on the gymnasium floor for the remainder of the hour and well into the next. Nearly forty-five minutes had passed since Mary had called her.

"What took you so long?" she snapped, glaring at Mary when she finally arrived.

"Your father wanted to read the article before I left the house. You know how he is about his paper."

"You could've picked up another copy on the way over."

"I could've, I guess. To be honest, I didn't think about that."

Katy took the paper from her while asking, "Will you keep an eye on the kids while I read this?"

"What if they want something?"

"I'll be right over there on the bleachers."

"Maybe you should wait until you get home."

"I'm not waiting several hours to find out what's been printed about me. Please just stand here and watch the kids."

Katy carried the paper to the bleachers and sat down. After glancing over the first two pages, she fixed her gaze on the picture at the bottom of Page 3. A smile spread across her face but then disappeared as Principal Hall came into the gym carrying his own paper.

"Oh, hey there," he called out to Mary as he passed by her, not appearing the least bit concerned that she was standing watch over the kids. As he approached Katy, he said, "What a great story! I wasn't sure if you'd seen the article yet, so I brought you a copy."

Without offering anything further he tucked his paper under his arm, waved his fingers at Mary and walked out of the gym.

Katy looked again at the photograph of her and Rachel and whispered, "Thank you, David."

Chapter 57

Rachel spoke with her sons the night she and Dani returned from the tournament. David's article hadn't come out yet, but after she filled them in on what was happening with her and Katy, combined with their dad's suspicions about them, neither was shocked by the picture in the newspaper the next morning.

Rion was first to respond by giving her a hug. Rafael congratulated her, telling her how proud he was that she was following her heart and choosing love. Both were glad to see a smile back on their mother's face and a glow that meant she was finally happy again. They shared with her how much they enjoyed the pizza "planting" day at Katy's and how they felt right at home with her starting from when they arrived until they left to go home. They liked Katy and already had a bond with Jason, her older brother and their coach and mentor, and were looking forward to becoming an extended part of the Hopkins' family.

Rachel met with George after his classes let out on Tuesday. He read the article the night before and, having seen the other story weeks earlier, wasn't as upset with the photo as he was with now having to come to terms with the fact that his and Rachel's marriage was beyond resurrection and that he had no other choice but to accept the fact that he would have to live his life without her in it. Rachel assured him she would always be a part of his life, if for no other reason than the sake of their children. However, her life was with Katy now and there would be no turning back from that.

Three days later, Katy and Rachel had their first official date and were inseparable from that moment on. They went everywhere together and not a single person in Lincoln, except Mildred Snodgrass, paid them any attention. If they did it was usually just to offer a smile or to congratulate Katy on the big win.

Frank and Mary were elated that their daughter had found happiness and threw a party to welcome Rachel into the family that just happened to coincide with her birthday. The invitation list included Katy's siblings and their spouses, Rachel's children, Nora and Steve, Laura and Rebecca, Martha and her husband, and, believe it or not, George. Beth made her famous spiked punch, but this time Katy paid attention to the number of drinks she consumed and stayed sober until night's end.

The relationship between Katy and George had a rough start but his resentment began to subside as time passed. The biggest reason for his hostility, he confided, was not so much losing Rachel to her, but the fear that his daughter would grow to love her more than him. Katy reassured him that she was there to add to the family, not take anything from it. Their mutual civility towards one another continued to strengthen, and at Rafael's graduation two and a half months later, they sat side by side as he walked across the stage to get his diploma.

Being a professor, George was adamant that his children continue their education past high school. Since he and Rachel were tied up with work schedules, Katy volunteered to drive Rafael around to check out college campuses in both Kansas and Missouri. Rion and Dani tagged along, forging an even tighter bond between the four of them.

During that first summer as a couple, Katy and Rachel, and more often than not all three kids, would relax on Katy's old blanket in front of the library to listen to the outdoor concert series, go to a movie or attend a live performance at the community theater. One weekend, they all traveled to Lake of the Ozarks where Katy not only taught the teenagers how to ski but to pilot a boat as well. Their outings together were always a blast, but if you asked the kids, they would tell you the activity they liked best was going to Luigi's for pizza eating contests and competing against Katy in the arcade. She routinely lost, prompting them to ask if she had done it on purpose, something she would neither admit nor refute.

Through it all, Katy remembered the thought she had the day they planted hedges where she wished that they were her family. And now, by all appearances, they were.

By mid-August, Rafael had decided on the college he wanted to attend and Rachel and Katy went with him to register and help him move his belongings into his new dorm room. A week later, Rachel turned her house back over to George and she, Rion and Dani moved in with Katy. Rion was quick to claim the western bedroom, leaving Katy and Dani to clear out what was her office to create a personal space of her own.

Everyone clicked from the start and respected each other's boundaries as they learned to navigate their new, conjoined living arrangements. It didn't take long for Rion to become a fan of Katy's as she took the time to listen to what he had to say and not pass judgment like his father sometimes did. She also let him drive her Jeep, which practically catapulted her to sainthood for that act alone.

Katy mounted a basketball hoop on the front of the garage and she and Dani would spend hours shooting baskets or playing one-on-one. Rachel and Rion would come out on occasion and pair off against them. Rion was an excellent basketball player and oftentimes equaled – and sometimes bested – Katy's skills on the court. Rachel was a good athlete as well and rivaled Dani point for point in their matchups.

Chapter 58

Six months into their relationship, around the same time as Katy's birthday. Katy proposed to Rachel and she accepted. Mary made several quick adjustments to the plans for her annual birthday bash to include an engagement party at the same time. The guest list brought back everyone that had been at Rachel's party months earlier.

Katy and Rachel followed the unofficial Hopkins' tradition and had their ceremony in her parents' back yard. Same-sex marriages weren't legal in Kansas at the time, so they opted for a commitment ceremony instead. Standing next to the minister, Katy's freshly manicured fingers fidgeted with the buttons on her linen suit as she swayed from side to side waiting for Rachel to make her appearance. Mary, seated a few feet away in the front row, watched her gnaw on her bottom lip as the bridesmaids and their escorts approached the altar. Beth and Ben took their positions first, followed by Emma and Mason, Nora and Jason, and, finally, Laura and Rion. Danielle, Rachel's Maid of Honor, came next, her tiny hands clinging tightly to Frank's arm as he accompanied her down the aisle. Beth scooted over for her to squeeze in beside her and patted her on the back to help calm her nerves.

Frank came forward to give Katy a kiss on the cheek then took his seat next to Mary. To the amazement of everyone he had shifted from his rigid, biblical stance to where he no longer condemned homosexuality as a sin. An even bigger impression he made on Katy was in personally inviting Rachel and Laura into his home after his threat to banish them forever. As for Mary? Well, she was beside herself that Katy was finally going to have the life – and love – she so rightfully deserved.

Frank caught Laura tugging at the front of her gown to raise it higher, the low cut apparently exposing too much cleavage for her comfort. He giggled as he pointed it out to Mary and she immediately reprimanded him by giving him the "straighten-up-right-now-or-I'll-bend-you-over-my-knee" scowl that Katy and her siblings knew all too well. This was witnessed by all four of their children, who had to turn their heads and cover their faces to keep from laughing out loud.

George had recently started dating and came with his new girlfriend, Beatrice. To avoid drawing undue attention to themselves, they claimed two seats on the back row next to Martha and her husband. Dani wiggled her fingers at him and he did the same in return. Katy was surprised – and impressed – that he had decided to come after all.

When the organist started to play the first few notes of the bridal march, attendees on both sides of the walkway stood and turned to look at Rachel. Katy gasped when she saw that she was wearing Beth's gown. Beth had never forgotten how much Katy admired the dress and packed it away for this very occasion, knowing it would be brought out again at her little sister's ceremony. Katy had no idea she had arranged with Rachel beforehand to wear it, and seeing her in it brought tears to both sister's eyes.

Rafael stood proud and tall beside his mother with his arm extended for her to hold as he led her down the aisle. Several heads tipped toward them while a handful of women clasped their hands and let out an audible sigh as they passed by. When the minister asked who would give her away, he and his siblings answered in unison, "We do." Rachel looked at them and mouthed the words, "I love you." Rafael then kissed her on the forehead and took his place between Katy and Rion.

After the ring exchange, Rachel and Katy read aloud messages they wanted to share with each other before the ceremony concluded. The minister moved aside as they turned to face one another.

"Rachel," Katy began. Her bottom lip was quivering as her mind raced to bring the words to her lips. Locking eyes with Rachel, she took a deep breath and exhaled slowly as she reached for her hands. "I have never loved anyone the way I love you. You are the only person in my heart, in my soul and in my dreams. Without a doubt, I will love you forever. I am beyond blessed to spend today, tomorrow and all of eternity by your side."

Rachel returned her gaze with a wink. "My Katy," she said, smiling as she squeezed Katy's hands. "I will treasure you always and in all ways. My heart is yours to keep, my hand is yours to hold, and now, my life is yours to share. I have loved you since the first day we met, and I will love you until time is no more."

When both had finished, they stepped aside to allow the minister to rejoin them.

"And now," he proclaimed loudly, "by the power vested in me by the great state of Kansas, I, Wilmer Snodgrass, licensed minister and – Katy asked me to add – President of the Lincoln School Board, now pronounce you, Katy and Rachel, life partners on this the 24th day of August, 2006. You may kiss your bride!"

Seeing David lower his camera after capturing the moment, he jokingly told Katy, "If that photograph ends up in the Herald Banner, I promise you can keep your job!" The off-handed remark sparked uproarious fits of laughter from the audience that didn't taper off until Katy and Rachel had walked down the aisle together. Whenever anyone brought it up at the reception, the hilarity would start all over again.

Katy's friends and family had conspired together before the wedding to plan their honeymoon with a surprise trip to New York City. Nora, Steve, Laura and Rebecca bought airline tickets, Frank and Mary made hotel arrangements, Katy's brothers and their wives made dinner reservations at several of the finest restaurants in the city, and, knowing how much both loved the theater, Beth and Ben gifted them with front row seats to the hottest show on Broadway. Rachel's kids, with a little financial assistance from George, arranged for a limousine to transport them from the airport to the hotel and back again. The only thing missing from the package was a ride to the Kansas City airport. To no one's surprise, Mary volunteered before anyone else had the chance.

Chapter 59

Watching Katy shoveling snow off the back deck from the kitchen window, Rachel smiled and gripped her coffee mug with both hands, warming her fingers with its radiant heat. What an incredible path their lives had taken, starting with a chance encounter and culminating in the most beautiful love story that anyone could ever dream of.

The journey leading to their union was entangled in a web of challenges, adversity, tenacity and perseverance, temporarily derailed by the scandal that followed an innocent, spontaneous kiss. Yet, here they were, nearly two years later, happier than ever and living their best life together.

With Rion now away at college with his older brother, Dani was the only child still at home. Katy began noticing changes in her behavior that were reminiscent of herself at that same age in that Dani showed absolutely no interest in boys, opting instead to occupy her time with only her female friends. Her style of dress had changed as well, her clothing from previous years replaced by outfits with a more masculine flair. Thinking she may be going through similar issues she'd had all those years ago, Katy encouraged her to open up to her one day while Rachel was at work.

"Hey, kiddo," she started. "Wanna go out and shoot some hoops with me?"

Dani, who was lounging on the couch watching TV and munching on potato chips, leapt to her feet and answered in an excited voice, "Sure!"

She hurried to her room to get her basketball, and, after donning their jackets, they walked outside. Once they were on the driveway, Katy restarted their conversation.

"We haven't really talked in a while," she said as Dani passed the ball to her. "How are things going with you?"

Katy pulled up for a jumper and Dani waited for it to clear the net before giving her an answer. Her response was brief and direct.

"Fine."

Katy continued to probe as she bounced the ball back to Dani.

"Anything exciting happening in your life lately?"

Dani dribbled to the basket and executed a layup. She grabbed the ball afterwards and turned to face her.

"I don't know," she muttered softly. "Maybe, I guess."

Katy goaded her into a game of one-on-one, guarding her from taking another shot while at the same time insisting, "Come on, Dani. Don't leave me hanging here!"

Dani tucked the ball under her arm and stared at her.

"You're not going to let this go," she grumbled. "Are you?"

"Absolutely not," Katy argued.

It was then that Dani started telling her about one of her classmates, a girl named Cheryl. She described how the two of them had been hanging out a lot and doing stuff that they "maybe oughta" shouldn't be doing.

Katy, curious to know more, asked, "What do you mean?"

"Well," Dani muttered and then stopped.

"Dani," Katy said in a low voice. Her tone was soft and sympathetic. "You know you can tell me anything."

Dani locked eyes with her and confessed, "I think I'm a lesbian."

Even though she already knew the answer, Katy inquired, "Why do you think that?"

"I really like being around this girl, Katy. I think about her all the time."

Katy moved beside her and put her arm around her shoulder.

"And how does Cheryl feel about you?"

"Same. She told me that yesterday."

"Is this a relationship you want to pursue?"

"Yeah. It just feels right, you know?"

"Then you should go for it. The heart knows what the heart wants, Dani."

"Are you gonna tell my mom?"

"No. I'm going to let you do that. I'll be there for support, if that's what you want."

"I'd like that. Thanks, Katy."

"Do it soon," Katy urged. "Before she finds out some other way."

That night, Dani sat down with Rachel and opened up about her sexual orientation. As Katy expected, Rachel wasn't surprised by the news either and gave her daughter a hug to show her approval and acceptance. Knowing she had both of their blessings, Dani called Cheryl before going to bed and asked her on a real date. Cheryl had the same talk with her parents the next evening and they also consented to the relationship. From that moment on, the teenagers were rarely seen apart.

The next family milestones were Dani's graduation from high school and Rafael's from college. At both events, Katy and Rachel sat alongside George and Beatrice, who was soon to become the kids' step-mother. Following in the spirit, Katy and Rachel redid their vows when same-sex marriages became legalized in 2014. At their request, Mr. Snodgrass performed the second ceremony as well. Their wedding, in addition to Rafael's marriage to his long-time girlfriend, Kelly, the next year, Rion's to his college crush, Carla, two years after that, and Dani's to Cheryl ten months later, were all held in the Hopkins' back yard.

And then came the grandbabies. George and Katy painted quite the picture sitting together in the Waiting Room when Rafael and Rion became dads for the first time, each realizing just how far they had come to get to that point. When Dani's wife, Cheryl, went into labor, Katy and Rachel were invited into the Delivery Room to help them welcome their baby into the world. Because Katy had such a positive influence on Dani's life, they named their daughter, Katherine, after her. The bond between Katy and that little girl was instantaneous. By the time Katherine was two, she was Katy's constant shadow whenever they were together.

When Katherine turned four, Katy volunteered at her Little League games, lending her skills to whatever role the coaches assigned her: bandaging boo-boos, fetching water, keeping score, etc. Rachel was there as well, cheering loudly from the sidelines. At each event, Katy noticed how much her "mini me" outperformed the other players.

In the years that followed, Katy and Dani continued to elevate Katherine's love of sports, sharing their knowledge, experience and passion, and, by her senior year in high school, she was being scouted by some of the top colleges in the nation with a choice to play either softball or basketball, or both. After selecting her alma mater, Katy and Rachel were there with her when she signed the acceptance letter. It was one of the proudest days of their lives.

Katherine was in her second year of college when Rachel was diagnosed with stage four ovarian cancer. Doctors gave her little hope, but she valiantly battled the disease until it ended her life two years later. Katy was with her through all of her treatments and never left her bedside during her final days in hospice. She fell into a deep, dark depression after Rachel died, and three months later, Dani, unable to reach her by phone for a day and a half, drove to the house and found her lifeless body on the living room floor. The official cause of death was heart failure, but everyone who knew her was convinced she died from a broken heart.

While going through her belongings to pick out items for her service, Dani found the messages she and Rachel had shared with one another at their commitment ceremony in 2006. Their expressions had little significance to Dani back then as a teenager, but now, as an adult with a wife of her own, they held much more value.

She took the time to read each one aloud, starting with Katy's.

Rachel – I have never loved anyone the way I love you. You are the only person in my heart, in my soul and in my dreams. Without a doubt, I will love you forever. I am beyond blessed to spend today, tomorrow and all of eternity by your side.

One tear followed another as she then switched her focus to her mother's message.

My Katy – I will treasure you always and in all ways. My heart is yours to keep, my hand is yours to hold, and now, my life is yours to share. I have loved you since the first day we met, and I will love you until time is no more.

A week later, Katy was buried next to Rachel. On their shared headstone, Rachel's children had inscribed, "Rachel and Katy: A love to last through all eternity."